科技英文寫作

Technical Writing in English

李開偉 編著

全華圖書股份有限公司

自序

　　全球化與國際化是產業與社會發展的主要方向，而國民英語能力的提升則是配合這種發展的要務之一。語文的能力可由聽、說、讀、寫四個層面來衡量，聽與說是人際直接溝通需要的技巧；而讀與寫則是知識取得與傳播所必備的能力。由於環境的不足，過去國內體制內之英語教育主要著重於閱讀能力的培養；聽與說僅是聊備一格、寫作更是不受重視。因此，撰寫英文的文件對於即使是受過高等教育的人士而言也多半是很困難的。

　　培養學生撰寫英文文件的能力是國內研究所教育非常重要又令人感到無力的一環，因為語言能力的培養是長期的工作，要想以一兩門課程的開設來讓學生脫胎換骨的想法是不切實際的；但是"做"勝過"不做"；"要求"必定強於"不要求"。筆者最近擔任本校研究所「科技英文寫作」課程之授課，深感適當教材的缺乏，遂將近年來從事研究工作曾經撰寫之英文文件整理並增加其他範例而成該課程之教材。這本科技英文寫作範例中的書信、電子郵件、備忘錄等文件大多是筆者與國外相關機構與人士直接往來之文件；為了尊重當事人的隱私，文件中大部分的人名、地址、電話均被修改，然文件中文句與內容則保持原有之面貌。在論文撰寫部分的範例許多都是個人發表論文曾用過文字；除了文句的撰寫，此部分也提及專業投稿與改稿要注意的事項，可視為研究方法的一部分。

　　語文是文化的一部分，語法是大多數人接受的文字呈現的方式，因此許多用法並無絕對的是非可言，只能說適當或不適當，因此有些主張可能未必為相關人士認同；例如筆者提到專業文件裡應避免使用 I,We 等第一人稱用語，此乃是許多專業外籍人士的建議，但在閱讀期刊論文時，有時仍會看到這類的用法。

　　科技領域內，各種專業領域的用語差異頗大。由於個人的背景的關係，書內範例的專業用語偏重於工業工程、工業管理、工業設計、職業安全衛生等領域。本書可做為相關科系大學部高年級暨研究所英文課程之教材，也可做為非工程背景而有志於從事工程、科技方面之英文文件撰寫或翻譯的人士的參考書籍。

　　本書付印前雖然經過多次校稿，然而誤謬可能無法完全避免；因此懇請讀者與各界人士惠予批評指教。

李開偉 謹識 於中華大學工業管理系

Contents

Chapter 1

論文與技術報告之文法

Chapter 2

英文的標點符號

Chapter 3

論文與技術報告之字彙與文句

Chapter 4

論文與技術報告之格式與內容

Chapter 5

論文投稿

Chapter 6

英文書信寫作

Chapter 7

履歷表與個人簡歷

Chapter 8

備忘錄、傳真暨其他文件

Chapter 9

常用字彙

參考資料

Chapter 1
論文與技術報告之文法

1-1 人稱

　　論文與專業文件之讀者為特定或非特定的一群人，文中之人稱應一律使用人稱代名詞或第三人稱，如 the author…、the employee（s）、the subject（s）、the interviewer …，而不使用第一、第二人稱如 I、me、we、us、you 等字：

> Irecommend that …（我建議……）中使用 I 並不適當，應改用 the author：
> The author recommend that…（筆者建議……）

　　當已敘述討論的對象時，可使用 they，例如：

> The subjects participated in a one-hour training before the experiment. They read and signed an informed consent form for the participation of the study.
> 受測者在實驗前參與了一個一小時的訓練，他們閱讀並簽署了一份參與研究的書面同意書。

　　英文中第三人稱（單數）之他（he, him）、她（she, her）與他的（his）、她的（her）及一些人稱代名詞（如 policeman, chairman, foreman, fisherman 等）均有性別的暗示，當文章裡提到的人物性別不明或同時包含了男性與與女性時不可使用這些字眼，較好的方式是使用不含性別暗示的人稱代名詞（如：police, chairperson, supervisor, fisher 等）；第三人稱可以複數取代單數：使用 they, them, their，若是不能使用複數時應他與她一起使用：he/she, him/her, his/her；he or she, him or her, his or her。

> After each experimental trial, the subject rated the slipperiness between the shoes and the floor on a five-point scale. She also rated the muscular effort on the right shank on a similar scale.
> 每次的實驗之後，受測者對鞋與地板間的滑溜性以一個五級的尺度來評分，她也對右小腿的負荷以一類似的尺度來評分。

特別注意

　　若本實驗的受測者全數為女性，則以上用法是正確的，若有部分受測者為男性則應將 She 改為 She/he 或 She or he；若用複數則無性別的困擾：

1. After the experimental trials, the subjects rated the slipperiness between the shoes and the floor on a five-point scale. They also rated the muscular effort in the right shank on a similar scale.

　　在實驗之後，受測者對鞋與地板間的滑溜性以一個五級的尺度來評分，他們也對右小腿的負荷以一類似的尺度來評分。

　　若參與者中有女性，下列句子主詞則不適當：

2. All the policemen in the city participated in this study.

　　本市所有的警察參與了這項研究。

　　應改為：All the polices in the city participated in this study.

1-2　英文字的詞性

　　英文字的詞性，依其功能，可分為以下幾種：

一、名詞noun

　　表示名稱的字，包括人的職稱、機構、場所、地名、機器、物質、學門、理論、方法等之名稱，如：manager, research institute, tablet, plastics, electronics 等。

1. The marketing personnel are using tablets to present to their customers.
   銷售人員正使用平板電腦向他們的客戶做簡報。
2. Hypothesis testing is widely used to analyze experimental data.
   假設檢定廣泛地被用來分析實驗性數據。
3. Two tablets were adopted in data collection.
   數據收集採用了兩台平板電腦。

代名詞 pronoun 亦為名詞的一種，分為人稱代名詞、不定代名詞、疑問代名詞和關係代名詞：

1. 人稱代名詞：指示人稱，如they, you, we等。

> (1) They were requested to respond to the questions on the survey.
> 他們被要求來回答問卷上的問題。

2. 指示代名詞：指示特定的人、事、物，如it, there, this, that等。

> (1) This was one of the assumptions of the study.
> 這是研究的假設之一。
>
> (2) It was their responsibility to complete their tasks in a timely manner.
> 適時地完成作業是他們的責任。
>
> (3) There are two commonly used approaches in determining the minimum traveling distance.
> 有兩種決定最小旅行距離的常用方法。

3. 不定代名詞：指示不確定的對象，如some, many, much, all, other等。

> (1) Some of the subjects did not complete the survey.
> 部分的受測者沒有完成問卷調查。

4. 疑問代名詞：如who, what, where, which。

> (1) Which method will be used depends on the sample size.
> 哪種方法將被採用會由樣本數決定。

5. 關係代名詞：具有連接詞作用之代名詞，如whichever, whatever, whoever等。

> (1) Whoever completed the task first was identified as subject 1.
> 第一個完成作業的人被指明為1號受測者。

1

二、動詞verb

　　動詞是表達動作的字，每個句子必須至少有一個動詞。動詞可分為及物動詞與不及物動詞，許多動詞可作為及物動詞與不及物動詞；另有許多動詞只能當及物動詞或不及物動詞。

1. 及物動詞transitive verb：動詞後必須接受詞，語意才完整者。若受詞後還需要受詞補語語意才完整者，稱為不完全及物動詞，不需要補語者可稱為完全及物動詞。

> (1) The research assistant screened（動詞）the data（受詞）upon completion of the study.
> 研究一完成研究助理就檢視數據。
>
> (2) All the undergraduate students complete（動詞）the course requirements（受詞）before they graduate.
> 所有的大學部生在畢業前完成課程要求。
>
> (3) The candidate of a degree must submit（動詞）a thesis draft（受詞）to file for an oral defense.
> 學位候選人必須繳交論文初稿以申請口試。
>
> (4) The nurse monitored（動詞）the patient's condition（受詞）carefully.
> 護士細心地監控病人的狀況。

2. 不及物動詞intransitive verb：動詞後不必接受詞，即可表達完整語意者。若還需要主詞補語語意才完整者，稱為不完全不及物動詞，不需要補語者可稱為完全不及物動詞。

> (1) A survey has been administered（動詞）.
> 一項調查被執行了。
>
> (2) The condition of the patient was carefully monitored（動詞）.
> 病人的狀況被小心的監控。
>
> (3) A thesis draft has been submitted（動詞）.
> 一份論文初稿已被繳交。
>
> (4) The data were analyzed（動詞）using the Microsoft Excel.
> 數據被使用微軟的Excel分析。

(5) The experiment stopped（動詞）when the subject was tired.
受測者覺得疲勞時實驗就結束。

(6) Most commercially available drones follow（動詞）a similar design.
大部分的商用無人機依循類似的設計。

(7) In the experiment, the participants stood（動詞）in the origin.
實驗時，參與者站在原點。

(8) An experiment was performed（動詞）to study the effects of footwear material on the coefficient of friction of floor.
一項實驗被執行來研究鞋具材料對於地板摩擦係數的影響。

三、形容詞adjective

　　形容詞是描述或修飾名詞的字，可在以下方面描述名詞的特性：人或物之數量多寡、人的生物（性別、年齡）、生理或性格特質、人或物的外觀特質；人、事、物之主觀感覺特質或客觀之狀態；物體或物質之物理、化學特質……其他特質。

1. Scientists have conducted much research on the developing of Organic Light Emitting Diodes(OLED).
科學家在開發有機發光二極體上進行了許多研究。（數量多寡）

2. Many studies have been conducted on the developing of Organic Light Emitting Diodes(OLED).
許多有機發光二極體開發的研究被進行了。（數量多寡）

3. The buying power of female college students was compared with that of their male counterpart.
女性大學生的購買力被拿來跟男性(大學生）相比（性別）

4. Even though colored monitored are available, monochrome displays are still common in industrial computers.
即使有了彩色的監視器，單色的顯示在工業電腦仍然很常見（外觀特質）

5. The once robust quality assurance system in the food industry in Taiwan now lies in ruins.
台灣食品工業一度十分穩健的品質保證系統現已崩潰。（系統特質）

6. Discharge of untreated waste water into the public drainage is prohibited.
排放未經處理的廢水到公共排水系統是被禁止的。（化學特質）

7. All the iPhone users are satisfied with this smart phone.
所有的iPhone使用者都對這款智慧型的手機滿意。（功能特質）

1

四、副詞adverb

　　副詞用來修飾動詞、形容詞、副詞、片語、子句、或整個句子的字,字尾常為 ly。

特 別 注 意

　　字尾為 ly 的單字不一定是副詞,例如 friendly 是形容詞。

1. All the proposals were reviewed rigorously.

　　所有的計畫書都被嚴格的審查。(「嚴格的」用來修飾動詞reviewed)

2. The experimental condition was strictly monitored.

　　實驗狀況被嚴密的監控。(「嚴密的」用來修飾動詞monitored)

3. The manuscript has been revised carefully.

　　稿件被細心的編修了。(「細心的」用來修飾動詞revised)

4. The parts have been machined automatically.

　　零件被自動的加工了(「自動的」用來修飾動詞machined)

5. The problems were resolved unexpectedly.

　　問題意外的被解決了。(「意外的」用來修飾動詞resolved)

6. Models A and B was significantly different.

　　模型A與B顯著的不同。(「顯著的」用來修飾形容詞 different)

7. Surprisingly, the cost of the project was only a half as what has been expected.

　　很意外的,計畫的花費只有先前預期的一半。(「意外的」用來修飾整個句子)

五、連接詞conjunction

　　連接詞用來連接單字、片語、子句、句子的字;常見的連接詞包括 and, or, but, so, for, if, than, that, because。

1. All the participants were college students and were right-handed.

　　所有的參與者都是大學生並且都是慣用右手的。

2. The temperature and humidity in the laboratory were recorded.
實驗室裡的溫度與濕度被記錄下來。

3. This aircraft has both a vision and a satellite positioning systems.
這架飛行器具備了一具視覺及衛星定位系統。

4. The invasions of UAVs into the airspace near airport have resulted in financial losses due to midair collisions or near collisions with the jet and delays and cancellations of commercial flights.
無人機入侵機場附近空域造成了因空中與噴射機碰撞或幾乎碰撞及商用航班的延誤與取消的經濟損失。

5. The idea of using a pilotless aircraft to retrieve information in hostile territories is attractive because there is no risk of losing human pilots.
使用無飛行員航空器來在敵方的領空擷取情報的想法是很吸引人的，因為那樣沒有損失人類飛行員的風險。

六、冠詞article

冠詞分為不定冠詞（a 或 an）與定冠詞（the）；冠詞通常放在名詞前表示單一、非特定、或特定的個體（包括人、事、物、概念等）一般非特定名詞前用 a，若名詞字首為母音則用 an。

1. An accelerometer was used to measure the acceleration of the target.
一具加速度計被用來量測目標物的加速度。

2. An aircraft was detected in the non-fly zone.
禁航區裡發現一架飛機。

3. A commercial aircraft was detected in the non-fly zone.
禁航區裡發現一架商用飛機。
（an表示一具；the指示「特定的」目標物）

七、介系詞preposition

介系詞是用來指明其後面的受詞與前面之名詞或動詞間關係的字，常放在受詞之前，故也稱為前置詞。常用的介系詞包括 on, in, to, of, off, from, before, after, by, up, upon, with, under, over 等，介系詞常出現在片語中。

1. Due to the limitation of the power supply of the drone, there were pauses when battery changes were required.

   由於無人機電源供應的限制，（實驗）在需要更換電池時暫停了（幾次）。

2. The operator replaced the battery and then had the drone flied back to the testing airspace again.

   操作員更換電池後讓無人機再次飛回測試空域。

3. The experiment was conducted under 12 material and temperature conditions.

   實驗室在12種材料與溫度狀況下進行的。

4. All the chips are vulnerable before they are packing.

   所有的晶片在封裝前都是易受損的。

1-3 片語 phrase 與子句 claus

一、片語phrase

由兩個或多個單字組合而成用來表示特定意思的詞，片語可代表一詞類（名詞、動詞、形容詞、副詞、連接詞等），但不足以形成一子句。

1. The employee satisfaction reflects the employee's level of job satisfaction.

   員工的滿意度反應了員工對工作滿意的水準。（名詞片語）

2. Global integration of economies over the past two decades has interconnected many of the countries and industries in the world.

   過去二十年間全球經濟體的整合使得世界上許多國家與工業能夠相互的連結。（名詞片語）

3. The capital asset pricing model was established by Sharpe in 1964.

   資本資產鑑價模式是Sharpe在1964年建立的。（名詞片語）

4. Portfolio theory has during many decades been considered as the holy grail of investment.

   （投資）組合理論幾十年來都被視為投資的聖杯（經典）。（名詞片語）

   holy grail: 耶穌在最後晚餐所拿的聖杯，比喻神聖。

5. <u>Unmanned aircraft vehicles</u>（UAVs）, or colloquially drones, have been used for decades in military missions as platforms carrying cameras, sensors, communication devices, and weapons.

<u>無人飛行載具</u>或通稱的無人機數十年來一直被用在軍事任務上當作攜帶照相機、感測器、通訊裝置、及武器的平台。（名詞片語）

6. For safety and security reasons, <u>no-fly zone</u> （NFZ） and <u>restricted fly zone</u>（RFZ） have been announced by the aviation administration authorities.

為了安全與保安的理由，民航管理當局公告了<u>禁航區</u>與<u>限航區</u>。（名詞片語）

7. Speculation (Babuse et al, 2013) <u>takes place in</u> an open environment where the future return distribution is not known.

投機<u>發生</u>於未來報酬分配為未知的開放環境（Babuse et al, 2013）。（動詞片語）

8. Organizations need to <u>be able to</u> generate a culture that facilitates and allows the conditions to develop and design new products and services.

組織需要<u>能夠</u>產生一個能促進並允許開發與設計新產品與服務的文化。（動詞片語）

9. Business organizations, due to rapid environmental changes, began to adopt organizational learning <u>so as to</u> attain outstanding performance.

由於快速的環境改變，商業機構開始採用組織學習<u>以便於</u>獲取突出的表現。（連接詞片語）

10. Some companies find work sampling applicable for establishing incentive standards on indirect <u>as well as</u> direct labor operations.

某些公司發現工作抽樣可應用在為間接<u>與</u>直接勞力作業之建立獎勵標準上。（連接詞片語）

11. <u>In addition to</u> the applications in industry, UAVs are becoming popular among the hobbyists for entertainment purposes.

<u>除了</u>工業的應用外，無人機也在娛樂用途上在業餘的愛好者之間風行了起來。（連接詞片語）

二、子句clause

是至少包含一個動詞的多個單字之組合，是句子中的句子。子句分為主要子句與從屬子句；主要子句意思完整，可單獨成為一個句子，從屬子句則意思不完整，無法單獨成為一個句子。

---

1. This type of learning does not achieve the competitive advantage of the organization, but <u>it is necessary for its survival.</u>

   　　　　主要子句

   這種學習無法獲致組織的競爭優勢，但它是組織存活必須地要素。

   主要子句：單獨看時意思依然完整，可獨立成為一個句子。

這個句子可改成兩個獨立的句子：

This type of learning does not achieve the competitive advantage of the organization.

It is necessary for its survival.

如此修改在文法上是可以的，但沒有 but 連接，語句讀起來較不順暢。

---

2. It was estimated that <u>the use of computer can save as much as 35 percentage of total cost.</u>

   　　　　　　　　　　　　　　主要子句

   據估計，<u>使用電腦可以節省高達35%的總成本</u>。

此句之獨立子句在文法上也可獨立成：

The use of computer can save as much as 35 percentage of total cost.

使用電腦可以節省高達 35% 的總成本。這樣說是表達一個客觀的事實。沒有了「據估計」的意思。

<u>Even if the model appeared to be reasonable from a theoretical point of view,</u>

　　　　　　　　從屬子句

several problems arise from its use in practice.

<u>即使從理論的觀點來看這個模式似乎是合理的</u>，它在實際的使用上卻引發多個問題。

從屬子句：單獨看時意思不完整。

這句話的重點在於後面的「它在實際的使用上卻引發多個問題」。

---

3. Although there is much evidence to suggest the benefits of an independent board of directors, 從屬子句

there are also benefits to having insiders.

雖然有許多證據建議一個獨立董事會的好處，擁有內部董事也有好處。這句話主要是說「擁有內部董事有好處」。

4. The basic design of a drone has a microcontroller that acts as a flight control, usually with four but up to eight motors and propellers, a radio receiver, electronic speed control, and a battery, built on a light plastic or metal frame.

　　　　　　　　　　從屬子句

無人機的基本設計包含了一具可當飛行控制的微控制器、四到八個馬達與槳葉、一個無線接收器、電子速度控制器、及一個電池，裝在一個輕的塑膠或金屬架上。

🔍 1-4　動詞的時式

　　論文中常用的動詞時式包括現在式、過去式、現在完成式、過去完成式及未來式；而以過去式最常用，因為在撰寫論文時研究活動幾乎都已結束了，使用過去式較簡單。各種時式的使用場合如下：

一、現在式

1. 敘述不變的真理或現象。

---

(1) Water has a lower viscosity than that of the engine oil.
水的黏滯性比機油低。

(2) The oxidation of silicon is the most critical manufacturing process in the deposition and growth stage.
矽的氧化是沉積與成長階段最關鍵的製程。

---

2. 敘述一般都接受的事實。

> (1) High-heeled shoes are commonly worn in the workplace and for leisure activities.
>
> 在工作場所與休閒活動中高跟鞋是普遍被穿著的。

3. 敘述現在的情況：在純數學模式推導，較不涉及時間概念的研究論文中常以現在式書寫。

句中is used是被動式而不是過去式，爲「被用來」之意。

> (1) An initial matrix is used to calculate the importance of the activities.
>
> 一個初步矩陣被用來計算活動的重要性。

二、過去式

1. 敘述其他文獻的內容。

> (1) Goodwin (1975) measured and compared cursor positioning performance among cursor keys, a light pen, and light gun while performing random and sequential pointing tasks.
>
> Goodwin (1975) 以執行隨機與循序的定點作業來量測與比較游標鍵、光筆、與光槍在游標定點作業的績效。

2. 敘述本研究的步驟與方法。

> (1) The plasma cleaning process for each gas was conducted by controlling the pressure, time, and gas flow rate on the PBGA substrates.
>
> 每一種氣體的電漿清潔是經由在PBGA基板上之壓力、時間與氣流速率的控制來進行的。

3. 敘述本研究的結果、討論與結論。

> (1) The present study identified several factors that were significantly associated with workers'ratings of floor slipperiness.
>
> 本研究找出了多個與工人對地板滑溜程度評分顯著關聯的因子。

三、現在完成式及過去完成式

　　敘述自己或他人已完成的研究事項，這些研究活動自過去的某個時間點開始，若持續到過去某時停止則用過去完成式，若一直持續到現在則用現在完成式；寫作者有時不易區分這兩種情況，簡單的決定方式是若文獻上的作者已退休甚至於已去世了，使用過去完成式，若作者仍然在從事相關學術研究則用現在完成式。若是對這兩種時式的使用仍然不確定則建議使用過去式。

1. Professor S. Thomson has established a model to represent the digitization process in switching the analog signal.
   S. Thomson 教授建立了一個模式來呈現將類比信號數位化的轉換過程。

四、未來式

　　敘述未來的研究。

1. Determination of the optimal control-display ratio to minimize the operation time for this interface design will be an important issue in the future.
   決定這種介面設計的最佳控制－顯示比以將操作時間最小化將是未來的一個重要的議題。

Chapter 2
英文的標點符號

🔍 2-1　常用的標點符號

　　英文寫作時常用的標點符號包括：句點 period (.)、問號 question mark (?)、驚嘆號 (!)、逗點 comma (,)、冒號 colon (:)、分號 semicolon (;)、雙引號 quotation mark (" ")、斜線 dash (/)、括弧 parenthesis ( )、連接線 hyphen (-)、省略符號 apostrophe (')、虛線 double hyphen (--)。

　　目前文字的處理幾乎都是以電腦文書處理輸入，然而在文書處理軟體檔中，Microsoft WORD 則是最常用的文書處理軟體，電腦都具備中英文的處理能力，習慣使用中文的使用者在處理英文文件時也容易犯一些錯誤。

特別注意

1. 許多人常在英文中錯用中文的標點符號。以下為中文的標點符號，英文中不可使用：。、『』「」【】。
2. 中文的逗點在中間，英文的逗點在下方，不可誤用。
3. 使用電腦中文輸入時，中文為全形輸入，每個符號均占兩格；英文全為半形輸入，每個字母與符號均占一格。
4. 逗點、句號、問號、驚嘆號、冒號、分號之後均需空一格才能接文字。

🔍 2-2　句點 . 問號 ? 與驚嘆號 ! 的使用

　　每個句子結束時必須要有句號、驚嘆號或問號。驚嘆號是用來表達情緒的符號，在正式的文件中很少使用。

1. 句點可用來標示圖或表的編號。

> (1) The results are shown in Figure 2.1.
> 　　結果顯示於圖2.1中。

2

2. 句點可用來標示數字中的小數點。例如：0.53, 12.50等。

3. 句點可用以標示縮寫。

a.m.	早上	p.m.	下午
W. K. Smith	first name 與 middle name 的縮寫	e.g.	例如（for example由拉丁文exempli gratia而來）
et al.	and others（由拉丁文et alii 與 et aliae 而來）	etc.	等等（and so forth由拉丁文et cetra 而來）
ex.	example	fig.	figure
i.e.	that is（由拉丁文id est而來）	lbs.	英磅
p.s.	post script 後記	Jr.	Junior（常見於人名中）
Ms.	女士	Mr.	先生
Mrs.	太太	Dr.	博士、醫師

Mon.	星期一	Tues.	星期二
Wed.	星期三	Thurs.	星期四
Fri.	星期五	Sat.	星期六
Sun.	星期天	Jan.	一月
Feb.	二月	Mar.	三月
Apr.	四月	Aug.	八月
Sep.	九月	Oct.	十月
Nov.	十一月	Dec.	十二月

4. 若是句尾的字具有縮寫的逗點，則原句點必須省略。

(1) The research personnel finished the experiment on 4:30 p.m..（ X ）

The research personnel finished the experiment on 4:30 p.m.（ O ）

研究人員於下午四點三十分完成實驗

2-3 逗點，

1. 用來分隔一連串的文字、數字、片語或子句，其最後一項常以等連接詞（and、or、but、for、yet等）來連接。

> (1) A research investigator may be a faculty member, a student, or a staff.
>   一個研究人員可能是大學教師、學生或者職員。
>
> (2) The mean scores were 3.37, 4.87, and 5.32, respectively.
>   平均分數分別為3.37、4.87及5.32。

2. 用於句首以年代為開頭標示於年代之後。

> (1) In 1963, researchers began a study to investigate the body's reaction to foreign tissue.
>   在1963年，研究人員開始調查身體對於體外器官的反應。

3. 用於形容名詞之二個以上之形容詞間。

> (1) The subject used a cylindrical, power-driven screwdriver.
>   受測者使用一把筒狀、有動力驅動的起子。

4. 用在句中表示附加說明之插入片語或子句。

> (1) Stevenson et al. (1989) indicated that DCOF under contaminated conditions, measured with a dynamic setup to simulate human slips, increases almost linearly with Ra, and increases only somewhat beyond certain Ra values.
>   Stevenson等(1989)指出以一個模擬人腳滑動的動態裝置，在有污染的狀況下量測到的DCOF值幾乎與Ra同步線性遞增，而在低於特定的Ra值之下只會稍為的增加。
>   句中 measured with a dynamic setup to simulate human slips是插入作為附加說明DCOF者。
>
> (2) Switchenko (1985), in a review of the research literature, found that icons might be useful and enhance performance only in some situations.
>   Switchenko (1985) 在一個文獻的回顧中發現圖像只有在某些情況下可能是有用的，並能提升作業績效。

(3) The comments from Dr. K. W. Li, a professor of Chung-Hua University, were very helpful.

中華大學的Dr. K.W. Li 的意見是非常有幫助的。

5. 在區隔句首有連接作用之副詞與句子。

(1) Certainly, the most important of these criteria is experience in the class of work being performed.

當然，這些準則中最重要的是執行中的工作分級經驗。

(2) Actually, all experienced time study men unconsciously follow the synthetic rating procedure to some extent.

事實上，所有有經驗的工時研究人員下意識的在某些程度上都會遵守綜合評比程序。

(3) Finally, the subject put down the tool on the workbench.

最後，受測者把工具放在工作臺上。

(4) Consequently, this function is often performed with the aid of modern computer systems.

結果，這項功能通常都是經由現代化電腦系統的輔助來執行的。

6. 用在日期是以月、日、年之順序中之日與年之間，如：January 15, 2019。

7. 若是日期是以日、月、年的順序，則不用逗點，如：15 January 2019。

2-4 冒號：

1. 用於引導句子之後欲說明的數項陳述（包括名詞、名詞片語或子句）。

(1) The functions of these two charts are:

　I. Man and Machine chart：Used to analyze idle man time and idle machine time.

　II. Operator process chart：Used to analyze workstation for proper layout and nest sequence of elements.

這兩份圖的功能分別是：

　I. 人機圖：用來分析閒置人員時間與閒置機器時間。

　II. 操作員程序圖：用在關於適當的布置與元件巢狀順序之工作站分析。

(2) Xerox has developed two visualization techniques: the cone tree for top-to-bottom hierarchies, and the cam tree for left-to-right hierarchies.

全錄公司開發了兩種視覺化的技術：由上至下層級的錐狀樹技術與由左至右層級的凸輪樹技術。

2. 用於引導句子之後欲引述他人之敘述處。

(1) The research personnel asked the worker: "Is the pair of shoes you are wearing right now, the shoes you normally wear at work?"

研究人員詢問工人：「你現在穿的鞋子是你平時上班穿的鞋子嗎？」

3. 用於表示時間，如：4:20 p.m.。

2-5 分號；

1. 可用來分開兩個以上之獨立子句。

(1) Using icons can utilize this good memory recognition for pictures; but the icons should be developed based upon the research on picture recognition.

圖像的使用可以利用這種很好的圖像記憶辨識的特質；但是圖像的發展必須根據圖像辨識的研究來做。

2. 用來分隔一連串之項目，而這些項目間又有子項目需以逗點來區分時。

(1) Guidelines for crank and handwheel radii are: light loads, radii of 3 to 5 inches; medium to heavy loads, radii of 4 to 7inches; very heavy loads, radii of more than 8 inches.

搖柄與手輪半徑的指引是：輕負荷時半徑3到5英吋；中到重負荷時半徑4到7英吋；非常重的負荷時半徑8英吋以上。

🔍 2-6 雙引號之使用 ""

1. 在句子中要突顯文字、片語或句子之特殊意義。

---

(1) The rating procedure known as " objective rating, " a method developed by M. E. Mendall, endeavors to eliminate the difficulty of establishing a normal speed criterion for every type of work.

由M.E. Mendall開發，並為吾人所知的「客觀評比法」，致力於消除對每種工作建立一個常態速度準則時的困難。

(2) This branch of the scientific study of worker and his environment is being recognized as "occupational physiology."

這個對工人與工作環境的科學化調查的流派，被公認為「工作生理學」。

(3) It does mean asking, "Should we change what we have chosen to define as reality to fit our model? and What might be the benefits of this change?"

它在問：「我們是否應該改變已經選取來真實的定義符合我們的模式的項目？及這個改變的好處是什麼？」

(4) Provide answers to questions such as "Should this plant implement JIT?"

提供有關於「這個工廠是否應導入JIT？」這類問題的解答。

---

2. 一字不改的引述他人的文字時。

---

(1) "Managers at all levels and in all organizations are striving to achieve results through people."

「所有組織的各級經理人，都是致力於經由人們的努力而獲得工作成果。」

特別注意

1. 部分國家之英式語法採用單引號 ' '，
2. 右邊的雙引號旁若有逗號、句號、問號等標點符號時，這些符號應置於引號之內，即其左邊。

2-7 連接線 -

1. 用來連接副詞及其後之形容詞以組成一複合形容詞。

better-prepared engineer	準備較佳的工程師
just-in-time system	即時系統
non-parametric	無母數的
well-defined	清楚定義的
well-managed organization	管理良好的組織

(1) Just-in-Time purchasing requires suppliers to deliver components to the purchaser's receiving dock, or sometimes directly to the production line, as they are required.
及時採購系統需要供應商運送元件到採購廠商的收貨口，有時會被要求直接送到生產線上。

(2) A non-parametric test was performed for the dependent variable.
對於應變數執行了一項無母數檢定。

(3) A well-managed organization should establish a set of well-defined organization goal.
一個管理良好的組織，應該建立一組良好定義的組織目標。

2. 用來連接由形容詞與形容詞組成之複合形容詞。

flat-soled shoes	平底鞋
high-heeled shoes	高跟鞋
right-handed	（慣用）右手的
two-tailed test	雙尾檢定
three-dimensional	三維的

(1) There are two commonly held beliefs concerning high-heeled shoes for females.
有兩個關於女性高跟鞋常見的信念。

(2) This might contribute to their finding that high heels were less slip resistant than flat-soled shoes.
這可能支持了他們對於高跟鞋比平底鞋較不抗滑的發現。

2

(3) Solid modeling requires three-dimensional thinking and visualization skills.
實體模型的建立需要三度空間的思考與視覺化的技術。

(4) A two-tailed test was performed to compare the difference between the two groups.
一個雙尾檢定的執行被用來比較兩個群體之間的差異。

(5) All the subjects were right-handed.
所有的受測者都是慣用右手者。

3. 用來連接由形容詞與名詞組成之複合形容詞。

all-or-none assumption	全或無假設
short-term memory	短期記憶
long-term investment	長期投資
low-back pain	下背痛
low-workload task	低負荷作業
lower-level	較低層次的
right-hand	右手的
real-time system	真時系統
real-world	真實世界
two-group design	兩群體設計

(1) A two-way analysis of variance (ANOVA) was performed on the COF values obtained from the friction measurement.
一個兩維的變異數分析被用來分析由摩擦量測得到的COF的數據。

(2) The MRP is a closed-loop system.
MRP是一個封閉迴路系統。

(3) Dispatching informs first-line supervision of the released order and their priority.
物料的派送能知會第一線關於訂單釋出與其優先順序的督導。

(4) Information in working memory is transferred to long-term memory by semantically coding it.
工作記憶裡的資訊是經由語意編碼來轉換成長期記憶。

4. 用來連接名詞及其後之形容詞以組成一複合形容詞。

AI-based	人工智慧基礎的
box-shaped	箱型的
bottom-up	由下而上的
component-dominant	元件支配的
computer-aided	電腦輔助的
computer-generated	電腦產生的
computer-integrated	電腦整合的
cost-competitive	有成本競爭力的
distribution-free	分布型式自由的
head-up	抬頭的
head-mounted	頭戴的

(1) Computer-aided design and computer-aided manufacturing systems have proliferated in the mechanical industries over the past two decades.
電腦輔助設計與電腦輔助製造系統在過去的二十年間，快速的在機械工業裡擴展。

(2) Computer-generated information displays do not necessarily improve the performance of the operators.
電腦產生的資訊顯示，不必然會改善操作人員的作業績效。

(3) The emergence of computer-integrated manufacturing (CIM) has increased the attention given to the use of integrated systems.
電腦整合系統(CIM)的產生增加了對於使用整合系統的注意力。

(4) The use of TQC methods in Japan has demonstrated that highly responsive and cost-competitive manufacturing can be done without much capital investment.
TQC方法在日本的使用說明了不需要大幅的資本投資就能達到有高度回應與有成本競爭力的製造。

(5) The head-mounted displays allow the pilot to retain a view of flight instruments while scanning the full range of the outside world for threatening traffic.
頭戴顯示器允許飛行員在全空域掃瞄外面世界有威脅性的交通狀況時能夠保留飛行儀表的影像。

2

(6) They concluded that high-heeled shoes were less slip-resistant and the commonly held belief that high-heeled shoes were less safe was true.

他們總結高跟鞋較不具抗滑性，而一般人相信的高跟鞋較不安全的想法是真的。

(7) The optimization is based on the trade-off between the cost of inspection and cost of defects.

最佳化是根據(產品)檢驗成本與瑕疵成本間的妥協來進行的。

(8) As parts move through various operations, the model processes them according to each machine operating characteristics and routes them according to the system situation-dependent control logic.

當零件經過不同的作業時，其模式根據每臺機器的操作特性來處理這些零件，並且系統根據狀況的控制邏輯來運送它們。

(9) Artificial intelligence (AI)-based approaches have been receiving much enthusiastic attention from industry.

人工智慧基礎的思考途徑在工業界受到了很熱烈的注意。

(10)There are four key conceptual elements of the framework for user-centered design.

以使用者為中心設計架構中有四個關鍵的概念單元。

(11)This is a good example of user-friendly design.

這是一個對使用者友善設計很好的例子。

(12)Predictions on the outcome of time-sharing real-world tasks are still relatively primitive.

對真實世界分時工作結果的預測，相對來說，仍然非常的原始。

(13)Top-down forecasting and bottom-up forecasting are general forecasting patterns used for predicting product demand.

在產品需求的預測上，由上至下與由下至上仍然是一般使用的預測形式。。

5. 用來連接對等之名詞以組合成一複合名詞。

accident-proneness	意外傾向
assembly-line	裝配線
data-base	資料庫
human-computer interaction	人-電腦互動

human-human communication	人際溝通
human-machine interface	人機介面
driver-fixture combination	驅動器-夾具組合
variance-covariance matrix	變異-共變矩陣

特別注意

若是前一名詞有修飾其後名詞之作用，則其間不用 -

1. work station
2. workstation
3. student worker

---

(1) Attempts to determine just what patterns of personality factors create accident-proneness have not been successful.
決定何種人格因子的類型會導致意外傾向的嘗試並不成功。

(2) The powered driver-fixture combination was proposed as an alternative to the traditionally used pliers for wire-tying tasks.
動力驅動器與夾具的組合被建議可當做傳統以鉗子來進行綁鐵絲作業的另外一種選擇。

(3) More recently, major advances have been made in data-base technologies.
最近，資料庫技術取得了主要的進展。

(4) A human-machine system is an arrangement of people and machines interacting within an environment in order to achieve a set of system goals.
人機系統是在為了達成一組系統目標的前提下，在環境中對於人與機器互動所做的安排。

6. 連接介系詞或連接詞等字以形成複合名詞。

from-to chart	由－至圖
in-depth	深入的
in-plant	廠內
in-process	製程中的
on-line help	線上輔助
on-site	現場
top-to-bottom sequence	上至下順序
What-if questionnaire	什麼－如果問卷

(1) The scope of this paper does not permit an in-depth discussion of this important topic.
本文的範疇並不允許對這個重要的議題做深入的討論。

(2) On-line reporting systems directly report events as they occur.
線上回報系統會在事件發生時直接回報。

(3) On-site measurement of floor slipperiness is very complicated.
現場地板滑溜性的量測非常複雜。

7. 連接兩個以上之人名以表示其共同的關係，如：

Box-Jenkins procedure

Graeco-Latin square

Kruskal-Wallis test

Mann-Whitney-Wilcoxon test

Silver-Meal algorithms

(1) The Box-Jenkins procedure is a systematic method that does not assume any specific model, but analyzes historical data in order to determine a suitable model.
Box-Jenkins程序是一種不假設特定模式，但分析歷史資料來決定適當模式的系統化方法。

(2) The Silver-Meal algorithms are simple heuristics for selecting replenishment quantities under conditions of deterministic time-varying demand.
Silver-Meal 演算法是在固定時間變動需求情況下選擇補充量的啟發式解法。

8. 表示分數。

one-third	三分之一
Two-fifth	五分之二
Three- eighth	八分之三

9. 表示範圍，如：參考文獻中需標明之頁數117-125。但正式的寫法是用to取代：
from page 117 to 125

2-8 斜線 /

1. 用來表示項目之間具有組合之關係；此種用法有時與連接線(-)是相通的

(1) The means and standard deviations for the shoe/floor combinations were summarized in Table1.
鞋與地板組合的平均值與標準差整理於表1中。

(2) Twisting wires can not be completed without the repetition of awkward hand/wrist postures.
扭轉鐵絲無法不以反覆的手與腕彎扭的姿勢來完成。

2. 表示二者之一的關係

(1) Contact your department/division manager.
聯絡你的部門經理。→表示部門可能是department或是division，寫作的人並不確定。

(2) He/she completed the task according to the instruction given by the researcher.
他/她依照研究人員給的指示完成了工作。→表示他可能是男性或女性。

(3) Spillage of water, oil, and/or mixtures of both are very likely especially in the fry vat and sink areas.
積水、積油或累積油水的混合是非常可能發生的尤其是在油炸區與水槽區。

(4) Order release initiates the execution phase of production; it authorizes production and/or purchasing.
訂單的釋出啟動了生產的執行階段；它授權生產或是採購作業的進行。

3. 表示分數或比值

> (1) Chang et al. (2001b) reported that the F_N/A^2 of Brungraber Mark II is the smallest (0.07 N/cm^2) among the four slip measurement devices compared.
>
> Chang 等(2001b) 報導Brungraber Mark II (量到)的F_N/A^2 值在四種被比較的摩擦量測器材中是最小的(0.07 N/cm^2)。

4. 用於單位中，如：m/sec。但文章裡較正式之用法是用per: meters per second

🔍 2-9　括弧 ( )

1. 用來補充說明其前之名詞、片語或子句。

> (1) The computer interprets the keystroke and determines its ASCII number (each character has a different ASCII code associated with it).
>
> 電腦詮釋輸入的觸鍵並決定它的ASCII號碼（每一個字母都有一個不同的ASCII號碼）。

2. 標示文獻或著作年代。

> (1) Another cognitive advantage for menu displays is that they can be designed to organize the decision making of the user (Koved, 1986)
>
> 另外一個選單顯示在認知上的好處就是它們可以被設計來組織使用者的決策（Koved, 1986）。
>
> (2) Koved (1986) indicated that another cognitive advantage for menu displays was that they could be designed to organize the decision making of the user.
>
> Koved （1986）指出選單顯示在認知上的另外一個好處就是它們可以被設計來組織使用者的決策。

3. 標示數值。

> (1) Forty females (71.4%) and 16 males (28.6%), out of 58 employees from all ten restaurants participated in the survey.
>
> 全部十家餐廳的58名員工中的40位女性（71.4%）與16位男性（28.6%）參與了這項調查。

(2) The means (±S.D.) of age, length of tenure, and working hour per week of the participants were 22.55 (±5.94) years, 13.12 (±13.28) months, and 37.86 (±9.55) hours, respectively.

參與者的年齡、任職時間與每週的工時的平均值（±標準差）分別為22.55（±5.94）歲、13.12（±13.28）月及37.86（±9.55）小時。

(3) A one-way ANOVA on friction coefficients in the seven areas across all restaurants indicated a strong statistical significance (p<0.001).

所有餐廳裡的七個區域的摩擦係數的單維變異數分析顯示了很強的統計上的顯著性（p<0.001）。

🔍 2-10　省略符號'

1. 用來表示縮寫。

(1) The subjects didn't know the weight of the load being handled.

受測者不知道其所處理之負荷物的重量。

正式的論文中應避免使用縮寫，因此此句宜改為：

The subjects did not know the weight of the load being handled.

2. 表示所有格。

(1) A Duncan's multiple range test was conducted if a significant result was obtained for any factor in the analyses.

分析中若任何一項因子得到顯著的結果則會再進行Duncan 的多重全距檢定。

(2) The correlations associated with the subjective ratings were calculated using Spearman's correlation coefficient.

（不同）主觀評比間的相關性是以計算 Spearman相關係數進行(分析)的。

(3) Pearson's correlation coefficient between the two variables was calculated to examine the correlation of the variables.

兩個變數間的相關性是計算Pearson相關係數來檢驗的。

🔍 2-11 虛線 --

2

1. 用來引導一連串的文字，其作用類似冒號但較不正式。

> (1) Several items need further study -- the shape, inclined angle, and the tool weight.
> 許多項目都需要進一步的研究-- 包括形狀、傾斜角與工具的重量。

2. 用來引導進一步的解釋。

> (1) Most dashes are equivalent to comma -- that is, they separate elements within a sentence.
> 大部分的斜線是和逗點對等的--也就是它們區分了句子裡的單元。

3. 在原文引述他人的文句並於其後標示作者的姓名。

> (1) "Give me liberty or give me death." --Patrick Henry.
> Patrick Henry 說：「不自由，毋寧死」。

Chapter 3
論文與技術報告之字彙與文句

🔍 3-1　基本句型

　　名詞、名詞片語、名詞子句在句子中常當作主詞或受詞。動詞是句子中表達動作意思的字彙,每個句子至少要有一個動詞,每個句子必須有至少一個完整的意思。

　　英文句子有基本的句型,這些基本句型可用連接詞(and, or 等)連接成複合句,或以補充說明來表達比較複雜的語意。

1. 主詞+完全不及物動詞

The subject stopped.(受測者停止。)
　　主詞　　動詞

2. 主詞+不完全不及物動詞+主詞補語

The subject felt tired.(受測者感覺疲勞。)
　　主詞　動詞　主詞補語

以上二句可用and結合成一個句子。

The subject felt tired and stopped.(受測者感覺疲勞並且停下來。)

(1) The sample size of the study was small.(本研究的樣本數很小。)
　　　　　　主詞動詞　　　主詞　補語

(2) The data were not normally distributed.(數據不是常態的分配。)
　　主詞　動詞　　　　　　主詞補語

以上兩句可以組合成一個句子:

The sample size of the study was small and the data were not normally distributed.

(此研究的樣本數非常小而且數據並非常態的分配。)

(3) All the subjects were female.(所有的受測者都是女性的。)
　　　　主詞　　　動詞　主詞補語

(4) All the subjects were college students and were healthy.
　　　　主詞　　動詞　　主詞補語　　　　動詞　主詞補語
　　(所有的受測者都是大學生且健康的。)

(5) The mean stature and body weight of the subjects were 168 cm and 57 kg, respectively.
     主詞   動詞 主詞補語

（受測者的平均身高與體重分別為168公分與57公斤。）

例句(4)、(5)可以連起來：

All the subjects were college students and were healthy. Their mean stature and body weight were 168 cm and 57 kg, respectively.

（所有的受測者都是大學生且健康的，他們的平均身高與體重分別為168公分與57公斤。）

第二句的受測者改成「他們的」，避免重複主詞，讀起來也會比較順。

或者將例句(3)、(4)、(5)合併：

All the subjects were female. All the subjects were college students and were healthy. The mean stature and body weight of the subjects were 168 cm and 57 kg, respectively.

此三句文法正確，但讀起來不順，改成下列句子後會好些：

All the subjects were female college students and were healthy. Their mean stature and body weight were 168 cm and 57 kg, respectively.

（所有的受測者都是健康的女大學生，他們的平均身高與體重分別為168公分與57公斤。）

3. 主詞+完全及物動詞+受詞

(1) The authors made three assumptions.（作者們做了三個假設。）
   主詞 動詞   受詞

(2) Murphy (1998) established a statistical model.
 主詞   動詞   受詞
（Murphy (1998)建立了一個統計模式。）

例句(1)、(2)可以連起來：

Murphy (1998) made three assumptions and established a statistical model.（Murphy (1998) 做了三個假設並建立了一個統計模式。）

(3) Li et al. (2007) conducted an experiment.（Li et al. (2007)進行一項實驗。）
 主詞   動詞   受詞

(4) Li et al. (2007) analyzed the experimental data and established a model.
     主詞   動詞   受詞   動詞   受詞
   （Li et al. (2007)分析實驗數據並且建立了一個模式。）

以上二句可連起來：

Li et al. (2007) conducted an experiment. They analyzed the experimental data and
established a model.
第二句的主詞改為They（et al. 為「等作者」，表示作者至少三人以上）讀起來
較順。

(5) Chang (2011) analyzed the fall-related injury cases during 2000 to 2010.
     主詞   動詞   受詞
   （Chang (2011)分析了2000至2010年間與跌倒有關的傷害案例。）

(6) Chang (2011) has published his results of fall-related injury cases during 2000 to 2010
     主詞   動詞   受詞
in *Ergonomics*.
   （Chang (2011)在Ergonomics （期刊名）發表了他在2000至2010年間與跌倒有關傷
害案例的結果。）

以上二句可連成一個句子：

Chang (2011) analyzed the fall-related injury cases during 2000 to 2010 and has published
his results in *Ergonomics*.
fall-related injury cases during 2000 to 2010在兩個句子中均出現，因此合併句後面即當
省略。

(7) Drones can reduce the degree of physical risk for rescuers locating
     主詞   動詞   受詞
missing people in hostile environments.
   （無人機可以降低在敵方環境下定位失蹤人員的救難者的身體風險程度。）

4. 主詞+完全及物動詞+受詞1+受詞2

(1) The research personnel gave the subjects an instruction.
   主詞   動詞 受詞1 受詞2
（研究人員給受測者一個指示。）

  若人是受詞2則其前面需要介系詞：

(2) The research personnel gave an instructionto the subjects.
   主詞   動詞 受詞1 受詞2

5. 主詞+不完全及物動詞+受詞+受詞補語

(1) Murphy (1998) established a statistical model with three assumptions.
 主詞   動詞   受詞   受詞補語
 （Murphy (1998)建立了一個有三種假設的統計模式。）

(2) Li et al. (2007) conducted a research to study the factors affecting floor
 主詞   動詞 受詞

slipperiness on workplaces.
   受詞補語
 （Li et al. (2007)進行一項研究來探討影響工作場所地板滑溜性的因子。）

(3) The authors found the phenomenon interesting.
  主詞動 詞受詞 受詞 補語
 （作者發現這個現象很有趣。）

以上二句可以連起來，把第二句的The authors改成They讀起來比較順：

 Li et al. (2007) conducted a research to study the factors affecting floor slipperiness on workplaces. They found the phenomenon interesting.

(4) Murphy (1998) established a statistical modelto describe the
 主詞   動詞 受詞

relationship between variables A and B.
    受詞補語
 （Murphy (1998)建立了一個統計模式來描述變數A與B之間的關係。）

(5) Wang (2013) reported a time series model to predict the demand of

　　主詞　　　　　動詞　　受詞

smartphone in the Asian market.

　　　　　受詞補語

（Wang (2013)報導了一個時間序列模式來預測智慧型手機在亞洲市場的需求。）

3-2　適當的字彙與例句

1. research, study, investigation 三者均可用來表示「研究」之意；前兩者可用於任何類型的研究，investigation則常用在有蒐集數據、加以分析並產生結果的研究，不蒐集數據只做純理論推演的研究則較少用。另外，research為不可數名詞，沒有複數的形式；study與 investigation為可數名詞，複數時字尾要以ies及加s顯示：

(1) In this study, a general method for finding the optimal hierarchy is developed.

In this research, a general method for finding the optimal hierarchy is developed.

（本研究開發了一個找到最佳層級的一般方法。）

(2) In a previous study, Culver and Viano (1990) determined the size, orientation and relative position of body segments of seated occupants.

In a previous research, Culver and Viano (1990) determined the size, orientation and relative position of body segments of seated occupants.

In a previous investigation, Culver and Viano (1990) determined the size, orientation and relative position of body segments of seated occupants.

（在之前的一項研究中，Culver與Viano (1990)決定了坐姿乘坐者的尺寸方位與身體部位的相對位置。）

(3) Much research has been done in examining the performance of positioning task under various visual display environments.

Many studies have been done in examining the performance of positioning task under various visual display environments.

Many investigations have been done in examining the performance of positioning task under various visual display environments.

（關於檢驗在各種視覺環境下定位作業的績效，已經有許多研究被執行了。）

2. researcher 與investigator均可用來表示「研究員」，research personnel為研究人員（包括所有參與研究的工作人員）；研究（計畫）的主持人則以principal investigator（簡稱P.I.）表示，共同主持人與協同主持人稱為co-principal investigator，簡稱co-PI；研究中被研究的人稱為(human) subject（受測者或研究對象），若已說明是研究的參與，subject也可以participant（參與者）代替：

(1) Parng (1988) is the only researcher who has separated the four interface components.

Parng (1988) is the only investigator who has separated the four interface components.

（Parng (1988)是唯一將四種介面元件分開的研究員。）

(2) Dr. Wang was the principal investigator of this research project.

（Dr. Wang是這項研究計畫的主持人。）

(3) The human subjects completed the experiment in the presence of the research personnel.

（受測者在研究人員面前完成了實驗。）

(4) All the subjects were paid NT100 per hour for their participation in the study.

All the participants were paid NT100 per hour for their participation in the study.

（所有受測者參與本研究都可得到每小時新臺幣100元的報酬。）

3. draft是「草稿」，而manuscript則指「稿件」，draft通常會再經過修改而成為可發表的manuscript。

(1) An article has been published based on a draft previously prepared.

（一篇根據之前準備的草稿而產生的文章已經被發表了。）

(2) This manuscript has been revised according to the questions and comments from the reviewers.

（這份稿件已經按照審查委員的問題與意見加以修改了。）

(3) Manuscripts which have been published elsewhere will not be accepted for publication.

（已經在其他地方發表過的稿子將不會被接受發表。）

4. 「研究計畫」英文為research project；進行研究計畫之前應該先撰寫研究計畫書 "research proposal"：

> (1) The National Science Council supports many research projects every year.
>   （國家科學委員會每年都贊助許多研究計畫。）
>
> (2) All the researchers were requested to work out their research proposals in two weeks.
>   （所有的研究員都被要求在兩週內完成他們的研究計畫書。）

5. 計畫書或稿件等文件的提出或投稿可用submit（動詞）或submission（名詞）表示：

> (1) The applicants need to submit their research proposals by December 31.
>   （申請人必須在十二月三十一日前提交他們的研究計畫書。）
>
> (2) An electronic version of the text should be submitted together with the final hardcopy of the manuscript.
>   （一份文字的電子版本（檔）應該與稿件的最後書面版本一併提交。）
>
> (3) Submission of an article implies that the work described has not been published previously and is not under consideration for publication elsewhere.
>   （文章的投稿暗示其內容以前未被發表過，也未被其他處所考慮出版中。）

6. 稿件或計畫書通常須經過審查(review)；審查者（委員）為reviewer或referee；一般學術審查是以同儕審查（即學者之間相互審查或peer review）為主：

> (1) Two reviewers will review these research proposals to determine the acceptance of the projects.
>   兩位審查委員將會審查這些研究計畫書來決定是否接受計畫。
>
> (2) Both of the two reviewers recommended acceptance with minor modifications.
>   兩位審查者都建議在小幅度修改後接受刊登。
>
> (3) The editor will determine whether to accept the manuscript for publication based upon the recommendations from the two referees.
>   主編會根據兩位審查委員的建議來決定是否接受稿件的刊登。
>
> (4) A commitment to peer-reviewed publication is at the heart of the Center's ongoing mission.
>   本中心進行中任務的核心就是對於同儕審查出版品發表的承諾。

7. literature 為「文獻」之意，為不可數名詞，不可使用複數型式；所有的論文都應該包括文獻的探討，文獻探討可用literature review表示：

(1) Surprisingly, however, reviews of the literature indicate that research on the factors that influence warning comprehension and memory is scarce (Young & Wogalter, 1990).
但是，另人驚訝的是文獻探討的結果顯示影響（人對）警示理解與記憶的因子方面的研究很少見(Young & Wogalter, 1990)。

(2) Similar results have been reported in the literature (Chang and Matz, 2001, Li et al., 2004).
類似的結果曾經被文獻報導過(Chang and Matz, 2001, Li et al., 2004)。

8. 研究或實驗的執行可用perform 或conduct 來表示，因為研究是被研究人員執行的，所以通常用被動的形式表達：

(1) Two studies were conducted to determine the adequacy of display/control gain as a metric for characterizing a control-display interface consisting an LCD display and a separate input device.
兩項研究被執行來決定顯示／控制增量在當做包含一個液晶顯示與一個分離輸入裝置的控制－顯示介面量化尺度的足夠性。

(2) The study was conducted in the laboratory.
The study was performed in the laboratory.
本研究是在實驗室中進行的。

(3) Li et al. (2004) conducted a research to investigate the floor slipperiness of ten western style fast-food restaurants in Taiwan.
Li 等學者(2004) 執行了一項研究來調查臺灣十家西式速食店的地板的滑溜性。

9. interview為訪問或訪談；訪問者（研究人員）為interviewer，而受訪者為interviewee，受訪者即為研究之subject：

(1) The interviewer explained the purpose of the study to the subjects before the interviews began.
訪問者在訪談開始之前向受測者解釋研究的目的。

(2) The interviewee was interviewed on a one-on-one basis.
受訪者是在一對一的方式下被訪問的。

10. 問卷調查或訪談通常都是用匿名的方式進行的以保障受訪者的隱私與個人權益，「匿名的」可用 anonymously（副詞）或anonymous（形容詞）表示：

> (1) The participants were interviewed anonymously.
> 參與者以匿名的方式接受訪問。
>
> (2) The comments from the two anonymous reviewers were very helpful.
> 兩位不具名的審查委員的意見非常有幫助。
>
> (3) The authors acknowledge the constructive suggestions for manuscript revision made by the editor and two anonymous referees.
> 作者感謝編輯與兩位匿名的審查委員對稿件修訂所提出具有建設性的建議。

11. informed consent 為「（書面）同意書」，許多涉及人員受測者的研究在進行前必需先取得受測者的書面同意方可開始進行。

> (1) All the subjects signed informed consent before they participated in the experiment .
> 所有的受測者在參與實驗前都簽署了書面同意。

12. confidential 為「隱私的、隱密的」，名詞為confidentiality：

> (1) All data obtained in this project will be kept confidential. Individual identifying information will not be disclosed in reports or publications resulting from the study .
> 本計畫的數據與資料都將被機密的保存，個人的識別資訊將不會在報告或者出版品中揭露。

13. randomized（隨機化的）或random（隨機的）常用於實驗順序或研究過程的安排，random（形容詞）、randomized（形容詞）、randomly（副詞）或randomization（名詞）通常暗示每種狀況出現的機率是相同的；arbitrary（隨意的）則用於一般非特定的敘述，此字沒有任何機率方面的含意：

> (1) A simple random sample of workers is selected. （○）
> A simple arbitrary sample of workers is selected. （✕）
> 一個簡單隨機的工人樣本被選取了。
>
> (2) A two-factor randomized experiment was conducted. （○）
> A two-factor arbitrary experiment was conducted. （✕）
> 一個兩因子隨機化的實驗被執行了。

(3) The employees were selected arbitrarily to join the project.

員工被隨意的（可能是隨便指派的）選出來參與這項計畫。

(4) The employees were selected randomly to join the project.

員工被隨機的（可能用抽籤或查亂數表的方式）選出來參與這項計畫。

(5) The work-in-process components were inspected randomly.

加工中的零件被隨機的檢驗。

(6) The work-in-process components were inspected arbitrarily.

加工中的零件被隨意的檢驗。

14. 許多研究都是根據一些基本的假設來做的，這些「假設」為assumption，其動詞為assume；另外，有些假設在研究中要以統計方法來決定是否成立，這類的假設為hypothesis（複數hypotheses）；hypothetical為「假設的」：

(1) This research was based on three assumptions.

本研究是根據三項假設來做的。

(2) It was assumed that linear relationship exists between the two variables.

假設線性關係存在於兩個變數之間。

(3) The hypothesis that the mean wage of female employees was not less than those of the males was rejected. In other words, the wages of the females were less than those of the males.

女性員工的平均薪資不少於男性的假設被否絕了；換句話說，女性的薪資是少於男性的。

(4) Three hypotheses were tested in this study.

本研究檢定了三項假設。

(5) A hypothetical model was adopted to simulate the operation of the assembly line.

一個假設的模式被用來模擬裝配線的運作。

15. theory為「理論」，theorem 則是可以經由公式推導證明成立的「定理」；「理論上的」為theoretical：

(1) The applicability of this theorem was discussed in the article.

本文討論了這個定理的應用性。

(2) One might ask how large a savings can be achieved in theory by the forgoing methods.

One might ask how large a savings can be achieved theoretically by the forgoing methods.

有人可能會問，理論上用前述的方法可以達到多大的節省。

(3) There is no theoretical upper bound on the optimal number m.
最佳m數並無理論上的上限。

16. 「差異」可用difference或者discrepancy表示；兩個項目之間之直接數據比較常用前者，discrepancy表示差異但常有矛盾的意思在內；difference 可表各種大小不同的差異，但discrepancy通常表示差距較明顯的差異；variation的意思是「變異」或「變化」，它可能發生在不同項目間，也可能發生在同一項目（的不同情況）上：

(1) The difference between males and females is not obvious.
男性與女性間的差異不明顯。

(2) The reason for the discrepancies between the two studies was unknown.
兩項研究間矛盾的原因並不清楚。

(3) Variations of product quality among the batches should be strictly monitored.
批量間產品品質的變異（化）應該嚴格的被監測。

17. illustrate、demonstrate 都是「說明」的意思，可交換使用；若有「解釋」的意思可以用explain代替：

(1) These findings demonstrate the possible effects of feedback and error correction on speech input tasks with a short-term memory component.
These findings illustrate the possible effects of feedback and error correction on speech input tasks with a short-term memory component.
這些發現說明了在有短期記憶的成分下回饋與錯誤修正對於語音輸入工作的可能影響。

(2) Moore (1972) demonstrated the squeeze-film effect between two neighboring surfaces using the following equation.
Moore (1972) illustrated the squeeze-film effect between two neighboring surfaces using the following equation.
Moore (1972) explained the squeeze-film effect between two neighboring surfaces using the following equation.
Moore (1972)用以下的公式說明（解釋）兩個鄰接平面間的薄膜壓縮效應。

3

18. significantly（顯著的）在學術論文中專指具有統計上的顯著性，多數的情況下，在肯定的敘述句中其後必須緊接統計之顯著水準（如p<0.001），若要表達同類的意思又沒有統計上的依據則可使用obviously（顯然的）、apparently（顯然的）或者clearly（清楚的）：

> (1) Type A and type B were apparently different.（✗）
>
> Type A and type B were significantly (p<0.05) different.（○）
>
> A型與B型是顯著(p<0.05)不同的。
>
> (2) Significantly, algorithm A is better than algorithm B.（✗）
>
> Apparently, algorithm A is better than algorithm B.　（○）
>
> Obviously, algorithm A is better than algorithm B.（○）
>
> 顯然的，A演算法比B演算法好。

19. significantly、obviously、apparently 三者均為副詞，若用形容詞則將字尾的ly去掉即可：

> (1) The difference between specimen A and specimen B was significant (p<0.05)（○）
>
> The difference between specimen A and specimen B was apparent (p<0.05).　（✗）
>
> The difference between specimen A and specimen B was obvious (p<0.05).（✗）
>
> The difference between specimen A and specimen B was clear (p<0.05).（✗）
>
> A樣本與B樣本間的差異是顯著的(p<0.05)。
>
> (2) It was obvious that route A provided better results than route B.（○）
>
> It was apparent that route A provided better results than route B.　（○）
>
> It was significant that route A provided better results than route B.（✗）
>
> 顯然A途徑比B途徑提供了較佳的結果。
>
> The superiority of model A was apparent.（○）
>
> The superiority of model A was obvious.（○）
>
> The superiority of model A was significant.（✗）
>
> A模式的優越性是很顯然的。
>
> (3) It is clear that this ratio approaches 100% as a maximum.
>
> 很清楚的是這個比率會趨近100%這個上限。

20. 雖然意思相同，affect 為動詞、effect為名詞，兩者不可混淆：

(1) The aging effects on the operating behaviors of the subjects were not clear.
   年齡老化對於受測者操作行為的影響並不清楚。

(2) Age is believed to affect the operating behaviors of the subjects.
   我們相信年齡會影響受測者的操作行為。

21. standard 通常指由特定機構發布的「標準」，如CNS、BSI、ASNI、ISO等標準，達到標準當然是比較好的狀況，未達標準則需加以改善；criterion（複數為criteria）是提供判斷或決定的「準則」，依準則決定的情況並無「好」或「不好」方面的暗示：

(1) A measured static COF of 0.5 was adopted as a safety standard in the USA.
   量測之靜摩擦係數0.5已被美國採用做為安全的標準。

(2) The footwear pad slip/non-slip judgment criterion between repetitive strikes followed the recommendations by Chang (2002).
   在重複的撞擊間鞋材測試片是否滑動的判斷準則是依據Chang (2002)的建議（進行的）。

(3) Some criteria must be established to determine whether to buy or to make.
   有些準則必須被建立來決定究竟應該外購或者自製。

22. quantitative是量化的，而qualitative則是質化的：

(1) Quantitative analysis was performed for these data.
   這些數據都以量化分析處理。

(2) Three qualitative variables were used to represent the three conditions in the experiment.
   三個質化的變數被用在實驗裡來代表三種情況。

23. comparable 是「可比較的」，comparative則是「比較的」：

(1) The results from the two experiments were not comparable.
   兩個實驗的結果是無法比較的。

(2) Comparative discussion was described in the following paragraph.
   比較性的討論敘述於下一節中。

24. between用於兩者之間的比較，超過兩者之間之比較則應among：

(1) The difference between the two samples was tested using a X^2 test.
兩個樣本間的差異是用卡方檢定來檢驗的。

(2) The difference among the workers was assumed to be negligible.
工人間的差異假設是可以忽略的。

25. empirical（根據經驗的）與experienced（有經驗的）意思不同，不可混淆：

(1) All the participants were experienced construction workers.
所有的參與者都是有經驗的營建工人。

(2) Empirical attempt has been made to identify the optimal hierarchy associated with a given set of function.
根據經驗的嘗試曾被用來找出在給一組函數下的最佳層級。

(3) Some empirical equations obtained from dimensional analysis of experimental results were summarized in Table 2.
表2整理了一些由實驗結果之因次（尺寸）分析所得之經驗公式。

26. equipment是直接可以使用的「設備」；apparatus 是「裝置」代表研究人員必須加以組裝、連結、安排之後才能使用者；device 是較簡單的equipment「儀器」；gauge 與meter則是最簡單的量表或量具：

(1) Most new manufacturing equipment, which once had only program logic controllers, now requires increasing amounts of computing power.
大部分新的製造設備，過去曾經只有程式邏輯控制器，現在需要愈來愈大的計算能力。

(2) The layout of the apparatus was shown in Figure 1.
研究裝置的布置顯示於圖1。

(3) Two commonly used friction measurement devices were used in the study.
本研究使用兩種常用的摩擦量測儀器。

27. condition 指特定的「狀況」，而situation則指非特定的「情況」，兩者是不同的：

> (1) The experimental conditions were under the control of the research personnel. （○）
>
> The experimental situations were under the control of the research personnel. （✗）
>
> 實驗的狀況在研究人員的控制之下。
>
> (2) Practical situations may be quite different from the experimental scenario of the current study. （○）
>
> Practical conditions may be quite different from the experimental scenario of the current study. （✗）
>
> 實際的情況可能會與本研究的情節相當的不同。

28. imply是「暗示」或「意味」的意思，名詞為implication；reveal則是「顯示」或「透露出」之意：

> (1) This implies that temperature was not an important factor in the experiment.
>
> 這意味著溫度在實驗中不是一個重要的因子。
>
> (2) The implication was that temperature was not an important factor in the experiment.
>
> 得到的暗示是溫度在實驗中不是一個重要的因子。
>
> (3) This reveals that temperature was not an important factor in the experiment.
>
> 這顯示溫度在實驗中不是一個重要的因子。

29. function當名詞時可解釋為功能、功用或函數，做為函數使用時應有至少一個數學式與其對應；function也可當做動詞，意思是「發揮功能」：

> (1) The probability distribution of y is often called the probability density function for y.
>
> y 的機率分布通常稱為y的機率密度函數。
>
> (2) The new machine has many powerful functions.
>
> 新機器有許多強大的功能。
>
> (3) The new machine did not function well in the past two weeks.
>
> 新機器在過去兩週功能發揮的不太好。

30. result與outcome 均爲結果之意，常可交換使用；有時敘述自己或他人的結果也可以使用finding（發現）；output 爲輸出或產出，不適合用來表示研究結果：

(1) The experimental results showed that both temperature and humidity affected the dependent variable significantly (p<0.05).
實驗的結果顯示溫度與濕度兩者都顯著的(p<0.05)影響應變數。

(2) The outcomes of the study indicated that both temperature and humidity were important factors affecting the dependent variable.
研究結果指出溫度與濕度兩者都是影響應變數的重要因子。

(3) The findings of Smith (2002) were not consistent with the results of the current study.
Smith (2002)的發現與本研究的結果並不一致。

(4) Based on the results of the experiments, there appears to be a strong positive correlation between the apparatus outputs and human experiment outcomes.
根據各項實驗的結果，似乎在儀器的輸出值與人類實驗結果間存在著強烈的正相關的關係。

(5) These findings illustrate a general problem faced by the designers of speech interfaces.
這些發現說明聲音介面設計者普遍會面臨的一個問題。

31. opportunity與chance 均可解釋成「機會」，但正式的文件中較少使用chance而較常使用opportunity：

(1) The subjects had the chance to practice before the experiment.（✕）
The subjects had the opportunity to practice before the experiment.（○）
受測者在實驗前有機會練習。

(2) There is a vast chance for new approaches of tackling this area.（✕）
There is a vast opportunity for new approaches of tackling this area.（○）
有很大的機會來針對這個領域開發新方法。

32. about與approximately 均可解釋成「大約」、「近似」，但正式的文件中較少使用about 而較常使用approximately：

(1) The appearances of the two samples were about the same.（✕）
The appearances of the two samples were approximately the same.（○）
兩個樣本的外觀幾乎是相同的。

(2) The times to complete the process for the two machines are about the same. （✕）

The times to complete the process for the two machines are approximately the same. （○）

兩臺機器完成這個製程所花的時間幾乎是一樣的。

33. appropriate與proper 均可解釋成「適當的」，但使用appropriate 比較正式些；同樣的道理improper與inappropriate「不適當的」比較起來後者較為正式，指物件的是否適當也可用suitable或unsuitable：

(1) It is not proper to use A as an indicator. （✕）

It is improper to use A as an indicator. （✕）

It is not appropriate to use A as an indicator. （○）

It is inappropriate to use A as an indicator. （○）

用A當作指標是不適當的。

(2) Various measures of performance are proper for this stage of analysis. （✕）

Various measures of performance are appropriate for this stage of analysis. （○）

不同的績效量度對於這個階段的分析都是適當的。

(3) This study provides valuable information for shoe designers in designing suitable female footwear concerning slip resistance and muscular load on the lower legs. (Li, in press)

本研究提供了鞋類設計師在考量抗滑性與小腿肌肉負荷之適當女鞋設計上很有價值的資訊。

(4) Figure 1 shows the general algorithm suitable for creating a subroutine for any modern type of CNC control. (Abbas, 2003)

圖1顯示了適合建立任何現代化CNC控制之次程序之一般演算法。

「適當的」若是當作副詞修飾動詞時，應使用properly：

(5) A variable lead-time can be accurately modeled if the delay is properly implemented, using a unique state variable to represent work-in-process (WIP).

如果延遲是適當的被導入－使用一個獨特的狀態變數來代表半成品，一個可變的前置時間的模式就能夠準確的被建立。

34. determine與decide 均爲決定之意，但是在技術文件中前者較爲常用：

(1) The function and performance of a product may be decided by an evaluation research. （╳）

The function and performance of a product may be determined by an evaluation research. （○）

一個產品的功能與操作表現可用評估研究來決定。

(2) Blade sharpness was decided by calculating the average of the down ward component of the cutting force over the entire test period. （╳）

Blade sharpness was determined by calculating the average of the down ward component of the cutting force over the entire test period. （○）

刀鋒的鋒利度是由計算整個測試期間向下切割力量的平均值來決定的。

(3) The Research Center aims to decide the causes of accidents and injuries and then proceeds to identify and validate interventions. （╳）

The Research Center aims to determine the causes of accidents and injuries and then proceeds to identify and validate interventions. （○）

研究中心致力於決定事故與傷害的成因進而找出並驗證介入事故與傷害預防的方法。

35. question與problem中文均爲「問題」之意，但是兩者是截然不同的；question是需要回答的問題，例如：How many subjects did you used in the experiment? 此爲一question 但不是一個problem。我們常聽到的青少年問題、社會問題、老人問題、機器的問題等均爲problem而非question。在對應的動詞上，需要回答（answer）的是question而需要解決（solve）的則是problem。

(1) The make-or-buy decision question is an interesting one because of its many dimensions. （╳）

The make-or-buy decision problem is an interesting one because of its many dimensions. （○）

由於問題的多向度特性，製作或買的決策問題是很有趣的。

(2) Any machine question should be reported to the supervisor immediately. （╳）

Any machine problem should be reported to the supervisor immediately. （○）

任何機器的問題均應立即報告領班。

(3) Slipping and falling are major occupational safety and health questions. （✗）

Slipping and falling are major occupational safety and health problems. （○）

滑跤與跌倒是主要的職業安全與健康的問題。

(4) The question to be answered is "Can the workers accomplish their tasks without using this tool?" （○）

The problem to be answered is "Can the workers accomplish their tasks without using this tool?" （✗）

需要回答的問題是「工人們能夠不用這個工具來完成它們的工作嗎?」

(5) One hundred man-years had been expended by the OR community in solving the minimum make-span scheduling questions. （✗）

One hundred man-years had been expended by the OR community in solving the minimum make-span scheduling problems. （○）

OR 領域的人已經消耗了一百人－年的資源在解最小工作時距的排程問題上。

36. 問卷調查的問卷是 "questionnaire" ，不可用 "a list of questions" 或 "a set of questions" ，一般的問卷調查也稱爲survey：

(1) Both basic and applied research frequently rely on surveys or questionnaires to measure variables.

基礎與應用研究都常仰賴問卷調查來量度許多變數。

(2) A questionnaire is a set of written questions or scales used for both experimental and descriptive research.

問卷是使用在實驗性與敘述性研究上的一組書面的問題或量度。

(3) The attitudes of the employees were measured using a list of questions. （✗）

The attitudes of the employees were measured using a questionnaire. （○）

員工的態度是用一份問卷來量度的。

(4) Questions are commonly used to measure people's attitudes and behavior. （✗）

Questionnaires are commonly used to measure people's attitudes and behavior. （○）

問卷常被用來量測人們的態度與行為。

(5) Answers to the questions would be quantified and submitted to statistical analysis. （✗）

Answers to the questionnaire would be quantified and submitted to statistical analysis. （○）

問卷的答案將會被量化並進行統計分析。

3

37. method（方法）、methodology（研究方法）與approach（研究途徑）：前二者用以說明研究的具體方法與過程，一般研究方法的敘述都用前二者；而approach則是強調探討問題之過程或是研究問題的思考方向：

> (1) Current OR-based approaches are either too simple in their assumptions or too complex to be readily solved or implemented. (Suri, 1988)
> 現行以OR為基礎的思考方向不是在假設上太過於簡單就是在解題與執行上太過於複雜。
>
> (2) Perhaps the solution lies in finding simple scheduling approaches that work well under these new conditions.(Suri, 1988)
> 或許解決之道在於找出能在這些新的情況下很好用的簡單排程的方式。
>
> (3) The American approach to dealing with large complex manufacturing operations has been to adopt material requirements planning (MRP) and manufacturing resource planning (MRP II).(Suri, 1988)
> 美國處理大型複雜製造作業的方式是採用物料需求計畫(MRP)與製造資源計劃(MRP-II)。
>
> (4) There are two approaches in establishing risk adjusted reorder points, depending on whether stockout costs are known or unknown.
> 視缺貨成本為已知或未知，有兩種建立經風險調整過之訂貨點的方式。
>
> (5) The method (methodology) of the study is described in Section 2.（○）
> The approach of the study is described in Section 2.（✕）
> 本研究的方法描述於第二節中。
>
> (6) Three different approaches to lead-time modeling are analyzed: first order delay, third order delay, and pure delay.（○）
> Three different methods to lead-time modeling are analyzed: first order delay, third order delay, and pure delay.（✕）
> 一階延遲、三階延遲及純延遲等三種不同方式的前置期模式的建立被加以分析。

38. 在敘述多種對象或項目的數字時，數字與其對應的項目間常用respectively（個別的）來連結。例如：

> (1) The mean age, stature, and body weight of the subjects were 25.3 yrs, 172.5 cm, and 63.2 kg, respectively.
> 受測者的平均年齡、身高與體重分別為25.3歲、172.5公分及63.2公斤。

(2) The weight of Model A,B, and C were 1.2,1.5, and 0.9 kg, respectively.

A、B、C三型的重量分別為1.2、1.5及0.9 kg。

(3) The mean (±S.D.) muscular discomfort scores for the three wires were 4.53 (±1.57), 5.17 (±1.32), and 5.63 (±1.22), respectively.

三種鐵絲下肌肉不適分數的平均值(±標準差)分別為4.53 (±1.57)、5.17 (±1.32)、及5.63 (±1.22)。

(4) The temperature and relative humidity during the measurements averaged 28.01℃ (±2.24) and 61.1% (±6.38), respectively.

量測期間的溫度與相對溼度的平均值分別為28.01℃ (±2.24)及61.1% (±6.38)。

(5) The means (±S.D.) of age, length of tenure, and working hour per week of the participants were 22.55 (±5.94) years, 13.12 (±13.28) months, and 37.86 (±9.55) hours, respectively.

參與者的平均(±標準差)年齡、任職時間與每週工時分別為22.55 (±5.94) 歲、13.12 (±13.28)月與 37.86 (±9.55)小時。

39. synchronize為「同步化」，名詞為synchronization：

(1) The two systems were synchronized using a photocell switch .
兩個系統是以一具光電開關來加以同步化（使同步運轉）。

(2) Synchronization of the two systems was achieved using a photocell switch.
兩個系統的同步化是以一具光電開關來達成的。

40. refer to為「指」，或者「關於」，名詞reference是指文獻的來源或出處：

In this paper, fatigue refers to the after-effects of the working day and working week on mood, performance, and physiological measures.
本文中，疲勞是指一天或者一週的工作之後人員在心情上、績效上、及生理上之量度值。

🔍 3-3 避免長句子

　　長句子通常不易閱讀，寫作時應該避免。在 A4 或 letter 的文件上，句子的長度宜以一至二行爲宜（以字級 12 級爲例），超過三整行的句子則爲長句子，應該將之分爲兩個以上的句子來敘述。

　　避免長句子的重要原則就是一個句子只敘述一件事情，盡量少用 and 來連接子句，以便文句精簡易讀。

> Mechanical engineers must study the properties of metals and alloys and must have an understanding of their behavior under stress and strain, expansion and ontraction, and friction, and the ways in which they can be changed by heat treatment.（季健，2002）
>
> 機械工程師必須研究金屬與合金的性質並了解它們在應力／應變、膨脹／收縮、摩擦下的行為與它們在經過熱處理後的改變方式。

1. 這個句子太長，應該至少分爲兩個句子才容易閱讀：

Mechanical engineers must study the properties of metals and alloys. They must have an understanding of these materials' behavior under stress and strain, expansion and contraction, and friction, and the ways in which they can be changed by heat treatment.

2. 第二個句子裡仍然用了太多and，再改爲：

Mechanical engineers must study the properties of metals and alloys. They must have an understanding of these materials' behavior under stress/strain,expansion/contraction, and friction. The ways in which the materials can be changed by heat treatment should also be comprehended.

　　stress/strain 中 expansion/contraction 以 / 取代 and 表示對等的關係。

(1) Applied science, on the other hand, is directly concerned with the application of the working laws of pure science to the practical affairs of life, and to increase human's control over his/her environment, thus leading to the development of new techniques, processes, and machines.（季健, 2002）

另一方面，應用科學是直接關切純科學上工作法則在實際生活的應用，並增加人類對環境的控制；以導致新技術、製程與機器的發展。

此句可改為：

Applied science, on the other hand, is directly concerned with the application of the working laws of pure science to the practical affairs of life. It increases human's control over his/her environment, thus leading to the development of new techniques, processes, and machines.

(2) The main focus of this paper is to present Expert Enhanced Coloured Stochastic Petri Nets (EECSPN) and to show their application in assembly/dis-assembly, assembly/disassembly planning, modeling and representation, parts and operation sequencing, and determination and optimization of a detailed plan.

本文的焦點在於呈現專家擴充顏色的隨機Petri網路並展示它們在組裝/拆卸、組裝/拆卸計畫、模式的建立與展現、零件與作業的排序及一個細部計畫的決定與最佳化上面的應用。

此句太長可改為：

The main focus of this paper is to present Expert Enhanced Coloured Stochastic Petri Nets (EECSPN) and to show their application in the following areas:

- assembly/disassembly
- assembly/disassembly planning
- modeling and representation
- parts and operation sequencing
- determination and optimization of a detailed plan

本文的焦點在於呈現專家擴充顏色的隨機Petri網路並展示它們在以下領域的應用：

- 組裝/拆卸
- 組裝/拆卸計畫
- 模式的建立與展現
- 零件與作業的排序
- 一個細部計畫的決定與最佳化

(3) Materials management is concerned with the flow of materials from suppliers to production and the subsequent flow of products through distribution centers to the customer and is responsible for the planning, acquisition, storage, movement, and control of materials and final products.
物料管理關切的是物料從供應商到生產的流通與後續的產品由配送中心到消費者的流動，並且負責物料與最終產品的規劃、取得、儲存、移動與控制。

此句太長，可修改為：

Materials management is concerned with the flow of materials from suppliers to production and the subsequent flow of products through distribution centers to the customer. It is responsible for the planning, acquisition, storage, movement, and control of materials and final products.

或是：

Materials management is responsible for the planning, acquisition, storage, movement, and control of materials and final products. It is concerned with the materials flow from suppliers to production and the subsequent products flow through distribution centers to the customer.

(4) The alternative that requires the minimum investment of capital and produces satisfactory functional results will always be chosen unless the first incremental cost associated with an alternative having a larger investment can be justified with respect to its incremental benefits. (Degarmo et al., 1984)
需要最小資本投資並產生令人滿意的機能結果的方案通常都會被採用，除非有第一遞增成本之較大投資之方案能夠被證實能產生相關之遞增利益。

此句可改為：

The alternative requiring a minimum investment of capital and producing satisfactory functional results will always be adopted. Exception can be made when the first incremental cost associated with an alternative having a larger investment can be justified with respect to its incremental benefits.

(5) The main objectives of this research were to determine the reasons for speed limit violations through a "self and other" approach, to define the factors underlying the various reasons for speeding, to determine the profile of those that exceed speed limits, and to discuss how the conclusions of these investigations could affect a relevant safety campaign.
(Kanellaidis et al. 1995)
本研究的主要目的在於經由「自我與他人」的方式來決定超速違規的原因、定義不同原因之下超速的因子、決定超過速限下之情境與探討這些調查的結果可能會如何的影響相關的安全活動。

此句太長可改為：

The main objectives of this research were:

• to determine the reasons for speed limit violations through a "self andother" approach,

• to define the factors underlying the various reasons forspeeding,

• to determine the profile of those that exceed speed limits,

• and to discuss how the conclusions of these investigations could affect a relevant safetycampaign.

本研究的主要目的在於：

• 經由「自我與他人」的方式來決定超速違規的原因

• 定義不同原因之下超速的因子

• 決定超過速限下之情境

• 探討這些調查的結果可能會如何的影響相關的安全活動

3-4 避免使用片語

專業技術文件的撰寫，在文字上應該精簡，因此能夠以一個適當的字表示的意思就應該避免使用片語，以避免不必要的增加文字的長度。在以下的例子中，使用左邊的片語不如使用右邊的單字來的精簡：

a large number, a huge number, a lot of, lots of	many
a number of	some
as soon as possible	immediately
at a rapid rate	rapidly
at the present time	now
at the same time	simultaneously
be able to	can
be aware of	know
conduct an inspection of	inspect
give instruction to	instruct
in reference to	regarding
in the near future	soon
prior to	before
on a personal basis	personally
take part in	participate
the majority of	most
make a decision	decide

1. Fifty college students took part in the study. (✗)

   Fifty college students participated in the study. (○)

   五十位大學生參與了本研究。

2. The research personnel cleaned the measurement device after the experiment as soon as possible. (✗)

   The research personnel cleaned the measurement device immediately after the experiment. (○)

   實驗之後，研究人員立即清理了量測器材。

3. A lot of employees reported discomfort on their low back after their works. (✗)

   Many employees reported discomfort on their low back after their works. (○)

   許多員工反應他們工作後感到下背不適。

4. The majority of the participants completed the experiment without difficult. (✗)

   Most participants completed the experiment without difficult. (○)

   大部分的參與者沒有任何困難的完成了實驗。

5. The research personnel conducted an inspection of the device and the experimental layout before the experiment. （✕）

The research personnel inspected the device and the experimental layout before the experiment. （○）

研究人員在實驗前檢查了實驗器材與布置。

6. If one is exposed to a number of these stressors at the same time then this cumulative effect may pose an additional risk. （✕）

If one is exposed to some of these stressors simultaneously then this cumulative effect may pose an additional risk. （○）

如果有人同時暴露在這些壓力源（全部或部份）當中，則此累積性的效應將會增加額外的風險。

3-5　避免語意不清

　　任何句子都必須只有一個清楚而明確的意思，會讓人產生混淆的語句應該避免：「負負得正」型的句子常會使文句的語法與邏輯變得複雜，應該避免使用；若等於的狀況根本不存在時「不小於」應該直接說「大於」。

1. The COF values on the terrazzo floors were not lower than those of the granite floors.

磨石子地板的摩擦係數值不低於花崗岩地板的值。（此句暗示磨石子地板的摩擦係數值可能等於也可能高於花崗岩地板的值。）

如果所有磨石子地板的值都高於花崗岩地板之值的話，此句最好改成：

The COF values on the terrazzo floors were higher than those of the granite floors.

2. All engineers are not required to submit reports.

語意不清，此句的可能意思有以下兩個：

Engineers are not all required to submit reports.

工程師不是全部都要交報告

No engineers are required to submit reports.

沒有一個工程師需要交報告

3. The operator told the supervisor several times he expected an accident.

語意不清，此句的可能意思有以下兩個：

The operator told the supervisor several times that he expected an accident.

操作員告訴主管好幾次，他預期會發生事故。

The operator told the supervisor that several times he expected an accident.

操作員告訴主管，他好幾次都預期會發生事故。

🔍 3-6 使用轉換詞

在撰寫文件時，有時一個敘述之後要立刻呈現與其不同想法的敘述，此時句子內或句子間必須使用具有轉換作用（transition）的字詞、片語或子句以引導後面的敘述。轉換作用可使文句讀起來更加的流暢而易懂。這些有轉換的字詞常放在句首，而使用哪一個連接詞需視前後句子的關係而定。

常見具有轉換作用的字與片語如下：

actually	實際上	as a result of	由於
also	也是	as previously noted	如前所述
and	及	in addition	再者
besides	然後	in other words	易言之
but	但是	for example	例如
consequently	結果	then	然後
finally	最後	so	所以
furthermore	再者	secondly	其次的
however	然而	moreover	再者
indeed	實際的	nevertheless	雖然如此
hence	因此	rather	反之、不如說

1. However, the main problem associated with adding a grinding spindle to a CNC lathe is that the control software is very complicated.(Abbas, 2003)

   然而，在電腦數值控制車床上增加研磨轉軸的主要問題是控制的軟體非常的複雜。

2. Consequently, the distribution of the lead-time can be determined by identifying the distribution of the waiting time.

   結果，前置期的分布能夠由等候時間的分布來辨識決定。

3. Consequently, excessive efforts in studying the best dispatching heuristics in various environments are unnecessary.

   結果，過多的投注於不同環境下最好的配送啓發式方法的研究努力是不必要的。

4. Nevertheless, all dimensions do not have the same significance, or the same impact on operational performance.

   雖然如此，所有的向度對於作業績效並非都有相同的重要性或相同的衝擊。

5. Hence, in order to build the scheduling knowledge base, training examples must have enough information to reveal this property.

   因此，為了建立排程知識資料庫，訓練案例必須擁有足夠的資訊來顯示這種性質。

6. In addition to neural network, some other approaches such as frequency domain transformation and stochastic modeling have been adopted in tackling the issue.

   除了神經網路外，其他方法例如頻率領域轉換與隨機模式也被用來處理這個議題。

Chapter 4
論文與技術報告
之格式與內容

4-1　研究成果與論文發表

　　學術研究的成果的發表形式包括學位論文、研討會論文、期刊論文、技術報告及專利。

1. authorship是著作具名，著作具名的結果是論文作者的標示：包括作者的姓名、排名順序、服務機關、及通訊作者（corresponding author or correspondence author）之聯絡資訊。作者（author）包括第一作者（first author）、共同作者（coauthor）。coauthor包括第二作者及排名之後的其他作者。作者排名應該反應每位作者的相對貢獻，first author當然是最主要的貢獻者，其貢獻通常包括擬定研究主要構想與撰稿；排名第三以後之作者，通常相對貢獻較低，僅針對研究的一部分提出協助；corresponding author是投稿時負責與期刊或研討會的editor聯絡的作者，由於first author對於整個研究的細節最了解，因此由first author擔任corresponding author的情況最普遍，當然作者團隊可以協調任何一人擔任corresponding author。

(1) Authors must meet all four conditions in order to be listed.

Substantial contributions to conception and design, acquisition of data, or analysis and interpretation of data. Drafting the article or revising it critically for important intellectual content. Final approval of the version to be published. Agreement to be accountable for all aspects of the work in ensuring that questions related to the accuracy or integrity of any part of the work are appropriately investigated and resolved.

作者必須滿足以下全部四條件方得掛名：

對於概念與設計、數據獲取、或數據分析與解釋有相當的貢獻，撰稿或在重要的智慧內容方面的修稿，同意最終版本的刊登，同意對於作品各方面牽涉到任何一部分的正確性或誠信之適當調查與解決問題負責。

(2) All authors will be contacted by email at submission to ensure that they are aware of and approve the submission of the manuscript, its content, and its authorship.

投稿時所有的作者都會以email聯繫以確保他們知悉並同意稿件投遞、稿件內容及著作的具名。

(3) The corresponding author is responsible to communicate with the editor concerning the submission of the paper.

通訊作者負責與主編聯繫關於投稿事宜。

(4) The corresponding author takes responsibility for and speaks on behalf of all authors.

通訊作者負責並代表所有作者發言。

(5) The corresponding author should ensure that all authors have seen the final draft of the manuscript before it is published.

通訊作者應確保所有作者在出版前有看過最終版本稿件。

2. affiliation 是「服務機關」，發表學術論文必需標示作者的服務機關，若是在學的學生則為就讀的學校與科系

(1) The authors will be required to provide their full names, the institutional affiliations and the locations, with an asterisk in front of the name of the corresponding author.

作者必須提供姓名全名及服務機關與地點，並在通訊作者的姓名前加一個星號。

3. thesis 是指論文，複數是theses；在美國，博士論文也常用dissertation表示，複數是dissertations.

(1) In academia, a thesis or dissertation is a document that presents the author's research and findings and is submitted in support of candidature for a degree or professional qualification.

在學術界，論文是用來呈現作者的研究成果並且提交做為學位或專業候選人資格的文件。

(2) A thesis is not required for the master's degree in the department.

本系的碩士學位不需要寫論文。

(3) In the USA, an oral defense is a type of final examination for a doctoral candidate. The candidate needs to respond to all the questions and comments properly concerning issue on his/her dissertation.

在美國，口頭辯護（口試）是博士候選人最終的考試的形式之一。候選人必須適當的回應論文中所有議題有關的問題與評論。

4. conference 是一群人聚在一起討論事情之意，學術研討會可稱爲academic conference 或者scientific conference，也常簡稱conference。但要多注意許多其他類型的聚會，例如商品展覽也可稱爲conference。事實上許多國外的大型學術研討會也同時有商品（如儀器設備、應用軟體廠商參展）與人員招募（就業博覽會）的展覽。在美國，球隊的聯盟也稱爲conference，這種conference代表這些隊伍會定期聚會比賽。

(1) An academic conference is a formalized event where researchers present their results in speeches and posters.
學術研討會是研究人員們以演講及海報展示來呈現他們的研究成果的正式場合。

(2) Researchers are encouraged to participate in scientific conferences to share their research findings with others.
研究人員都被鼓勵參與科學的研討會以和他人分享其研究成果。

5. forum 原意是開放空間的意思，後來衍生爲開放討論的空間，國內常翻譯爲「論壇」，許多學術研討會也用forum這個字，forum也常用於大型團體（國際性或全國性）政治、經濟、環保等議題的討論，而這類的討論會往往不限於學術性的討論。

(1) There will be an international forum on global warming which will be held next January.
明年一月將會有一場關於全球暖化的國際論壇。

6. symposium 是古希臘的一種社交活動，參加者聚在一起喝酒並談論或是辯論一些議題，後來衍生爲聚會之意，國內也常翻譯爲「論壇」，許多學術研討會也用symposium這個字；跟forum一樣，symposium也常用於大型團體（國際性或全國性）政治、經濟、環保等議題的討論，而這類的討論會不限於學術性的討論。

(1) An international symposium will be organized for researchers to present their latest findings on the innovation of semiconductor manufacturing technologies.
一項國際性論壇將會被舉辦讓研究人員來發表他們在半導體製造技術創新方面最近的研究成果。

7. theme: 許多conference會訂定研討主題，稱爲theme，主題的範圍可能很廣泛，也可能很特定。

(1) The theme of this conference is "New-era Industrial Engineering and Management Innovation."
本研討會的主題是「新世紀的工業工程與管理創新」。

8. oral presentation：

「口頭報告」之意，這是學術研討會中發表論文最主要的方式。論文發表人通常需製作投影資料，以口頭說明配合投影資料的呈現來敘述研究的內容與成果。一般研討會安排論文發表人口頭報告的時間大約介於十到三十分鐘之間，視發表人的多寡而定。報告之後發表人必需回應現場聽眾所提的問題與意見。國際性學術研討會幾乎都要求以英文投稿、與口頭報告，因此投影資料也必需以英文製作，Microsoft的Powerpoint幾乎是目前絕大部分人使用的簡報製作與顯示的軟體。由於國人大多缺少以英文做口頭報告的經驗，因此若無充分之準備很容易遇到尷尬的場面。

製作Powerpoint投影資料是口頭報告準備工作最重要的一環。Powerpoint投影片的多寡會視大會所提供之報告時間而定，筆者個人的經驗是每一分鐘製作一張投影片，因此若有十五分鐘的報告時間，則製作十五張投影片。投影片的製作應該以文字搭配圖表或相片來呈現較佳的視覺效果。由於報告的時間非常短，因此報告應將重點放在這個研究的目的、方法與成果，論文中的文獻探討通常都省略，討論也只能提出最重要的部分。

資深而且英文底子深的研究人員通常能依投影片的排列而做一個適度的口頭說明，但新進的學者要直接以投影資料做英文的口頭報告往往還有困難。因此，投影片製作完成之後，最好能夠配合投影資料寫個講稿，然後以講稿配合投影片試講，練習試講中若發現投影片太多講不完、太少、或內容必須調整，則必須修改投影片。修改完之後再試講，一直到感覺自己可以從容不迫而很有自信的把整份投影資料說明完畢爲止，若是實在無法不看講稿侃侃而談，則發表人可以攜帶講稿上台備忘，完全照講稿唸是很不好的方式，但也是實在沒有辦法的辦法。口頭報告之前最好也能思考一下聽眾可能提出的問題及如何來回應這些問題，這樣在有人提問題時才不至於手足無措。完成這些工作後，口頭報告的準備工作才告一段落。oral presentation的準備工作流程如下圖所示。

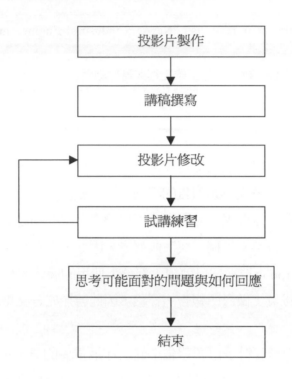

9. poster presentation：

「海報展示」之意，有些學術研討會的論文發表人數過多，無法安排每位發表人做口頭報告，因而安排部分的論文以海報展覽的方式來發表。poster presentation的主要準備工作在於海報的製作。因為篇幅的限制，海報上內容通常都非常的精簡，其設計可以文字搭配圖表以呈現較佳的視覺效果。

研討會的主辦單位通常會規定海報的規格與展示的時段，論文發表人應按照規定的格式製作，並且在預定的時段將海報張貼於指定的位置上。一般的慣例，論文發表人應在海報張貼時段站在海報旁回應參觀者所提的問題與意見。

(1) Poster presentation sessions will be organized to present the most recent research findings in biotechnologies.
海報展示場次將會被安排來呈現生物科技領域最近的研究發現。

10. proceeding 是指「會議記錄」之意，學術會議的紀錄通常主要就是參與者所發表的論文，這種論文即為研討會論文（conference paper）；研討會論文通常是由許多論文集合成冊，因此一般多用複數proceedings，稱為論文集。傳統的研討會的論文集通常以書本的形式出版，現在的論文集多半以隨身碟收錄為主。有些研討會只收錄oral presentation的論文，而有些則oral與poster presentation的論文都收錄到proceedings中。

(1) In academia, proceedings are the collection of academic articles that are published in a conference. They are usually distributed as printed books or compact discs after the conference has closed. Proceedings contain the contributions made by researchers at the conference. They are the written record of the work that is presented to fellow researchers.

   在學術界，論文集是在研討會中發表的學術性的文章的集合，它們通常是在研討會結束後以印刷書籍或是光碟的形式分發給參與者，論文集涵蓋了研究人員在研討會中所做的貢獻，它們是對於同僚呈現研究成果的書面記錄。

11. workshop是「工作場所」或「工作坊」之意，許多研討會也開設小型的workshop，此種workshop是人員培訓的教育訓練課程，在國內通常翻譯成「講習會」，通常必須另外付費參與。

(1) A workshop is a gathering or training session which may be several hours to several days in length. It emphasizes problem-solving, hands-on training, and requires the involvement of the particpants.

   人員培訓講習會是可能長達數小時至數日的人員聚集或訓練的場合。它強調問題的解決與實作，並要求參與者的投入。

12. seminar 是教育訓練課程設計的一種，其實施的方式是由一位主講人對一特定議題提出報告，然後所有的參加者分別針對該議題提出自己的看法與評論，有時參加者必須輪流上台進行報告；seminar國內各學校多半翻譯為「書報討論」。

(1) A seminar is a form of academic instruction, either at a university or offered by a commercial or professional organization. It has the function of bringing together small groups for recurring meetings, focusing each time on some particular subject, in which everyone present is requested to actively participate.

書報討論是學術課程的一種形式，通常由大學或者商業或專業的機構開設。其運作是將小組成員多次聚集，每次聚焦於特定議題的討論，而每位參加者必須主動的參與。

13. technical report 是技術報告，它是公民營機構在完成一項研究之後所做的書面記錄，該記錄內記載了研究的目的、方法、結果與建議。例如研究人員在完成了研究計畫之後必須向委託機關或服務機關繳交之結案報告即為技術報告。在國外，許多機構的技術報告也稱為technical memorandum或技術備忘錄，但許多技術備忘錄不一定是一項研究的記錄，它可能是研究或技術人員針對特定研究或是工程議題所撰寫提供機關內部人員參考或閱讀的文件。

(1) All principal investigators need to submit technical reports upon completion of their research projects.

所有的研究計畫主持人在計畫完成的時候必需提交技術報告。

(2) Some research staffs are responsible for writing technical memorandums.

某些研究人員負責撰寫技術備忘錄。

(3) Technical memorandums are unpublished internal documents within an organization which provide solutions and recommendations for engineering and technical staffs.

備忘錄是組織內部未經正式出版的文件，這些文件提供工程與技術人員解決方法與建議。

14. patent是政府核發的專利，專利申請必須撰寫專利申請之相關文件，文件除了技術與設計方面的專業敘述外還包括法律方面的宣告。

---

(1) The United States Patent and Trademark Office is the government agency responsible for examining patent application and issuing patents.

美國的專利與商標事務局是負責受理專利申請與核發的政府機關。

(2) A design patent application may only have a single claim. Designs that are independent and distinct must be filed in separate applications since they cannot be supported by a single claim.

一項設計專利的申請只能提出一項宣告，互為獨立而不同的設計必需分開來申請專利，因為它們無法由單一宣告來支持。

(3) The term of a new patent is 20 years from the date on which the application for the patent was filed.

一項新專利的期限是自專利申請收件開始計算共20年。

🔍 4-2 論文撰寫的步驟

　　一篇學術論文的撰寫可能需要數個月甚至於數年才能夠完成，文章的撰寫若能依循特定的步驟與原則，應該能夠排除寫作的障礙並提高寫作的效率。以下為投稿期刊論文供讀者參考的步驟，這些步驟是在研究者完成所有的資料與數據分析之後才開始的：

1. 工欲善其事，必先利其器。開始寫作前應先收集寫作需要的所有材料，包括所有的文獻（期刊論文、研討會論文、學位論文、技術報告等；未公開出版的文獻應避免採用）所有的數據分析的結果、所有的圖表、相片等。

2. 選定要投稿的期刊，研讀投稿需知以了解該期刊的題材範圍與撰稿格式與其他要求，收集一、兩份該期刊最近出版的文章以熟悉其格式、篇幅等。

3. 擬訂題目（參考下一節）。

4. 擬訂章節。傳統的論文章節可以分為研究背景與目的、研究方法、研究結果與討論、結論等，每一個部分也可再區分為若干節。

5. 擬訂章節的標題。

6. 開始撰寫。作者可以由某一章開始（不一定是由研究背景與目的開始）。寫作需要靈感，作者可以由自己大腦中最清楚的部分開始寫。只要有靈感，作者可以把任何一章節有關的東西用文字寫下並將其放在該標題之下。例如若讀者剛完成數據分析並且繪了許多的圖表，此時可以先挑出自己覺得最重要的圖表，然後以文字來敘述這些圖表所傳達的訊息，當然這些段落文字可放在研究結果與討論的標題之下；若讀者很清楚研究的方法與過程，此時可以用文字寫下來，這些段落文字可放在研究方法的標題之下。若是撰寫研究背景，則必須不斷的參考所蒐集的文獻，將其精要而相關的部分以自己的文字寫下來。一個章節或段落完成後，繼續進行下一個。記得寫作需要靈感，若是實在寫不出東西就應該去找別的事（例如讀文獻、檢視數據或者運動）做，有靈感的時候再回來寫。作者可能要花費相當長的時間在這個步驟，這個步驟完成時文章的主體應該已然完成了。

7. 檢視圖表的標題與配置是否恰當，進行必要的替換與修改。

8. 開始撰寫摘要。文章的主體完成之後再寫摘要，此時只要將目的、方法、結果、結論等各部分取主要的兩至四個句子加以排列組合再潤飾即可。

9. 整理參考文獻。

10. 全文修飾與潤飾。作者常常在讀每一個版本的稿子時發現不同的內容與文字的問題，因此一篇稿子要自己修改多次，才漸漸的呈現出較為嚴謹而具可讀性的面貌。

11. 請他人修改與潤飾。可請共同作者修改，也可請專業人士做英文文字的編修。

12. 撰寫致謝（acknowledgements）。

以上有些步驟的順序是可以互換的（如 6、7、8），而這些步驟可能要經過多個循環才能夠成就一篇好的文章。在開始寫初稿時不要太注意諸如文法拼字這些小節，這類問題在後續的修改與潤飾再處理即可。

4-3　標題 Title

　　論文的標題通常使用名詞片語或是簡短的句子以顯示這篇文章要介紹或談論的主題，而以片語較為常見。例如：

Ergonomic design and evaluation of wire-tying hand tools 綁鐵絲手工具的人因工程設計與評估	片語
Effects of display resolution on visual performance 顯示解析度對於視覺績效的影響	片語
Locating warehouses in a logistics system 一個後勤系統之倉庫配置	片語
Assessing floor slipperiness in fast-food restaurants using objective and subjective measures 以客觀與主觀評量來評估速食店內地板之滑溜性	片語
Cutting moments and grip forces in meat cutting operations and the effect of knife sharpness 肉品切割作業中切割的力矩、握力與刀鋒利度之影響	片語
Intelligent scheduling controller for shop floor control systems: a hybrid genetic algorithm approach 現場控制系統之智慧排程控制器：一個混合遺傳演算法	片語
What makes internet users visit cyber stores again? 什麼會使得網路的使用者會再次造訪網路商店？	短句
Are body dimensions affecting working posture? 身體的尺吋會影響工作姿勢嗎？	短句

4-4 摘要 Abstract

　　論文或報告的開頭處依慣例必須撰寫摘要，摘要必須以精簡的文字將此論文做一敘述，許多期刊都會規定字數，一般摘要的字數介於 250 到 350 字之間。摘要的內容主要是論文的目的、方法與結果。由於字數的限制，作者必須扼要的說明這些項目，讓讀者讀完摘要後就能夠大致的了解這篇文章討論的內容。摘要後通常需加上三到五個最能顯示這篇文章內容的關鍵字（keywords）或詞。

1. The abstract should state briefly the purpose of the research, the principal results and major conclusions. An abstract is often presented separate from the article, so it must be able to stand alone.
   摘要必須簡要的敘述研究目的、主要的結果與結論。摘要通常必須和文章分開，因此它必須能夠單獨呈現。

(1) Abstract

Using metal wire to tie components together is common on constructionsites. The wire-tying task, accomplished using pliers, involves repetitive forceful exertion and awkward wrist postures. In this research, the use of a powered screwdriver with a specially designed fixture for clamping and twisting metal wires was introduced. The powered driver-fixture combination was proposed as an alternative to the traditionally used pliers for wire-tying tasks. A laboratory experiment to simulate the wire-tying task using two power screwdriver-fixture combinations was performed. The experimental results showed that the normalized EMG of the flexor digitorumsuperficialis muscle and flexor carpi ulnaris muscle of the right arm were significantly reduced when using the powered driver-fixture combinations compared to using pliers. Using the powered driver-fixture combinations requires only 28% of the time to complete each wire-tying compared to using pliers. The numbers of awkward wrist postures, including extension and ulnar deviation were also significantly decreased when using the powered driver-fixture combinations. The subjective response of the subjects, including muscular exertion level, muscular discomfort, ease of use, and total satisfaction all favored the powered driver-fixture combinations, compared to pliers in performing the wire-tying task

Keywords: fixture, hand tool design, wire-tying task (Li, 2003)

4

摘要

使用鐵絲把物件綁起來在營建工地是很常見的，用鉗子進行的鐵絲捆綁作業牽涉到反覆的施力與手部不自然姿勢。本研究介紹了以電動起子配合一個特殊設計可以夾緊並扭轉鐵絲夾具的使用，電動起子-夾具的組合被建議當做傳統上以鉗子來進行綁鐵絲作業的另外一種選擇。研究在實驗室裡執行了一個使用兩種動力起子－夾具模擬綁鐵絲作業的實驗。實驗結果顯示，與使用鉗子相較，使用兩種電動起子－夾具的組合時（受測者）右手臂屈指淺肌與尺側屈腕肌常態化的肌電值會顯著的下降。與使用鉗子相比，使用兩種電動起子－夾具的組合只需要28%的時間即可完成一件綁鐵絲作業。使用兩種電動起子－夾具的組合時，不良的手腕姿勢，包括伸展與尺偏也都顯著的減少。與使用鉗子執行綁鐵絲作業，受測者的主觀反應包括肌肉施力水準、肌肉不適、使用容易性與整體滿意度全部都偏好電動起子－夾具的組合。

關鍵詞：夾具、手工具設計、綁鐵絲作業。

(2) Abstract

A field study was conducted to investigate the sensitivity of human participants in detecting the invasion of a drone in the airspace. A Phantom 4 quadcopter was remotely controlled to hovering at air locations inside or outside of a stadium. Twenty participants were requested to determine whether the drone has invaded in the test field or not on a fiv-point scale. The participants also responded whether they have heard the sound of the drone. The nonparametric measures of the sensitivity of drone invasion detection, or P(A), were calculated. The results indicated that the distance between the drone and the boundary of the airspace significantly affected the P(A) while the effects of drone altitude were not significant. The participants were not unbiased detectors. They tended to respond "probably yes," in general, when they spotted a drone near the airspace. The hearing of the sound of the drone provided partial cues in drone invasion detection.

Keywords: airspace invasion, rating scale task, response bias, signal detection, unmanned aircraft vehicle.

摘要

本研究進行了一項實地研究以調查人類參與者在偵測無人機入侵空域方面的敏感度。一架Phantom4四軸飛行器被遙控懸停在體育場內外的空中位置。20名參與者被要求以五等第評分來判斷無人機是否入侵測試空域。參與者還要回答他們是否聽到無人機的聲音。研究計算了無人機入侵偵測靈敏度(P(A))的無母數量度。結果顯示，無人機與空域邊界之間的距離顯著影響P(A)，而無人機高度的影響不顯著。參與者不是無偏差的偵測者。一般來說，當他們在空域附近發現一架無人機時，他們傾向於回答「可能有」入侵。無人機聲音的聽覺為無人入侵偵測提供了部分線索。

關鍵詞：入侵空域、尺度評分、反應偏差、信號偵測、無人飛行器。

4-5　前緣與研究背景 Introduction&Background

　　一般論文在開頭時應說明研究的背景、為何要做這個研究、此研究有何價值及專業術語的定義。說明這些項目最好的方式就是引用他人的文獻，因此論文的Introduction 常常是以文獻探討為主。在文獻探討時，必須敘述他人的著作；而敘述他人的著作時英文必須使用過去式或過去完成式。但若是他人的研究成果或主張已成為被廣泛接受的公理或普遍存在的現象，則可用現在式。引用文獻必須依原著的意思將句子加以改寫，應避免將原文句子照抄，否則就變成了抄襲了。一個句子的書寫方式有許多種，作者可以多方嘗試來找出最適當的句子。

　　論文或技術報告中常需要引用其他文獻，引用文獻時必需標示該文獻之來源，常見的作法是將作者姓氏或機關名稱（非個人作者）與出版年分標出（如 Leamon, 1992 或 IOSH, 1998）與標示文獻編號（如 [20]），而以前者較為多見，因為標示作者的姓氏乃是對其貢獻的肯定，同時也方便讀者識別；文獻編號標示的方式讓讀者在閱讀時必須參照文後得文獻目錄才能了解作者是誰。若是文章需經過投稿與審查的程序，則文獻的標示必須依照投稿須知的要求來做。

　　引用文獻的標示時，若作者有二人時，則二人的姓氏都必需標明。若作者有兩人以上，通常僅標示第一作者，然後再加上 et al. 表「等」之意。每一被引用之文獻之詳細資料均需列於文件最後的參考文獻中。

al 之後有一句點,但不表示句子的結束。

4

每個句子有多種寫法,請參考以下範例,讀者可自行練習改寫句子。

1. Survey research is "the systematic gathering of information about people's beliefs, attitudes, values, and behavior" (Sommer&Sommer, 1986).（定義）(Sanders & McCormick, 1993)

   問卷研究是「關於人的信念、態度、價值觀與行為的系統化之資訊蒐集」(Sommer與 Sommer, 1986)。此句可改寫為:

   According to Sommer&Sommer (1986), survey research is "the systematic gathering of information about people's beliefs, attitudes, values, and behavior".

   根據Sommer與Sommer (1986)的主張,問卷研究是「關於人的信念、態度、價值觀與 行為的系統化之資訊蒐集」,或改成:

   Sommer&Sommer (1986) indicated that survey research is the systematic data collection about people's beliefs, attitudes, values, and behavior.

   Sommer與Sommer (1986)指出問卷研究是關於人的信念、態度、價值觀與行為的系統 化之資訊蒐集。

2. The term flexible manufacturing system (FMS) has come to denote a computer-controlled group of numerically controlled machines linked by pallet transport and a load-unload system.（定義）(Tipnis, 1988)

   彈性製造系統(FMS)這個名詞被用來代表一個電腦控制棧板傳輸與上下貨系統連結之 數位控制機器組合。此句可改寫為:

   A computer-controlled group of numerically controlled machines linked by pallet transport and a load-unload system may be termed as a flexible manufacturing system (FMS).

   一個電腦控制之與棧板傳輸與上下貨系統連結之數位控制機器組合可以稱為彈性製造 系統 (FMS)

3. The term "work ability" was first introduced in Finland in the 1980s and was defined as: "how good is the worker at present and in the near future, and how able is he/she to do his/her job with respect to work demands, health, and mental resources?" （定義）

「工作能力」這個詞最早是在芬蘭在1980年代被提出並被定義為「工作者目前與未來預期的表現如何，以及工作者自我掌握其工作效能與身、心健康的能力。」

4. Critical path method(CPM) and project evaluation and review technique(PERT) are the two most commonly used approaches in project management.（說明現況）

臨界路逕法(CPM)與計畫評估與審查法(PERT)專案管理最常用的兩種方法。此句可改寫為：

In project management, the two most commonly used approaches are the critical path method (CPM)and project evaluation and review technique (PERT).

在專案管理中，兩種最常用的方法是臨界路逕法(CPM)與計畫評估與審查法(PERT)。

5. Webster's Third International Dictionary of the English Language (1981) defines comfort as a "state or feeling of having relief, encouragement, and enjoyment." （定義）(Zhang et al., 1996)

英文之韋氏第三國際字典（1981）定義舒適為「具有放鬆、支持與享受之狀態或感覺。」此句可改寫為：

Comfort is defined as a "state or feeling of having relief, encouragement, and enjoyment" in the Webster's Third International Dictionary of the English Language (1981). (Zhang et al.,1996)

舒適在韋式第三國際字典（1981）中被定義為「具有放鬆、支持與享受之狀態或感覺。」

6. There are many symptoms associated with MSDs. Frequent muscular fatigue is one of them. Muscular fatigue can be defined as "reduction in the ability to exert force under specific forceful exertion condition." （定義）

有許多症狀與MSDs有關，頻發的肌肉疲勞是其中之一。肌肉疲勞可定義為「在特定施力條件下施展力量能力的下降。」

7. Simulation is the process of creating a representation or model of the operation of a production system on a digital computer. （定義）(Grant, 1988)

模擬是在數位電腦上建立一個生產系統運行之顯示方式或模式的過程。

8. Leamon and Murphy (1995) reported that slips and falls resulted in the second most frequent claims and were the most costly claims in restaurant industries in the USA. （說明問題之重要性）

Leamon與Murphy (1995)報導滑跤與跌倒造成了美國餐飲業第二頻繁與最多支出的保險理賠申請。此句可改寫為：

Slips and falls resulted in the second most frequent claims and were the most costly claims in restaurant industries in the USA (Leamon and Murphy, 1995).

滑跤與跌倒造成了美國餐飲業第二頻繁與最多支出的保險理賠申請(Leamon與Murphy,1995)。或改成：

According to Leamon and Murphy (1995), slips and falls rcsultcd in the second most frequent claims and were the most costly claims in restaurant industries in the USA.

根據Leamon與Murphy (1995)之報導，滑跤與跌倒造成了美國餐飲業第二頻繁與最多之出的保險理賠申請。

9. Research has identified slips or trips as a contributing factor for low back injuries while carrying a load in over 30% of all such cases (Leamon, 1992). （說明問題之重要性）

研究指出滑跤與絆倒在30%的所有的物品搬運而造成了下背傷害中是（主要）貢獻因子(Leamon, 1992)。此句可改寫為：

Slips or trips were identified as a contributing factor for low back injuries while carrying a load in over 30% of all such cases (Leamon, 1992).

滑跤與絆倒被指出是30%的所有的物品搬運而造成了下背傷害中的（主要）貢獻因子(Leamon, 1992)。

10. An epidemiological study of construction workers showed that low back pain was a major health problem among these workers (Damlund et al., 1982). （說明問題的重要性）

一項營建工人的流行病學調查顯示，下背痛是這些工人的主要健康問題。(Damlund et al., 1982)。此句可改寫為：

Damlund et al. (1982) indicated that low back pain was a major health problem among construction workers, according to an epidemiological study.

Damlund等學者(1982)指出，根據一項流行病學調查，下背痛是營建工人主要的健康問題。

11. The results from Chang and Matz (2001) indicated that different samples of the same material could lead to significantly different friction values.（說明文獻之發現）

Chang與Matz(2001)指出相同材料的不同，樣本可能得到顯著不同的摩擦值。此句可改寫為：

According to Chang and Matz (2001), the friction values of different samples of the same material could be different significantly.

根據Chang 與Matz(2001)的結果，相同材料不同，樣本的摩擦值可能會顯著的不同。或改成：

The friction values of different samples of the same material could be different significantly (Chang and Matz, 2001).

相同材料的不同，樣本的摩擦值可能會顯著的不同（Chang 與Matz, 2001）

12. Contaminants such as grease and water are common in the kitchen floors of restaurants.（普遍的現象，不必引用）

諸如水與油污的污染物在餐廳廚房的地板上是常見的。此句可改寫為：

Grease or water contaminated floors are common in the kitchens of restaurants.

被油污或水污染的地板在餐廳的廚房是常見的。

🔍 4-6　研究目的與假設 Objective(s)

在敘述過本研究要探討的問題與相關文獻的介紹之後，作者必須用明確的文字來敘述本研究的目的，目的可用 objective purpose 或是 aim，但以前二者較為常見。

1. The purpose of this study is to develop an automatic LED inspection system which could replace current traditional inspection system.

本研究的目的是要開發一套能夠取代目前傳統檢測系統的自動化LED檢測系統。

2. The purpose of the present research is to develop a concise list of terms that most individuals who are less skilled with the English language are likely to understand.

本研究的目的是要發展一個能為多數非精通英語的人士能夠了解的精確的項目清單。

3. The objective of this study was to identify the ergonomic risk factors related to the musculoskeletal symptoms among the construction workers.
   本研究的目的是要辨識與建築工人肌肉骨骼傷害風險有關的人因工程風險因子。

4. The objective of this study was to assess the slip resistance of four commonly used female shoes in terms of the static COF of the sole materials. (Li, in press)
   本研究的目的是以鞋底材料的靜摩擦係數來評估四種常用女鞋的抗滑性。

5. The aim of this study was to develop an ergonomically designed hand tool for use in the wire-tying task. (Li, 2002)
   本研究的目的是要發展一種用於鐵絲捆綁作業的人因工程設計的手工具。

若是研究有兩項時可以在同一個句子裡用 and 連接；若目的有許多項時則可以用條列的方式來撰寫，但一篇研究報告裡的研究目的最好不要超過五項，以免分散了研究的主題：

1. The purposes of this study are to provide new evidence to consolidate previous findings and to offer guidelines for managers working in this field. (de Cerio, 2003)
   本研究的目的是提供新的證據使過去的研究能發現更為穩固並且提供此領域內之經理人的指引。

2. The research aims are to discover whether the implementation of QM practices has an impact on improvement in operational performance and to identify the areas where the influence is greatest. (de Cerio, 2003)
   本研究之目標在於是否發現品質管理實務的落實以對於作業績效的改善會有衝擊並找出受影響最大的領域。

3. The purposes of this article are to examine (1) performance-importance analysis and (2) customer-driven improvement models. (Garver, 2003)
   本文之目的在於檢驗：(1)績效－重要性分析 (2)客戶牽引改善模式。

4. The objectives of this study were:
   - to measure the COF of five commonly used floor tiles on a university campus under one dry and four liquid-spillage conditions;
   - to measure the roughness of the selected floor tiles;
   - to investigate the perceived floor slipperiness by human subjects for the floor-contaminated conditions; and
   - to discuss the correlations between the measured COF and perceived floor slipperiness. (Li et al., in press)

本研究之目的在於：

- 量測一所大學之五種常用地磚在乾與四種液體濺溢情況下之摩擦係數值。
- 量測選取地磚之表面粗糙度。
- 調查地板一污染情況下受測者對地板滑溜性之認知。
- 討論量測摩擦係數與地板滑溜性認知間的相關性。

5. The goal of this study was to examine the relationship between mouse use and upper extremity musculoskeletal symptoms among computer users. The specific aims were to:

　i　determine whether the prevalence of neck and upper extremity musculosk-eletal symptoms is related to intensity of mouse use (hours per day).

　ii　explore the relationship between musculoskeletal symptoms and individual , postural, psychosocial and organizational risk factors identified in the literature.

　iii　investigate the association between musculoskeletal symptoms and computer mouse usage when risk factors identified as significant in this study are considered. (Cook et al., 2000)

本研究的目標是檢驗電腦的使用者在使用滑鼠時與上肢肌肉骨骼傷害症狀間的關連性。具體而言，本研究的目的在於：

　i　決定頸部與上肢肌肉骨骼傷害症狀的盛行與密集的滑鼠使用是否有關。

　ii　探索肌肉骨骼傷害症狀與文獻上提出的個人、姿勢、社會心理、組織風險因子間的關係。

　iii　當本研究考慮的風險因子被證實為顯著時，調查肌肉骨骼傷害症狀與電腦滑鼠使用的相關性。

不以 objective　purpose 或是 aim 等字眼來說明研究目的情況也有，但比較少見。

1. In this study, a general algorithm has been created that can be used to generate a grinding subroutine suitable for use on a hollow spindle NC lathe.(Abbas, 2003)
本研究建立產生了一個適用於空心軸數值控制車床，研磨程序的一般演算法。

此句可改為：

The objective of this study was to establish a general algorithm that can be used to generate a grinding subroutine suitable for use on a hollow spindle NC lathe. (Abbas, 2003)

2. This paper summarizes the development of the SATRA Friction Test for footwear and floor surfaces, and describes three areas of applications of the test. (Wilson, 1990)

本文簡要的說明了SATRA對於鞋與地板表面摩擦測試的發展,並介紹此測試在三個方面的應用。

此句可以改為:

The purpose of this paper was to summarize the development of the SATRA Friction Test for footwear and floor surfaces, and to discuss three areas of applications of the test.

有些研究的目的是在於檢驗某些研究假設是否成立,此研究假設可以在研究目的之前或之後敘述。

1. The hypothesis of this study was that Machine A generates lower readings as compared to that of the Machine B and the difference between the two machines are more pronounced under high pressure conditions. The purpose of the study was to test this hypothesis.

本研究的假設是與B機器相比,A機器會產生較低的讀數。兩種機器間的差異在高壓力的情況下會更明顯。本研究的目的就是要檢驗這個假設。

2. The purpose of this study was to evaluate the differences in wrist and forearm postures while subjects typed on six different keyboards. The null hypothesis was that there were no differences in wrist extension among keyboard conditions. A secondary null hypothesis was that there were no differences in typing speed among keyboard conditions.

本研究的目的在於評估受測者以六種不同的鍵盤打字時手腕與手臂的差異。研究的虛無假設是不同鍵盤狀況間的(受測者)手腕伸展的情況沒有差異,第二個需無假設是不同鍵盤狀況間的(受測者)打字速度沒有差異。

4-7 研究方法 Method

　　研究方法是說明數據取得的所有相關的訊息,包括研究使用的儀器、設備、材料、參與人員、數據的取得方式與過程、及數據分析的方法;這些項目可以分小節或者分段的方式來說明。某些研究的主要在於發展演算方法或特別的邏輯而不涉及儀器、設備、材料與人員,此類的研究則以說明方法的發展為主:

This study was conducted in 10 western fast-food restaurants in Taiwan. 本研究在臺灣十家西式速食店進行。	調查場所
Work ability was measured by the Work Ability Index (WAI) questionnaire developed by Ilmarinen and his colleagues. 工作能力的量測是採用由Ilmarinen及其同僚開發的工作能力指數(WAI)來進行的	說明工具
The Phantom 4 was operated via a remote controller where an iPhone 6 Plus smartphone was connected as the display panel. Phantom 4是以一具遙控器操作並連接一只iPhone 6 plus 智慧型手機當作顯示板	器材操作
The participants pulled the handle statically during the trials using two hands. The pulling strength was measured using a strength measuring apparatus. 測試時參與者以雙手靜態的拉握把，拉的力量以一副力量測裝置來量測	量測方式與器材
After the strength measurement, the participant put the handle down on the floor and jointed a simulated truck pulling task. 力量量測後，參與者將握把放到地上並參與一項模擬拉車作業	量測過程
A suspension rail was installed overhead to support a safety harness along the walkway to provide safety precautions for the gait. 沿著步道上方安裝了一具懸吊的滑軌來提供步態的安全的預防	說明裝置
Two Brungraber Mark II testers, each operated by only one operator, were used in the friction measurements. 分別由一位操作員操作的兩臺Brungraber Mark II測試器被採用摩擦量測上。	使用量測器材
Themeasurement protocol recommended by Chang (2002) was adopted. 研究採用Chang (2002)建議的量測過程。	採用量測過程
To assess floor slipperiness perceived by the workers, a floor slipperiness survey developed by the research team was conducted at ten restaurants. 為了評估工人認知的地板滑溜性，一個地板滑溜性問卷被研究團隊開發出來並被用在十家餐廳的調查上。	敘述調查項目與方式

Forty females (71.4%) and 16 males (28.6%), out of 58 employees from all the restaurants participated in the survey. 所有餐廳五十八位員工中的四十位(71.4%)女性與十六位(28.6%)男性參與了這項問卷調查。	敘述調查人數與性別
A questionnaire was developed and administer-red to a total of 800 employees in three semi-conductor manufacturers in the Science Park, Hsin-Chu. 一份問卷被開發並在新竹科學園區三家半導體製造公司總計800名員工的調查上。	敘述調查方式與對象
Each subject answered the questions on the survey anonymously. 每位受測者以匿名的方式回答問卷上的問題。	問卷填寫的方式
Descriptive statistics and an analysis of variance (ANOVA) were conducted for the friction measurement data collected. 敘述統計與變異數分析被用在所蒐集到之摩擦量測的數據分析上。	敘述統計方法
Duncan's multiple range tests were performed if significant differences were found in different areas. 如果不同區域間被發現有顯著的不同則會進行Duncan多重全距檢定。	敘述統計方法
Subjective ratings of floor slipperiness were tested using the Kruskal-Wallis test among different areas. 不同區域間地板滑溜性之主觀評比是採用Kruskal-Wallis檢定來分析。	敘述統計方法
Rank-based multiple comparison tests between the areas were also performed to determine if significant results were obtained. 如果得到顯著的結果，則區域間的比較也會以排序基礎的多重比較檢定分析。	敘述統計方法
Regression analyses were conducted to establish the MET models. These models were verified by comparing measured data, predicted data of our models and that of the models in the literature. 迴歸分析被用來建立MET模式，這些模式經由比較量測數據、我們模式的預測值及文獻上模式的預測值來驗證	敘述統計方法

4

Data were electronically collected and converted to a SAS 6.0 format for statistical analysis. 數據是以電子的方式收集並且轉換成SAS 6.0 的格式以供統計分析之用。	敘述數據收集與處理的方法
Aback-propagation technique, aminimum distance algorithm and a maximum likelihood classifier were used in the current study. The performances of these three conventional classification models were compared. 本研究使用了向後擴散技術、最小距離演算法、及最大可能區分法，並比較這三種傳統的分類模式的操作績效。	敘述採用之演算方法與比較
Curves generated by different production lines were randomly selected as system training and testing samples. 本研究隨機的選取了由不同生產線產生的曲線當作系統訓練與測試的樣本。	敘述採用之樣本
A radial segmentation method together with a thinning algorithm was adopted to process the image data of a signature. 簽名影像數據的處理是採用放射區段配合薄化演算法進行的。	敘述採用之影像處理方法
Verification was achieved by examining whether a test signature was within the threshold boundary for a cluster generated. 實證的進行是經由檢驗測試的簽名是否會落在產生叢集的閾值範圍內。	敘述採用之驗證方法

4-8 結果 Results

　　研究結果的部分以敘述本研究所得到的結果爲主。對於量化分析的研究，此部分主要是敘述研究的數據：以文字說明配合圖表呈現（敘述統計）所探討現象的特質；以進階的統計分析（ANOVA 分析、迴歸分析、各種檢定）來呈現研究對象與主題的特質。

1. The mean ($\pm$S.D.) muscular discomfort scores for pliers, B&D-fixture, and Talonfixture tools were 3.83 ($\pm$1.15), 5.50 ($\pm$1.11), and 6.00 ($\pm$1.05), respectively. (Li, 2003)
   鉗子、B&D-夾具及Talon夾具的肌肉不適的平均（$\pm$標準差）分數分別為3.83 （$\pm$1.15）、5.50 （$\pm$1.11）、及6.00 （$\pm$1.05）。

2. The LSD multiple comparison tests showed that the time for the pliers was significantly (p<0.0001) higher than that for the B&D-fixture and the TalonÒ-fixture. The difference between the latter two was not significant. (Li, 2003)

LSD多重比較檢定結果顯示鉗子的時間顯著的(p<0.0001)高於B&D-夾具與TalonÒ-夾具，而後兩者之間的差距則未達到顯著水準。

3. The analysis of variance was executed for the NEMG(%) for the four muscles groups. Significant results were found for both wire and tool factors. The interaction effects for all muscle groups were not significant.

本研究對四個肌群執行了NEMG(%)的變異數分析，鐵絲與工具因子都得到了顯著的結果；所有肌群的交互作用則不顯著。

4. The results of the Kruskal-Wallis test for the surface conditions due to contaminants were significant (p<0.001).

污染物在不同表面狀況下結果之Kruskal-Wallis檢定結果是顯著的(p<0.001)。

5. The rank-based multiple comparison test results indicated that Shoes A and B (both 2.68) were significantly (p<0.05) higher than Shoes C (1.88) and D (2.14).

以排序為基礎的多重比較檢定結果顯示A 與B 鞋（均為2.68）顯著的(p<0.05)高於C鞋(1.88)與D鞋(2.14)。

6. The Spearman's correlation coefficient (r) between the subjective ratings for shoe/floor slipperiness and muscular effort in the right shank was 0.61 (p<0.05).

對鞋/地板間滑溜性的主觀評分與右小腿的肌肉施力間的Spearman's 相關係數(r)為0.61(p<0.05)。

7. The paired-sample t-test shows that the hypothesis is rejected at a significance level of 95% for all control strategies.

成對樣本的t檢定顯示在所有控制策略下，假設在95%之顯著水準下是被拒絕的。

數字的敘述：在常討論到數字之文件裡，一般均直接使用阿拉伯數字。然而要注意，句首不可使用阿拉伯數字，必須使用文字。

1. 136 employees participated in this study.（╳）

One humdred and thirty six empioyees participated in this study.（○）

一百三十六位員工參與了本研究。

一般數字若超過四位以上，由右邊向左每三位要標示一逗點，以利視讀，年代則不可加逗點。

　　若數字小於 10，則句子中應使用文字而不使用數字（與其他單位一起使用或表示特定編號或有小數點時例外），但若文中部分大於 10，部分小於 10，則可統一用阿拉伯數字：

1. Smith (1999) made two assumptions about the distribution of the lead time.（○）
   Smith (1999) made 2 assumptions about the distribution of the lead time.（✕）
   關於前置期的分布，Smith (1999)做了兩個假設。

2. The control cursor was represented by a red line one pixel wide and 80 pixels high.
   控制游標是用1個光點寬、80個光點高的一條紅線來表示。

3. The density of the specimen was 0.75 g/cm^3.
   樣本的密度是0.75 g/cm^3。

4. This effect of input modality on recognition was not found in Experiment 1.
   這種輸入感覺型式對認知的影響在實驗1中並未發現。

　　用來表達數字之單位（如℃、kg、cm）或性質的符號（如 $）或字母（如 USD、NTD）可依慣例使用。

1. Because of the expense and time involved, true negotiation normally will not be used unless the dollar amount is quite large; USD 50,000 or more is the general minimum set by some organizations.
   因為牽涉到的花費與時間，除非金額非常大否則通常不會真正的議價；50,000美元或者更高是某些機構所訂定的最小值。

　　在多數的量化分析裡，圖表是數據表現的非常好的工具。以視覺效果而言，圖的效果又比表好，然而以數據的複雜程度而言，圖能夠呈現的數據比表要少。一般常用的圖包括長條圖（bar chart）、直方圖（histogram）、比例圖或圓形圖（pie chart）、線圖（line chart）、數據散布圖（scatter plot）等。使用圖表時必須記得一件事：圖表是輔助文字說明的工具，文字才是文章的主體，一篇文章可以沒有圖表，但卻不能沒有文字。

1. Table 1 shows the means, standard deviations, and correlations of all the variables included in the model.
   表1顯示了所有包括在模式裡的所有變數的平均值、標準差、與相關係數。
2. Tables 2, 3, and 4 show the results of the Duncan multiple range tests for floors, footwear materials, and surfaces, respectively.
   表2、3、4分別的顯示了地板、鞋材與表面狀況的Duncan多重全距檢定結果。
3. The results of the regression analysis, which are summarized in Table 2, provide a closer insight into the relationships between the variables.
   整理表2的迴歸分析結果對變數間的關係提供了進一步的了解。此句可改為：
   Table 2 shows the results of the regression analysis which provide a closer insight into the relationships between these variables.
   表2顯示了迴歸分析的結果，這些結果對於變數間的關係提供了進一步的了解。
4. Figures 2, 3 and 4 show the two-way interactions of the three factors.
   圖2、3、4顯示了三個因子的兩向交互作用。此句可改寫為：
   The two-way interactions of the three factors are shown in Figures 2, 3, and 4.
   這三個因子的兩向交互作用顯示於圖2、3、與4。

4-9 討論 Discussion

　　在研究結果之後，應對研究結果進行討論。論文中的討論應針對研究得到的結果做進一步的分析、推理與其他文獻的結果比較或探討可能的未來應用。所作的推論應該合理─邏輯正確、有數據或是其他文獻為依據，不可在沒有任何依據的情況下僅依個人主觀的想法來作推論。

1. Females reported higher floor roughness ratings than those of males. This was not unexpected as it was a common belief that females have finer skin than males. （解釋）
   地板粗糙度的評分，不意外的是女性比起男性的評分更高，因為一般認為女性的皮膚比男性的皮膚細膩。
2. However, the reason a reduction was found with pulling and pushing is not clear. （解釋）
   然而，推與拉的情況下數值降低的原因並不清楚。

3. The discrepancy between the two studies might be caused by the different friction measurement protocols. （解釋）

兩個研究間的差異可能是由摩擦量測程序的不同所造成的。

4. The base areas of the heel of the shoes in their experiment were small compared to ordinary shoes. This might contribute to their finding that high heels were less slip resistant than flat-soled shoes. (Li, 2003) （解釋）

他們實驗的鞋根的底面積與一般鞋子比較起來很小，這可能是造成他們發現高跟鞋較平底鞋不抗滑的原因。

5. With no differences between conditions for ratings of perceived exertion, it is possible the differences in force production at the feet were not apparent to subjects. （推論）

由於研究狀況間認知施力的評分間並無差異，腳間力量產生的差異可能對受測者並不明顯。

6. Human subjects seemed incapable of differentiating the slipperiness of different floor materials. （推論）

受測者似乎無法分辨地板材料間光滑程度的差異。此句可改寫為：

It seemed that the subjects could not differentiate the slipperiness of different floor materials.

似乎受測者無法區分不同地板材料的光滑程度。

7. The ranking of subjective scores for both the floor and contaminated conditions seemed to lack consistency with the COF measured by the slip tester. （本研究數據間之比較）

地板與污染狀況主觀分數的排序似乎與滑動測試器所量的摩擦係數值不一致。

8. This was consistent with the findings of Chang and Matz (2002). （與其他文獻比較）

這和Chang與Matz(2002)的發現是一致的。

9. The maximum acceptable trolley loads (410-439 N) found in the present study were lower than the maximum acceptable horizontal forces measured by Snook and Ciriello (1991). (Ciriello et al., 2001) （與其他文獻比較）

本研究所發現的推車載重(410-439N)最大可接受水平推力比Snook與Ciriello (1991) 量得的最大可接受水平推力要低。

10. The results of the study indicated a strong linear correlation between the CR-10 rating and grip force. This was consistent with the findings in the literature (Borg, 1990; Park and Yun, 1996). （與其他文獻比較）

本研究的結果顯示CR-10評分與握力之間有強烈的線性相關，這與文獻的發現一致。

11. This study provides an example of using the SDT in quantifying the sensitivity of human participants in detecting the drone invasion in a low-altitude airspace.（說明貢獻）

本研究提供使用SDT量化人類參與者偵測無人機入侵低高度空域靈敏度的案例。

12. The implication of these results is that horizontal distance of the drone to the borderline should be considered in planning the visual monitoring system for drone invasion detection. （進一步說明結果的意義）

這些結果的意義是在規劃無人機入侵視覺監控系統時應考慮無人機至邊界的水平距離。

13. In Figure 7, the P(A) values at the distance of 40 m were higher than those at 20 m at all drone altitudes. This was consistent with what has been expected. The insignificance of the drone altitude was, however, unexpected.（說明結果與預期相符與不符）

圖7中在所有無人機的高度下，距離為40米的P(A)值皆高於20米之值，此與先前的期望相符。不過無人機高度的不顯著性卻不是我們所期望的。

14. The approach and the information of this study will be beneficial in the assessments of the performance of the monitoring system of a low-altitude airspace and the planning of the ground security system concerning drone invasion.（說明貢獻）

本研究的方法與訊息對於低空域監測系統的表現及地面關於無人機入侵方面安全系統的評估是有幫助的。

🔍 4-10 研究限制 Limitations of the Study

許多研究都是在特定的限制條件下進行的，如果這些條件可能會影響研究結果的解釋與應用的範圍，則必須清楚的在論文中敘述。若是研究的限制只有很簡短的敘述，則這部分可放在 Discussion 的後面，若是研究的限制的敘述佔了相當的篇幅（一大段文字或兩段文字以上）則可單獨成立一節，標題即為 Limitations of the Study。

1. Due to the difficulties in quantifying and controlling the environmental conditions, conducting a field study of drone invasion detection is extremely complicated.（研究限制）

   由於環境量化及控制的困難，執行一項無人機入侵偵測的實地研究非常地困難。

   上句也可改：

   Conducting a field study of drone invasion detection is extremely complicated because of the difficulties in quantifying and controlling the environmental conditions.

2. In addition to weather and atmospheric conditions, this study was limited as only one drone was adopted. A white Phantom 4 drone was tested.（研究限制）

   除了天氣與大氣狀況外，本研究也受限於只有一具無人機被採用。一具Phantom 4無人機被測試。

3. With the limitations mentioned above, the results of our study may not be generalizable and were applicable only under our experimental conditions.（研究限制）

   有了上述的限制，本研究的結果無法一般化並只能應用於與實驗狀況類似的條件。

4. In our simulated pulling experiment, walking was not considered due to the limitations of the space and technical difficult in data collection in the laboratory. Human gait could have cyclic effects on pulling force exertion. Such effects were, however, not considered in the current study and may be research topics in the future.（研究限制與建議未來研究主題）

   在我們的拉（車）實驗中，因為實驗室空間與數據收集技術困難的限制，（所以）走路未被考慮。人性類的步態對於拉力施展可能有週期性的影響。然而這樣的影響在本研究中未被考慮，可以當作未來研究的主題。

5. A limitation of this approach is that it has difficulty in handling the situation where there is severe intrapersonal variability.

   這種方法的侷限在於處理人與人之間有太大的變異情況時會有困難。（說明研究的價值與貢獻）

6. A limitation of this study was that the COF values were measured without sanding the footwear pads using abrasive papers as recommended in the literature. This was because sanding could alter the depth of the tread grooves on the footwear pads.

   本研究的限制之一是摩擦係數的量測並未如文獻上的建議使用砂紙來研磨鞋材測試片，這是因為研磨可能會改變鞋材測試片上紋路的深度。

7. There were limitations to this study. First of all, the results of the study should be taken as indicative because of the relative small sample size. Secondly, the walking velocities were estimated using the velocities of six tasks, three at the beginning and three at the end of each session. Variations of walking velocity might exist among the tasks performed in each session which might affect the estimated energy expenditure. Thirdly, the subjects were required to lift and lower the box using a squat posture. However, it was difficult for the subjects to maintain the same squat posture for all the tasks lasting for one hour. Some of the postures might be somewhat between squat and free styles.

本研究有些限制。首先，由於樣本數較小的關係，本研究的結果只應視為象徵性的；其次，走路的速度適用每節開始與結束時各三次，總計六次的作業來估計的，每節當中走路速度的變異可能存在於不同的作業中並影響能量支出的估計；第三，受測者被要求以蹲姿來抬起與放下箱子，然而在持續的一個小時當中要以相同的蹲姿來執行所有的作業是很困難的，某些姿勢可能介於蹲姿與自由的姿勢中。

4-11 結論 Conclusion

以文字對本研究做一總結的敘述，此部分的敘述應該精簡；結論中的敘述不需要詳細的解釋或進一步的說明，因為這些應該在討論中已經敘述過了。conclusion 中的敘述應該依據研究結果來回應研究目的中敘述的事項，有些學者主張這部分應對未來的研究提出建議，然而此部份應依文章的性質而定。

1. This study provides a scientific basis for shoe designers in designing suitable female footwear concerning slip resistance and the muscular load on the lower legs. (Li, 2003)（說明研究的價值與貢獻）

   本研究提供了在考量抗滑性與小腿肌肉負荷上適當女鞋設計之科學基礎。

2. 簡短的結論

   Conclusion

   This study showed that the wire-tying task, which is normally performed using pliers, could be accomplished using a power screwdriver if a proper fixture for clamping the metal wires could be designed. Replacementof pliers by a power driver-fixture assembly to tie metal wires has a number of benefits: reduced muscular effort, less performance time, reduced repetitive wrist motion and better user ratings. (Li, 2003)

結論

本研究顯示通常以鉗子來進行的綁鐵絲作業可以用電動起子來完成，如果一個能夠夾緊鐵絲的夾具能夠被設計出來。以電動起子－夾具的組合來取代鉗子來綁鐵絲有幾個好處：降低肌肉施力、較少的操作時間、減少手腕重複動作及較佳的使用者評比。(Li, 2003)

3. 較長的結論

CONCLUSION

High-heeled shoes are commonly worn in the workplace and for leisure activities. It is a common belief that high-heeled shoes produce a higher muscular load on the lower extremities. In this research, wearing high-heeled shoes resulted in higher NEMG (%) in the tibialis anterior, soleus and peroneus longus. This was consistent with the subjective ratings for muscular effort in the leg. The subjects felt higher muscular effort when wearing high-heeled shoes compared to flat-soled shoes. It was, therefore, concluded that high heels resulted in higher muscular load of the shank. High muscular load in the shank could cause fatigue in the lower extremities. It is also a belief that high-heeled shoes are more liable for slipping accidents. The COF measurements indicated that shoe A (rubber-soled) was the least slip-resistant shoe and shoe B (PU-soled), conversely, was the most slip resistant shoe. The COF measurement using a BM II tester simply tests the slip resistance of the sole material. The effects of the sample area and raised heel were not considered. Discrepancies, therefore, might exist between the friction coefficients and the subjective ratings for shoe/floor slipperiness. Based on the COF measurement data and the gait experiment, the two high-heeled shoes are not recommended. The flat-soled shoes, either shoes C (TPU-soled) or shoes D (PVC-soled) are a better choice for female to achieve both proper slip resistance and lower shank muscular load. This study provides valuable information not only for females in selecting proper shoes but also for the shoe designers in designing suitable female footwear concerning slip resistance and muscular load on the lower legs. (Li, 2003)

結論

高跟鞋是工作場所與休閒生活中常被穿著的鞋子，一般人都相信高跟鞋會在小腿產生較高的腿部肌肉負荷。在本研究中，穿著高跟鞋在小腿的脛骨前肌、比目魚肌與腓骨長肌導致較高的NEMG(%)值，這些是與腿部肌肉施力之主觀評比是一致的。與穿平底鞋相較，受測者在穿高跟鞋時會感到較高的肌肉施力；因此，可以做出高跟鞋造成小腿肌肉較高負荷的結論，較高的小腿肌肉負荷可能會導致下肢的疲勞。一般也相信高跟鞋較容易造成滑倒事故，本研究摩擦量測的部分指出橡膠底的A鞋最不抗滑，相反的PU底的B鞋最抗滑。使用BMII的摩擦係數量測只量鞋底材料的抗滑性，並不考慮樣品的面積與提高的角度。因此，鞋/地板間的摩擦係數與主觀滑溜性評比結果間的差異是可能存在的。根據摩擦係數量測與步伐實驗的數據，本研究推薦兩種高根跟鞋：平底的C鞋（TPU底）與D鞋（PVC底）能夠對女性提供適當的抗滑能力與較低的腿部負荷。本研究對女性選取適當的鞋具與女鞋設計師在考量抗滑性與小腿肌肉負荷時的女鞋設計上提供了寶貴的資訊。(Li, 2003)

4-12　誌謝 Acknowledgement

在論文的最後，作者通常可用簡短的文字來表達對於贊助本研究的機構或是個人感謝之意，機構的贊助通常包括研究經費的提供、儀器設備、場地的借用或是資料收集上的配合。國內許多研究是由國科會 (National Science Council) 或是其他政府機關以委託研究計畫的方式執行的，這類的成果發表時必須感謝經費的贊助並指出研究計畫的編號。個人對於研究的協助包括資料蒐集、資料分析、文書處理、圖表製作、校稿等，作者應敘明協助者的姓名、所屬機構並表達感謝之意。

4-13　參考文獻 Reference

Reference 中列出論文或報告中所引用過的每一篇文獻的出處，文獻排列的常見方式包括以作者（第一作者）姓氏的字母順序排列及依文中出現順序的編號排列兩種。若是機關出版物（非個人作者），則以機關名稱置於文獻的開頭處。

1. References

(1) American Society for Testing and Materials, F-1677-96, 2001. Standard method of test for using a portable inclinable articulated strut slip tester (PIAST), Annual Book of ASTM Standards. vol. 15.07. West Conshohochen, PA, American Society for Testing and Materials.

(2) Andres, R.O., Chaffin, D.B., 1985. Ergonomic analysis of slip-resistance measurement devices. Ergonomics 28, 1065-1079.

(3) Brungraber, R.J., 1967. An overview of floor slip-resistance research with annotated bibliography (NBS Technical Note 895). Washington, DC: National Bureau of Standards.

2. REFERENCES

American Society for Testing and Materials, F-1677-96, "Standard method of test for using a portable inclinable articulated strut slip tester (PIAST)," Annual Book of ASTM Standards, vol. 15.07, West Conshohochen, PA, American Society for Testing and Materials (2001).

Andres, R.O., Chaffin, D.B., "Ergonomic analysis of slip-resistance meas-ureementdevices," Ergonomics, 28, 1065-1079 (1985).

Brungraber, R.J., "An overview of floor slip-resistance research with annotated bibliography (NBS Technical Note 895)." Washington, DC: National Bureau of Standards (1967).

Chapter 5
論文投稿

5-1　作者與投稿

　　論文撰寫完畢即可準備投稿，投稿前必需確認作者具名與順序（authorship），若作者超過一人，則該研究最主要的貢獻者為第一作者（first author），其他作者則依照對研究的貢獻分別為第二作者（second author）、第三作者（third author）等。此處所說的貢獻是指心智上的貢獻為主，並不是每位參與研究的人都可列為作者。許多研究助理與學生在教授的帶領下做研究，若他們的工作完成是完全依（如數文獻與數據之蒐集與整理、資料之分析整理、繪圖等）指導教授指示進行的，則這些參與的人不必然為作者。第一作者以外的其他作者統稱為共同作者（co-author）。

　　作者當中必須有一位負責投稿與跟期刊主編聯絡的通訊作者（corresponding author），通訊作者必須寫投稿與連絡之信函（參閱 Chapter 6 之範例）、撰寫對於審查委員意見之回應（responses to the reviewers' comments）、投寄修正稿、與跟出版商（稿件校對、訂購抽印本等）之連絡事宜。一般的學術慣例是以第一作者為通訊作者，因為第一作者對於研究所有的問題都比其他作者熟悉，因此與主編連絡時對於各種問題比較能快速而且適當的回應。當然也有以共同作者之一擔任通訊作者的例子，例如第一作者可能會因為換工作而有一般郵件與電子郵件之地址變更之慮，這樣可能會耽誤與主編的連絡事宜。

　　傳統的投稿方式是通訊作者以一封投稿信（cover letter，請參考第二單元書信寫作的範例）並附上若干份數（通常二至四份）的論文紙本寄給期刊主編。現在的期刊都改用電子投稿的方式收稿，此時通訊作者在網際網路上登入投稿資訊（作者、論文標題、聯絡地址、論文所屬領域等），然而再上傳投稿信與論文的檔案。電子投稿免去了郵寄所需的時間與避免郵件遺失的風險，讓稿件審查的速度比傳統的方式快了許多。稿件被主編接受之後，主編會寄一份接受刊登的正式信函給通訊作者，然後將最後論文的版本交給出版商。

　　出版商在稿件排版完成之後，會寄一份排版後的稿件（proof）給通訊作者校對，此時只容許類似打錯字等問題的修正而已，作者不得再要求做大幅度的變更。出版之前，出版商也會寄一份版權轉移同意書請作者簽署，通常只要第一作者代表所有作者簽署即可，簽署這份同意書代表作者同意將論文的著作權移轉給出版商或者是發行人（學會或其他機構）。若是作者任期於政府機關或是私人企業，而這個研究是由機關或是公司的經費贊助的，則簽署這份同意書之前應該徵求機關或是公司的同意，以免日後衍生出法律糾紛。多數期刊在登出論文後，會針對該論文單獨裝訂提供給作者，此單獨裝訂的論文稱為抽印本（reprint 或 offprint），出版商可能免費提供若干份抽印本給作者，作者也可付費增訂抽印本。

出版商完成排版並經作者校稿之後的稿件稱為「付印中稿件」（article in press），付印中稿件為完成所有出版程序之稿件，這些稿件依序的等待出版中。許多國際期刊的等待出版時間可能長達一年甚至於更久，為了快速的提供讀者最新的資訊，許多期刊都將付印中稿件直接上網讓電子期刊訂戶的讀者可以讀取，紙本期刊的訂戶則必須等待出版之後才能看到。付印中稿件和正式出版之稿件唯一的差別是稿件上尚無出版的年份、卷數、頁數等資料。

某些期刊因為出版經費不足而要求作者支付全部或者部分出版的費用，這種費用通常稱為 page charges 或者 publication fee，因為這類的費用常以出版頁數計算，有些期刊除了頁數外也對文章裡面的圖表另外在收費，也有些期刊只對彩色圖表收費而黑白圖表不收費的。Page charges 通常必須在稿件出版前付款，作者投稿前應先了解期刊是否收取 page charges 及收費的金額與方式為何，以免造成日後的困擾。目前要收費的國際期刊，每篇文章的費用大致介於 200 美元至 1000 美元之間。

傳統期刊最初都是印行紙本的，紙本期刊投稿一般作者不須付費刊登，期刊經由訂戶（各機構及大學圖書館）支付的訂費及顧客購買單行本的收入來支應經營期刊所需費用。

在網路普及後，許多期刊開始發行電子期刊。這類期刊通常稱為 Open Access 期刊。Open access 期刊與傳統期刊的差異在於前者刊登後直接上網，讀者可在網路上閱讀甚至下載全文而無須付費，期刊發行商則向作者收取刊登費用。多數傳統期刊均有 Open access 出版選項，當作者收到接受刊登後可選擇 Open access 出刊或傳統出刊，選擇 Open acccss 出刊應先繳刊登費，不選擇 Open access 出刊一般皆默認傳統出刊。目前也有電子期刊僅發行 Open access 論文而無紙本期刊選項的，作者投稿前應先確認是否願意選擇 Open access 出版。Open access 出版與傳統出版的主要差異在於 Open access 期刊審稿及刊登速度較快，一般 Open access 期刊通常可於兩個月內審查完，接受刊登的稿件通常在必要的校稿、繳費後數日即可上線刊登。不過 Open access 期刊刊登費用昂貴，例如 Plos One 期刊每篇論文刊登收費美金 1,595 元，Plos Biology 則收費美金 3,000 元。

5-2 投稿須知

論文投稿之前，作者必須先閱讀刊物的投稿須知 (Guide for Authors)，以了解該刊物對稿件的內容與格式的要求。一般期刊對投稿的要求不外乎：

- 主題：符合期刊要求主題
- 內容：具有原創價值或是實務、應用價值
- 篇幅：字數或頁數之限制
- 章節、段落之訂定
- 字型
- 字體大小
- 圖表要求
- 參考文獻的標示與條列

1. 某國際期刊之投稿須知（或作者指引）

Guide for Authors

刊登稿件類別

The journal publishes:

- original full-length articles reporting on experimental and theoretical basic research
- case studies and short communications
- general surveys and critical reviews
- book reviews
- a FOCUS section, in which the following are included: reports of meetings, conference announcements, etc.

Authors interested in writing State-of-the-Art Review Papers and Ergonomic Guidelines（稿件品質） should contact the Editor-in-Chief and suggest possible topics.

All papers are refereed and are expected to attain a high standard of content, clarity and conciseness.

投稿收件人與地址

Papers should be submitted to the Editor-in-Chief, Professor A. Mital, University of Cincinnati, Ergonomics and Engineering Controls Research Laboratory, Cincinnati, OH 45221-0116, USA.

稿件份數與格式

Four copies of the manuscript should be submitted in double-spaced typing on pages of uniform size with a wide margin on the left. The top copy should bear the name and full postal address of the person to whom proofs are to be sent. The second page should contain the following information (in order): abstract (100-200 words), relevance to industry (25-50 words), and keywords (5-6).

參考文獻格式

The list of references should be arranged alphabetically by author, giving the complete source citation. Journal titles will be abbreviated in accordance with the Engineering Index system. Authors unfamiliar with this system may give full titles without abbreviation. In the text, references should be cited by author's name and year.

圖表格式與注意事項

All illustrations and tables should be numbered consecutively and separately throughout the paper. Line drawings should be in a form suitable for reproduction, drawn in Indian ink on drawing paper. They should preferably all require the same degree of reduction, and should be submitted on paper of the same size, or smaller than, the main text, to prevent damage in transit. Photographs should be submitted as clear black-and-white prints on glossy paper. Each illustration must be clearly numbered. Legends of the illustrations must be submitted in a separate list.

語文

The principal language of the journal is English.

校稿注意事項

Authors will receive proofs by e-mail, which they are requested to correct and return within 48 hours. No new material may be inserted in the text at the time of proofreading.

資料來源：International Journal of Industrial Ergonomics.

5-3 論文審查

一般期刊的編輯在收到稿件後,會將稿件送交兩位學者專家進行審查,這種審查稱為 peer review。審查完畢後,編輯會通知作者審查的結果;審查的結果不外乎以下四種之一:接受刊登 (acceptance as it stands)、接受刊登但必須小幅修改 (acceptance with minor modifications)、需大幅修改之後再審查 (resubmit with major modifications)、退稿 (reject)。期刊論文稿件審查的重點不外乎:

- 題目是否合乎期刊的要求
- 研究是否有(學術)創新或是應用的價值
- 文章的架構與範疇是否合理
- 文字的撰寫是否清晰、合乎邏輯
- 研究方法與結果之敘述是否合理
- 格式、文字是否合乎要求

若是稿件的題目或文章的範疇不合期刊的要求或是沒有任何學術或實用價值,一般都會遭到退稿的命運。研究方法是否合理與文字的撰寫是否清晰、合乎邏輯,視其程度而異,可能分別被退稿(常見的是方法錯誤或不合理)、要求大幅或小幅修改。格式不合要求或是錯別字通常需要小幅修改。

若是被要求修改,作者在投寄修訂稿時應該另外針對審查者提出的意見一一的說明每項的修改或是處理的情況。

許多 reviewer 都會以條列式的方式提出審查意見,如果是合理而又有對提昇論文的品質有幫助的意見,作者當然必需按照意見修改,如果作者自認有很好的理由不按審查意見修改,則必需提出很好的理由與說明來回應該審查意見。審查意見的多寡不應該是判斷該論文最後是否可能被接受的標準,許多年輕的學者在看到審查多達幾十點之後往往感到異常的挫折,並產生了打退堂鼓的念頭,這是不必要的。審查意見雖然很多,但若都是輕微的修改的意見,則該稿件依意見修改後被接受刊登的機率蠻高的。有時審查意見雖少,但每條都明顯的指出稿件所述研究不嚴謹、文字的撰寫不合期刊的要求,則該稿件最終被接受的機率不大。

基於學者的風範及基本的禮儀，有些期刊的主編在退稿時並不直接使用退稿（reject or rejection）的字眼，他們可能用間接的方式告訴投稿人諸如「這篇文章的範疇似乎和本刊的領域不符」或「如果您能考慮將本文依審查意見做大幅度的修改，那我們將歡迎您重新投稿」等，此時投稿人應該了解這篇文章被該期刊接受了可能性非常的低了。

1. Both reviewers suggested that the content of this manuscript doesn't fit the scope of this journal. I agree with them.（退稿）
   兩位審查者都建議這篇稿子的內容不符合本刊的範疇，我同意他們的看法。

2. Both reviewers have provided detailed comments for the authors' reference.
   兩位審查者都提供了詳細的意見以供作者參考。

3. A comprehensive editing for sentence structuring and grammar would be necessary.
   句子結構與文法的完整而徹底的編修是必須的。

4. Based on the reviewers' comments, the manuscript needs a major revision before it can be considered for publication.（大幅修改）
   根據審查者的意見，這篇稿子需要先大幅修改才能被考慮刊登。

5. The above paper has now been assessed by our referees. While the paper is basically acceptable for publication, there are a number of points that require clarification before we can proceed. I am enclosing these comments for your attention.（小幅修改）
   上述文章已經被我們的審查者審查過了。該文章基本上是可以被接受發表的，但是在我們進一步處理之前，有幾點（問題）必須要先釐清，我把這些意見附在信中供你參考。

6. I believe that if you can address the comments and the editorial changes suggested by the reviewers, we could have a worthwhile publication for this journal.（小幅修改）
   我相信如果你能夠對審查委員提出的意見與編修方面需要的改變做適度的處理，這個期刊將有一份值得出版的出版品。

7. I am pleased to inform you that the Editor in Chief has confirmed final acceptance of your paper. The paper has now been forwarded to the publisher for publication. PDF proofs will be sent out to you in due course and your paper will appear in the next available issue.（正式接受）
   我很高興的通知你，主編已經確認你的稿件的（最終的）接受。這篇文章已經被送到出版商那裡準備出版，PDF格式的校稿將會在適當的時候寄給你，而你的文章將出現在（本刊的）下一期當中。

8. It is a pleasure to accept your manuscript entitled FACTORS INFLUENCING RESTAURANT WORKER PERCEPTION SLIPPERINESS in its current form for publication in the Journal of Occupational & Environmental Hygiene. The comments of the reviewers who reviewed your manuscript are included at the foot of this letter.（正式接受）

我很高興的通知您，您所投稿到Journal of Occupational & Environmental Hygiene期刊的標題為 "影響餐廳工人對於地板光滑程度認知的因子" 的稿件已被接受以現在的形式（版本）刊登，審查者的意見列於信末（以供參考）。

9. 審查意見

Comments：

(1) The literature cited in page 3-De Jong et al., 2002 was not found in the References.

(2) On page 5, the authors described the three types of pliers used in the study. But the details and differences among the pliers were not clear. The authors should provide more details about these pliers in Section 2.1 and describe the differences among these pliers. Special components of the pliers, such as the return spring in pliers type 3 should be identified in the figures (2, 3, and 4.)

(3). On the top of page 8, "The subjects were also asked to make direct comparison between the pliers…" How were the subjects asked to do that? Did they do the pair-wised comparison?

(4) In Section 2.3.4, why not randomize the order of offering the 3 types of pliers and the thin and thick wires?

意見：

(1) 第三頁所引用的文獻－De Jong et al., 2002 在參考文獻中並未找到。

(2) 在第五頁，作者描述在研究中使用的三種鉗子，但這些鉗子間的差異與細節並不清楚。作者應在2.1節中提供更詳細的資料並描述這些鉗子間的差異；鉗子的特殊組件，例如第三種鉗子的返回彈簧，應該在圖(2, 3, 4)上標示。

(3) 在第八頁的上端，「受測者被要求來直接的比較鉗子……」受測者是如何被要求那樣做的？他們做成對的比較嗎？

(4) 在2.3.4節，為何不隨機的安排三種鉗子與細與粗鐵絲供應的順序？

10. 審查意見

Reviewer #1

(1) I think that a certain part of discussion-style text should be moved from results to discussion, including especially the parts of page 14 where a reference is mentioned in the text of results chapter.

(2) I would suggest that one or two photos of experiments could be added for enhancing illustrative features.

Reviewer #2

(1) This is a comprehensive field investigation both objectively and subjectively taking into consideration of several factors affecting slipperiness. Authors have made a lot of efforts on the large number of field measurements.

(2) Objectives should be stated in the Abstract.

(3) You used objective COF measurement and subjective slipperiness evaluation. Which one is more valid in terms of the measurement of floor slipperiness? It seems that you assessed the validity of subjective slipperiness evaluation based on the COF. Can you do it another way, i.e., can you assess the validity of COF based on subjective evaluation of slipperiness?

(4) Page 18, line 15-16: "The analysis of perceived floor slipperiness scores showed that the subjects were capable of visually discriminating floor slipperiness under different surface conditions." I wonder based on what you have your argument?

(5) Page 11 line 15: "all three factors were statistically significant" should be "the effects of the three factors on the COF were statistically significant".

(6) Page 13 line 11: "among the four floors" shouldbe "among the five floors."

(7) Page 19 line 18-19: "no matter what type of liquid was present." You have investigated four types. Don't you think the statement is over generalized?

(8) In conclusion, page 20 line 3-6: "but performed poorly at rating … footwear pad." These tow conclusions seem contradictory.

審查委員#1

(1) 我想特定部分的討論形式的文字應該由結果移到討論，特別是包括第十四頁結果章中提到參考文獻的文字部分。

(2) 我建議增加一兩張實驗的相片來強化說明。

科技英文寫作

審查委員#2

(1) 這是一個綜合了多項影響光滑程度因子考量的主觀與客觀的現場調查。作者費了很大的力氣來做大量的現場量測。

(2) 目的應該在摘要中敘述。

(3) 你使用客觀的COF量測與主觀的光滑程度評估，在量度地板的滑溜程度上哪一種比較正確？似乎你是根據COF來評估主觀滑溜評分的效度的，你是否可以用另外一種方式來做，換句話說，你是否可以根據主觀滑溜評估來評估COF的效度？

(4) 第十八頁，十五到十六行，「認知地板光滑程度的分析顯示受測者能夠以目視來區分不同表面情況下地板的光滑程度。」我想知道你是根據什麼作出這樣的主張的？

(5) 十一頁十五行：「所有三個因子都是統計顯著的」應該是「三個因子對COF的影響應該是統計顯著的」。

(6) 十三頁十一行：「在四種地板中」應該是「在五種地板中」。

(7) 十九頁十八到十九行：「不管有哪一種液體。」你調查了四種，你不認為這個陳述過度一般化了嗎？

(8) 在結論裡，二十頁三到六行「但是在評分上表現很差……鞋墊。」這兩個結論似乎是矛盾的。

11. 作者對審查委員的回應

針對審查委員 #1 提的 2 點意見及審查委員 #2 提的 8 點意見，作者的回應如下：

Response to the first reviewer's comments:

(1) On page 14, 7th line, moved "The negative correlation…" till the end of the paragraph to page 18th as a new paragraph before Section 4.3.

(2) A picture has been added as Figure 1.

Response to the second reviewer's comments:

General comments

(1) No response is needed.

(2) The Abstract will be too long if we put the objectives in it.

(3) Both COF and perception are commonly used as a measure of slipperiness although each has its own shortcomings. However, COF is more widely used than the perception evaluation, especially in field environments.

(4) The sentence was re-written as "The perceived floor slipperiness scores were significant (p<0.001) under different surface conditions."

112

(5) revised the sentence as indicated.

(6) revised as indicated

(7) revised as "no matter what type of liquid used in this study was present"

(8) The very last sentence has been changed to "For the five floor tiles studied, subjective scores may reasonably reflect the COF measured with the Brungraber Mark II slip tester with a Neolite footwear pad."

對第一位審查委員意見的回應

(1) 第十四頁第七行，將「負相關……」到本段結束移到第十八頁作為4.3節前的一個新段落。

(2) 新增一張圖當作圖1。

對第二位審查委員意見的回應

(1) 不需回應

(2) 若將目的放入的話，摘要將會變得太長。

(3) 雖然個有個的缺點，COF與認知兩者都常被當作光滑程度的度量；但COF比主觀評估更廣泛的被使用，尤其是在現場環境中。

(4) 句子被改寫成「地板認知光滑程度的分數在不同的表面情況下是顯著的($p<0.001$)不同。」

(5) 如文所示改寫句子。

(6) 如所示修改。

(7) 修改成「不管有哪一種本研究使用過的液體。」

(8) 最後一個句子改成「對於五種研究的地板，主觀分數能夠合理的反應由Brungraber Mark II 滑動測試器以Neolite鞋墊量得的COF值。」

12. 審查意見之回應

以下為另外一篇論文投稿時之審查意見回應。

Response to the comments of reviewer #1:

(1) The metal wire used in the study was standard wire (#16, #18, #20) purchased from a local hardware store. The length and the diameter were measured using an ordinary ruler and a caliper.

(2) The wire-tying tools designed in this study were based on our observation on local construction sites where pliers are the most common hand tools used to wrap and tie metal wire for various construction jobs. So, the experiment was conducted to compare our new designs and the pliers as wire-tying hand tool.

(3) Two additional photographs showing the wrist postures when performing the task are included in Figure 4 as example of wrist posture category.

(4) Amplitude plots of EMG (RMS) of flexor digitorumsuperficialis of one subject, using 4 different tools, performing the wire-tying task are added as examples (Figure 6).

Response to the comments of reviewer #2:

(1) The dependent variables are included in the revised manuscript.

(2) A sampling rate of 32 Hz is not high; however, it's believed to be acceptable since much lower sampling rates (20 Hz and 10 Hz) had been used in studying forearm muscular activities in some literature such as Hägg, G.M., Öster, J., Bystrom, S., 1997. Forearm muscular load and wrist angle among automobile assembly line workers in relation to symptoms, Applied Ergonomics, 28(1), 41-47. and Cook, T.M., Ludewig, P.M., Rosecrance, J.C., Zimmermann, C.L., Gerleman, D.G., 1999. Electromygraphics effects of ergonomic modifications in selected meat-packing tasks, Applied Ergonomics, 30, 229-233.

(3) Original sections 3.2 and 3.5 are combined as section 3.4. The original sections 3.3 and 3.4 are revised as sections 3.2 and 3.3, respectively.

(4) Notes describing whether the differences are significant are added under the Table 7 and Table 8.

(5) Notes describing the scale and the meaning are added under Table 10.

對第一位審查委員意見的回應：

(1) 本研究使用的鐵絲是由當地的五金店購買的標準鐵絲（16號、18號、20號）；鐵絲的長度與直徑是使用一般的尺與游標尺量的。

(2) 本研究設計的綁鐵絲工具是依據本地建築工地各種作業最常使用鉗子來綁鐵絲的觀察設計的，所以實驗的進行是以我們的新設計與當做綁鐵絲工具的鉗子來做比較。

(3) 另外兩張顯示執行工作時手腕姿勢的相片也被放在圖四中當作手腕姿勢分類的例子。

(4) 一位執行綁鐵絲工作之受測者使用四種不同的工具時之屈指淺肌EMG(RMS)變化圖被加入當例子（圖六）。

對第二位審查委員意見的回應：

(1) 修訂稿中已將應變數加入。

(2) 32 Hz的抽樣頻率並不高；但卻應該是可被接受的，因為更低的頻率（10 Hz到 20 Hz）在研究手臂的肌肉活動中曾被使用，例如Hägg, G.M., Öster, J., Bystrom, S., 1997. 汽車裝配線工人上臂肌肉負荷與手腕角度與症狀的關係, Applied Ergonomics, 28(1), 41-47. 與Cook, T.M., Ludewig, P.M., Rosecrance, J.C., Zimmermann, C. L., Gerleman, D.G., 1999. 選取之肉品包裝作業人因工程改善之肌電效應, Applied Ergonomics, 30, 229-233.

(3) 最初的3.2與3.5節合併成3.4節，最初的3.3與3.4節分別改為3.2與3.3節。

(4) 表7與表8下方分別增加描述差異是否顯著的說明。

(5) 表10下方增加了敘述尺度與意義的說明。.

Chapter 6
英文書信寫作

6-1　書信格式

　　英文書信的書寫方式是由左至右、由上至下。由於西方人士沒有保留信封的習慣，因此通常會在信上書寫地址。常見的書信格式是先書寫收信人的地址，然後開始寫信的主體，最後加上問候語，以下是常用的問候語：

Sincerely,
Sincerely yours,
Truly,
Truly yours,
Regards,
Best regards,
Very best regards,

　　問候語之後則是寄信人的署名，個人的職稱可列於姓名之後，問候語與寄信人的署名可放在信本文的左下方或者右下方。寄件人的地址與日期可寫在信的右上方或正上方；也有許多人將寄件人的地址寫在寄信人的姓名與職稱之後的。

　　英文書信中常用的縮寫字包括：

c/o	in care of 的縮寫，意思是「給」或「轉交」。
Ref.	Reference 的縮寫，為書信或討論案件的編號。
Re.	Regarding 的縮寫，意思是「關於」。
SUB	Subject的縮寫，意思是「主旨」。
CC	carbon copy的縮寫，意思是「副本」。
Encl.	Enclosure的縮寫，意思是「內含附件」，

　　現在電子郵件使用的頻率已經超過了傳統的郵件，e-mail 與一般信件的不同處，包括不使用信封投遞 e-mail 的信頭最好寫明主旨（subject）讓收信人打開信件之前能先了解此信的目的。主旨不需要寫完整的句子，只要用少許的文字來標示本信的主要目的即可，常用的主旨包括：

Say hello	問候
Inquiry	詢問
Asking for catalog	索取目錄
Application submission	提出申請
Paper submission	投稿

6-2 求職信

在郵寄履歷表、申請書、稿件或是其他文件時，必須撰寫一封信來說明投寄的事由，這種信稱為 cover letter。求職信裡應提及的事項包括應徵的職位、個人條件與資歷符合該職位的要求及隨函附上履歷表。

範例1

57 Ming-Hu Road

Hsin-Chu 300

Mr. Yung Ming Chen

Human Resource   May 20, 2003

Chun-Tsan Inc.

8F-2, 135 Fu-Hsing N. Road

Taipei 106

Dear Mr. Chen:

I am a graduate student in Industrial Management at Chung-Hua University, and I will be awarded a M.S. degree in June 2004. I am currently looking for a position related to job evaluation and design in the IE department of a major company.

At Chung-Hua, I am working with Dr. K. W. Li on injury prevention and risk management investigations that aimed to establish a healthy working environment. I have participated two research projects investigating the job evaluation and design of electronic factories. With this strong background, I certainly believe that I am competent to meet challenging tasks and can make a good contribution to your company.

Enclosed is my resume, which indicates my personal information, education, and working experience. I sincerely hope that my qualification is of interest to you and that an interview might be arranged at your convenience.

Thank you for your consideration. I look forward to hear from you soon.

Sincerely yours,

Jane Jane Lai

300新竹市名湖路57號

2003年5月20日

陳永明先生
人力資源部
中山公司
106 臺北市復興北路135號8樓之2
新愛的陳先生：
　　我是中華大學工業管理系的研究生，並將於2004年6月獲得碩士學位，個人目前正在尋找一份企業中IE部門與工作評估和設計有關之職位。
　　在中華，我正與李開偉博士致力從事於健康作業環境之傷害預防與風險管理方面之研究，個人曾參與二件調查電子廠內之作業評估與設計。有了這方面堅實的背景，個人確信能勝任具有挑戰性的工作，並能對貴公司做出很好的貢獻。隨函檢附顯示個人資料、學、經歷之個人履歷表，個人誠摯的希望，您會對本人之資格產生興趣並能在您方便的情況下安排面試。
　　感謝您的考慮，並期望能很快的聽到您的回音。
誠摯的
賴真珍

範例2　地址省略

Dear Mr. Chen:

I am replying to your advertisement of August 21, 2003, on *United Daily News*, offering a position as quality assurance engineer.

As my resume demonstrates, I have my bachelor degree in industrial management and have been working as quality control supervisor in the past two years. I am a Certified Quality Control Technician (CQCT) issued by the *Chinese Quality Control Society.* Your adspecified an interest in knowledge of ISO 9000 series. I am one of the coordinators in the establishhment of corporate ISO 9000 system on my current position.

Enclosed you may find my resume showing my detailed education, training, and working experience. I will be happy to answer any question concerning my qualification for your recruitment.

Best Regards,

Jane Jane Lai

親愛的陳先生：

　　本人欲申請貴公司於2003年8月21日聯合報提供之品保工程師之職位。

正如個人履歷表上所述，本人擁有工業管理學士學位並在過去二年擔任品管課長之職。個人也是中華民國品管學會所認可之品管技術師(CQCT)，貴公司之廣告表明了對ISO9000系列之興趣與知識（之需要），個人目前正是公司內部導入ISO9000系列的協調員。

　　隨函檢附顯示個人詳細學、經歷之履歷表，個人將很樂意回答任何與應徵資格有關之問題。

敬致

賴真珍

6-3 徵稿

1. 研討會論文徵文

Dear Colleagues:

Papers are invited for Symposia sessions on the topics of "Slips, Trips and Falls," sponsored by the International Ergonomic Society (IEA). The conference will be held August 24-29, 2003 at COEXASEM Convention Center, Seoul, Korea.

The objectives of symposia sessions are to provide an international forum to exchange information about recent advances in test methods, and findings on the causes and prevention of slip, trip and fall accidents.

In order to participate in the conference, all prospective authors/presenters must submit a 250-300 word preliminary abstract to the special session chairs by October 31th, 2002. The abstract should state the objective, methods, results, and applications. Author(s) will be notified by January 31th, 2003 regarding the acceptability of the papers for the symposia session presentation. Papers for conference proceedings are due April 30th, 2003. Each presentation in the symposium will be allotted four pages in the congress proceedings.

For further information, please contact symposia organizers.

Thedore Smith
Associate Professor
ISE
VPI&SU

親愛的同事：

　　由國際人因工程協會（IEA）贊助的論壇現在邀請「滑倒、絆倒與跌倒」方面主題的稿件，本研討會將會在2003年8月24～29日於韓國漢城的COEXASEM會議中心舉行。

這些論壇場次的目的在於提供一個國際的研討來交換最近在測試方法的發展、滑倒、絆倒與跌倒事故之成因和預防研究發現方面之資訊。

為了參與本研討會，所有的未來的作者／報告人必需在2002年10月31日前提交一份250~300字之初步摘要給特別場次之主持人，摘要應該敘述目的、方法、結果與應用，作者將會在2003年1月31日前接到關於是否能在論壇場次報告的接受通知，研討會論文集之稿件將於2003年4月30日前截稿，論壇的每一件報告將在研討論文集中預留四頁的空間。

更多的資訊請洽論壇的承辦人。

Theodore Smith

副教授

ISE

UPI&SU

2. 研討會論文徵文

Dear Colleagues,

We are pleased to announce a slip, trip and fall symposium at the next UK Ergonomics Society Annual Conference in 2004.Please see below and the attached announcement for details.In addition to the technical sessions, this conference also offers great opportunitics for networking and discussions of research.We certainly hope that you can present your latest work on this topic at this symposium. Thanks!

Harvey McGrory

親愛的同事

我們很高興的宣布下一次於2004年英國人因工程學會年度研討會之滑倒、絆倒與跌倒研究的論壇，詳情請參閱以下附件。除了本技術場次外，本研討會也提供了網路連結與研究討論的絕佳機會，我們當然希望您能在此議題上於論壇展示您最近的工作，謝謝。

Harvey McGrory

3. 研討會提醒投稿人投稿期限

Dear Colleagues,

This e-mail is a reminder that our symposium paper submission deadline is fast approaching ! (end of April).

Please let me know if you need further assistance. Additionally, I am forwarding an e-mail of instruction from IEA.

Best Regards,

Theodore Lockhart, Ph.D.

Associate Professor

Department of Industrial and Systems Engineering

Virginia State University

親愛的同事

　　本電子郵件是提醒您論壇投稿的截止期限快要到了！（四月底）

　　如果您需要任何協助請通知我。另外，我也轉寄了一份由IEA來的說明的電子郵件。

敬致

Theodore Lockhart, Ph.D.

副教授

工業與系統工程系

維吉尼亞州立大學

6-4 投稿與論文審查信

1. 期刊論文投稿信

October 22,2002

Professor C. Masten

Department of Industrial Engineering

State University of New York at Buffalo

Buffalo, NY 14260-2050   June 16, 2006

Rc: Slipping of the hand when handling a heavy weight

Dear Professor Masten,

On behalf of all authors, I'm submitting the above mentioned manuscript to you for publication in Applied Ergonomics. This article, an original research paper, describes one of our studies in handle design using an ergonomic approach. It has not been published and is not under consideration for publication elsewhere.

We are looking forward to work with you in the paper reviewing process. Thank you.

Best regards,

Kai Way Li, Ph.D.

Department of Industrial Engineering

Hsin-Chu

Taiwan

Tel: +886-3-523-6539

Fax: +886-3-523-6594

Email: kw.li@chu.com

Professor C. Masten

Department of Industrial Engineering

State University of New York at Buffalo

Buffalo, NY 14260-2050   June 16, 2006

事由：處理重物時手的滑動

親愛的Masten教授，

　　本人謹代表所有作者將上述稿件投稿至Applied Ergonomics期刊給您。這是一篇原創性的研究論文，它描述了我們使用人因工程方法來做握把設計的研究之一，這篇文章沒有被發表過，目前也未被其他刊物考慮發表中。

　　隨函謹附上三份稿件，我們期望在審稿的過程中與您合作，謝謝。

　　祝福您。

Kai Way Li, Ph.D.

Department of Industrial Engineering

Hsin-Chu

Taiwan

電話: +886-3-523-6539

傳真: +886-3-523-6594

電子郵件: kw.li@chu.com

2. 投稿Safety Science期刊（投稿人非通訊作者）

October 22,2002

Professor J. Sari

Norway Institute of Occupational Health

Yopeliukkatu 41 aA

NOR-00220 Stockholm

Norway

Dear Professor Sari :

We would like to submit the enclosed manuscript, entitled "Floor slipperiness measurement: friction coefficient, roughness of floors, and subjective perception under spillage conditions," to Safety Science for publication. I am submitting this manuscript on behalf of all authors. Dr. Li is the correspondence author for this manuscript. Please communicate with Dr. Li directly on matters related to this manuscript. We look forward to working with you in the review process.

Thank you very much.

Sincerely,

Ming S. Chen

CC: Dr. Kai Way Li
2002年10月22日

J. Sari教授
挪威職業健康署
Yopeliukkatu 41 aA
NOR-00220 斯德哥爾摩
挪威

親愛的Sari教授：
　　我們想要投遞標題為「地板光滑程度的量測：在液體濺溢下之摩擦係數、地板粗糙度，與主觀認知」的稿件至Safety Science以供發表，我代表所有的作者投稿，李博士是本稿件的通訊作者，關於此稿件的所有事務請直接與李博士連絡，我們期望在稿件的審查上與您合作。
非常感謝您
誠摯的
Ming S. Chen
副本：李開偉博士

3. 研討會論文收稿

Dear Dr Li

THE ANNUAL CONFERENCE 14-16 APRIL 2004 UNIVERSITY OF WALES, SWANSEA.

Thank you for sending an abstract for a Slips Workshop entitled A survey of floor slipperiness in fast food restaurants in Taiwan by Kai Way Li. We received your paper on 03-Sep-03. Your paper's reference number is 92 and you should quote this in any correspondence. The organisation that you are affiliated with is Chung-Hua University.

The keywords you have supplied for your paper are: slipping/falling, floor slipperiness, perception, fast-food restaurants. These may be used as index entries in the proceedings.

We will send all correspondence regarding the paper to the above address. From the information you have provided us, we understand that Kai Way Li will be presenting the paper. If any of this information is incorrect, please contact me at the above address as soon as possible.

Your paper will be sent to the selection committee during the summer and you will be informed of their decision to accept or reject your paper by 7 October 2003. A provisional programme and booking form will be distributed in November. If you have not heard from us by the end of October, please contact me. Once your paper has been accepted you will be sent an author pack which gives details of what is required for the submission. Should your abstract be selected, your paper will be published in the proceedings subject to the following conditions:

(1) The paper is submitted before the deadline for the receipt of papers which is 19 December 2003.

(2) The paper meets all layout and other criteria specified in the authors pack.

(3) Someone will present the paper at conference.

(4) The conference fee has been paid by 19 December 2003.

All queries should in the first instance should be address to me at the above address. Where appropriate I will pass your query onto Paul McCabe the Annual Conference Programme Secretary

We use an electronic database to administer the conference and to store your details. We will use this database to contact you regarding the Annual Conference and also to advise you of any further events run by the Society that we think you may be interested in. We will not give your details to third parties. By submitting an abstract you are agreeing to the storage of this information on our database. If you do not wish your details to be stored on our database, you may chose to remove your abstract by contacting me in writing with the request to delete all contact details from the database.

We look forward to seeing you at the conference.

Yours sincerely,

Judy Hull.
Conference and Marketing Officer
The Ergonomics Society
2003年9月3日

親愛的李博士：
2004年4月14日至16日於SWANSEA威爾斯大學之年度研討會
感謝由李開偉博士您寄來標題為「臺灣速食餐廳地板光滑程度之調查」於滑倒討論會的摘要，我們在2003年9月03日收到您的文章，您文章的編號是92號，您在所有的連絡中應寫明這個號碼，您的服務機關是中華大學。
您提供的論文的關鍵詞是：滑倒、跌倒、地板光滑程度認知、速食餐廳，這些可能被用在論文集中當作指數輸入。
我們將關於本義的所有連絡寄發至上述地址，由您所提供的資料，我們了解李開偉將會報告這篇論文，如果這些資訊有不正確的，請儘快以上面的地址與我們連絡。

您的論文將會在夏季被送到評選委員會，並在2003年10月7日前接到委員會接受或拒絕決定的通知。一份暫時的議程與登記表，將會在11月寄出，如果您在10月底前未接獲連絡，請通知我。一旦您的論文被接受之後，您將會收到一份投稿所需詳細資料的作者套件。如果您的摘要入選了，您的論文在下列情況下將會被登載於論文集中：

(1) 論文在收稿截止日，也就是2003年12月19日前寄達。

(2) 論文滿足作者套件中指定之格式與其他準則。

(3) 有人會在研討會中報告。

(4) 研討會的費用在2003年12月19日前繳交。

所有詢問應儘快的寄到上面的地址給我，若需要的話我將會將您的問題傳送給年會議程祕書 Paul McCabe。我們使用電子資料庫來管理研討會並存有您的詳細資料，我們將會使用此資料庫與您連絡關於年會事項並提供您可能會有興趣關於學會的進一步活動。投稿代表您同意我們存有您的資料，我們不會將您的詳細資料交給第三者看。若您不希望您的詳細資料存在我們的資料庫裡，您可以書面與我連絡，我們將會移除您的摘要並在資料庫中刪除您所有的資料。

我們期待在研討會中與您見面。

誠摯的

JudyHull.

年會與行銷辦公室

人因工程學會

4. 投修訂稿信

Dear Dr. Rammy,

I have revised my manuscript entitled "Ergonomic Evaluation of a Fixture Used for Power Driven Wire-Tying Hand Tools" following all the comments from the reviewer. In the revised manuscript, I removed a figure and some descriptions that the reviewer felt were redundant. There are also some minor language modifications. Enclosed you may find four copies of the revised manuscript and an original with the reviewer's comments on it. Thank you for your kind assistance making this manuscript publishable to IJIE.

Very Best Regards,

Kai Way Li, Ph.D.
Associate Professor
Department of Industrial Management
Chung-Hua University

親愛的Rammy博士

　　我已經依照審查委員所有的意見修訂了我標題為「一個用於動力鐵絲捆綁手工具之夾具的人因工程評估」之稿件；在修訂稿中，我移除一件圖與一些審查委員認為不必要的敘述，也做了一些小幅度的文字修飾，隨函檢附四份修訂稿與一份上有審查意見之原始稿。感謝您對這份稿件在IJIE上發表提供的協助。

敬致
李開偉
副教授
工業管理系
中華大學

5. 投修訂稿信

Dear Dr. Rammy:

Thank you for your letter of January 4, 2002 concerning the manuscript "Ergonomic Design and Evaluation of Wire-tying Hand Tools." The comments from the two reviewers are very helpful and I have carefully considered the comments from the reviewers.

Enclosed you may find three copies of the revised manuscript, one original manuscript, and the comment sheets. The manuscript was revised following all the comments from the second reviewer (#2) and comments 3 and 4 from the first reviewer. Comments 1 and 2 from reviewer #1 are explained in the summary sheet. Summary of my response and explanations are enclosed in two separate sheets.

Please let me know if something else needs to be done to make the manuscript acceptable to the journal. I appreciate your kind assistance in processing this manuscript. Thanks.

Very Best Regards,

Kai Way Li, Ph.D.

Associate Professor

Department of Industrial Management

Chung-Hua University

親愛的Rammy博士：

感謝您在2002年1月4日來函有關於「鐵絲捆綁手工具之人因工程設計與評估」的稿件，來自兩位審查委員的意見非常有幫助，我也很仔細的考量了審查意見。

隨函謹附三份修訂稿，一份為原始稿與審查意見頁，而稿件的修訂是依照第二位審查委員之所有意見與第一位審查委員的意見3與意見4進行的。第一位審查委員之意見1與意見2之處理說明於整理頁中。個人對審查意見之回應與解釋附於分開的二頁當中。

如果有其他的稿件而有助於期刊上的發表，請讓我知道，個人感謝您所提供之稿件處理協助，謝謝。

敬致

李開偉

副教授

工業管理系

中華大學

6. 通知暑假期間稿件之聯絡地址

Dear Dr. Rammy:

How are you doing? I like to thank you for your help in publishing my manuscript "Ergonomic Design and Evaluation of Wire-tying Hand Tool" (which is in press) in IJIE. I'm really very appreciated. My second manuscript entitled "Ergonomic Design and Evaluation of a Fixture used For a Power Driven Wire-Tying Hand Tool" is still under review process. Again, I'll need your kind support for the publication of this manuscript.

I have been selected as the 2002 visiting scholar in a Boston-based laboratory. I am working with four researchers of Liberty Mutual on a slips and falls research project. I'll work in the Center as a research staff during June 20 to September 27. So please use the following address if you need to mail something to me:

71 Frankland Road

Framingham, MA 01728

USA

Best regards,

Kai Way Li, Ph.D.

Department of Industrial Management

Chung-Hua University

親愛的Rammy博士：

　　您好，感謝您對於個人稿件「鐵絲捆綁手工具之人因工程設計與評估」發表於IJIE（付印中）之協助，真的很感謝，我的第二份標題為「使用於動力鐵絲捆綁手工具之夾具的人因工程設計與評估」的稿件仍然在審查的過程中。再一次地，個人仍將需要您這份發表的文稿提供支持。

　　我已經被一所波士頓之實驗室選為2002年的訪問學者，個人正與Liberty Mutual的四位研究員進行滑倒與跌倒之研究計畫，並將於6月20日至9月27日在該研究中心擔任研究人員，所以若要郵寄東西給我，請使用以下地址：

71 Frankland Road

Franingham ,MA01728

U.S.A

敬致

李開偉

工業管理系

中華大學

7. 投修訂稿信

Dear Dr. Rammy:

I came back to Taiwan last Wednesday (Sep. 25th) after a three-month tenure at a Boston-based laboratory during the summer. I worked with four other researchers on a restaurant floor slipperiness study. We have finished all the data collection and are working on a first manuscript. The visit was very fruitful.

Upon receiving the comments of my fixture design manuscript (from the two reviewers) from you, I have discussed with two of my colleagues here about the manuscript. Substantial changes have been made on the manuscript, including the removal of 4 tables and 5 figures and re-write the text on the original manuscript.

Enclosed you may find three copies of the revised manuscript entitled "Ergonomic Evaluation of a Fixture used For Power Driven Wire-Tying Hand Tools." I like to re-submit this manuscript to International Journal of IndustrialErgonomics. Please have this manuscript re-reviewed. Thank you for your kind assistance.

Very best regards,

Kai Way Li, Ph.D.
Department of Industrial Management
Chung-Hua University

親愛的Rammy博士：

　　在一所波士頓的實驗室為期三個月暑期的訪問後，我已於上星期三（9月25日）返回臺灣。我與其他四位研究員進行一項餐廳地板光滑程度的調查，我們完成了所有的數據收集並正在寫第一份稿件。此次訪問成果豐盛。

　　在從您那收到我的夾具設計稿件的意見（二位審查者）後，我與此地的兩位同僚討論過，並對稿件做了大幅度的修改，包括移除4個表與5個圖且重寫原稿中的文字。

　　隨函檢附三份標題為「用於動力鐵絲捆綁手工具之夾具的人因工程評估」的修訂稿三份，我想再將此稿投給International Journal of Industrial Ergonomics。請再審查此份稿件，謝謝您的協助。

謹致

李開偉博士

工業管理系

中華大學

8. 編輯通知稿件接受並請做小幅度修改

07 May 2003

Dear Dr. Li,

I have received two reviews of your manuscript entitled "Floor slipperiness measurement: friction coefficient, roughness of floors, and subjective percepti-

on under spillage conditions."

The reviews were positive and recommended publishing with minor modificat-

ions.

I have enclosed the reviewers' comments. Please, read them carefully and ap-

ply to the manuscript as you consider relevant. The other reviewer makes a comment about using discussion style and references in the results section. I agree with this comment.

I am sure you can do the modifications easily. I would appreciate receiving a letter with the final manuscript explaining your perceptions about the comme-

nts.

Please, proofread your manuscript carefully. I noticed some typos in the refer-

ences. Also check that the style of references corresponds to the requirements of Safety Science.

Sincerely,

Prof.dr. Jor Sari

Editor

Norway Institute of Occupational Health

Topeliukkatu4laA

00220 Stockholm

Norway

2003年5月7日

親愛的李博士：

　　我收到了您標題為「地板光滑程度之量度：在濺溢情況下的摩擦係數、地板粗糙度及人員主觀認知」稿件的二份審查意見。

　　審查的結果是正面的，並推薦再做小幅修改之後，接受刊登。

　　我附上了審查委員的意見，請仔細閱讀並在您考慮適當的情況下應用在稿件（的修訂）上，另外一位審查委員提出在結果部分加上討論之型式與引用文獻（的問題），我同意這個看法。

　　我確信您能輕易的修改，我將對會收到的定稿及您這些意見解釋您看法的信件表示讚賞。

　　請仔細的校對稿件，我注意到了一些參考文獻中的打字錯誤。請檢查參考文獻須符合Safety Science要求之格式。

誠摯的

Jor Sari教授

主編

挪威職業健康署

To peliukkatu 41 aA

00220 斯德哥爾摩

挪威

9. 編輯通知接受稿件刊登

Dear Dr. Li,

Re: Floor slipperiness measurement: friction coefficient, roughness of floors, and subjective perception under spillage conditions.

Your above-mentioned manuscript has been accepted for publication in *Safety Science.* Thank you very much for submitting your manuscript to *Safety Science.*

Yours truly,

Prof. Jor Sari

Editor

Norway Institute of Occupational Health

Topeliukkatu4laA

00220 Stockholm

Norway

2003年8月20日

親愛的李博士：

關於「地板光滑程度之量度：在濺溢情況下的摩擦係數、地板粗糙度及人員主觀認知」。

您的上述稿件已被*Safety Science*接受刊登，感謝您投稿到*Safety Science*。

真誠的

Jor Sari教授

主編

挪威職業健康署

To peliukkatu 41 aA

00220 斯德哥爾摩

挪威

10. 出版商通知接受稿件暨作者配合排版事宜

Our reference: ERGON 1227

Editorial reference: 02-24

Re：Ergonomic evaluation of a fixture used for power driven wire-tying hand tool

To be published in: International Journal of Industrial Ergonomics

Dear Dr. Li,

We have received your above-mentioned article for publication. On behalf of Elsevier Science, I would like to take this opportunity to thank you for choosing International Journal of Industrial Ergonomics as your publishing medium.

From the details supplied by the journal editor we have logged your address, and your e-mail, phone and fax numbers if available. Please check that the details are correct so we can contact you quickly, if necessary.

Any attachment to this e-mail is in PDF format. To view and print an attachment you will need Acrobat Reader from Adobe. This program is freely available and can be downloaded from http://www.adobe.com/. The Acrobat reader is available for a whole series of platforms which include PC, Mac and Unix. If you would prefer to receive the forms by fax or mail then please inform us immediately by replying to this e-mail with full fax details.

Unfortunately, it appears that your manuscript is not complete. Please see the attached form for details of the missing component(s).

We have noted that color artwork is included in your article. Please note that there is a charge for color reproduction (see attached form). Alternatively, the artwork can be reproduced in black and white for which there is no charge. Could you please let us have your decision by fax as soon as possible to avoid any unnecessary delay in publication. If you choose to have the artwork reproduced in color, then please complete the attached form, with your original signature, and return by mail to the address below.

We are proceeding with the publication of your article on the explicit understanding that you will sign and return an unaltered copy of the attached Transfer of Copyright form. A fax or copy of the signed form is sufficient for us to proceed in good faith; however, for legal reasons we still need you to mail us the form with the original signature present. If you have any doubts about your ability to do so, or if your employer has asked you to return a different form, it is essential that you contact us immediately to avoid difficulties at a later date.

If we have not heard from you within 15 days of the date of this e-mail we will publish the article with an Elsevier Science copyright line, or, in the case of Society journals, with the appropriate Society copyright line

To track the status of your article online from the Author Gateway please visit http://authors.elsevier.com/TrackPaper.html. You will need to provide the following details:

- Our reference ERGON 1227
- Corresponding author's surname Li

If you are a registered user of the Author Gateway you can track the status of your article from your personalized homepage and receive e-mail alerts onprogress. All you need to do is add your article's details to your list of accepted articles from your personalized homepage. Alternatively you can track your article without setting up a profile, but you won't be able to receive e-mail alerts or create your own ersonalized homepage.

Please bear in mind that it may take up to 24 hours after registration before your article is visible on the tracking system.

The Author Gateway is the new integrated online entry point for all your submission needs. The service provides access to author-related information and services from Elsevier Science.

Please only fax us the offprint order form if you wish to order additional offprint or the billing address is different from the address given at the top of the form; otherwise there is no need to return it.

The number of printed pages of your article is estimated at 11 (this has been calculated using the average number and size of figures for this journal.)

Elsevier will do everything possible to get your article corrected and published as quickly and accurately as possible. In order to do this we need your help. When you receive the proof of your article for correction, it is important to ensure that all of your corrections are sent back to us in one communication. Subsequent corrections will not be possible, so please ensure your first sending is complete. Note that this does not mean you have any less time to make your corrections, just that only one set of corrections will be accepted. Thank you.

If any questions or problems arise, please do not hesitate to contact us, preferably by fax or e-mail quoting ERGON 1227 in all correspondence.

Yours sincerely,

Elsevier Science NL

J. Baker

Sara Burgerhartstraat 25

105 KV Amsterdam

Netherlands

編號：ERGON 1227

編輯參考：02-24

關於：使用於動力鐵絲捆綁手工具之夾具的人因工程評估將登載於：International Journal of Industrial Ergonomics

親愛的李博士：

　　我們收到了上述您要出版的稿件，本人謹代表Elsevier Science公司，利用這個機會，感謝您選擇International Journal of Industrial Ergonomics當作您出版的媒體。

　　由期刊主編提供的細節，我們記錄了您的地址、電子郵件、電話、傳真等資料。請檢視這些資料是否正確，以便我們在必要時能很快的與您連絡。

　　這封電子郵件的附件都是PDF格式的。要看與列印附件，您將須用Adobe Acrobat Reader（軟體）這個程式。可以免費的由 http://www.adobe.com/ 下載，Acrobat Reader可以在整個系列平臺上系統使用，包括Pc、Mac與Unix。如果您想經由傳真或郵寄收到這些表格，請立即使用這份電子郵件的回覆來通知我們，並附上詳細的傳真資料。

　　很不幸，您的稿件似乎並不完整，請在附件中檢視缺件的部分。

　　我們注意到您稿件中有彩色的圖表，請注意彩色印製是要收費的，（見附件）。圖表也可以使用不收費的黑白印製，請儘快的以傳真通知我們您的決定以避免在出版上不必要的延誤。如果您選擇彩色印製，請填寫所附之表格並簽名後郵寄至下述地址。

　　我們出版您的論文是根據明確的理解來處理，因此您將會簽署並寄回一份所附的未經修改版權轉移表。影印或傳真表格，是足夠證明我們處理的很好。但是，基於法律的原因，我們仍須請您寄回有原始簽名的表格。如果您有疑惑，您是否能如此做，或是如果您的僱主要求您寄回一份不同的表格，則您立刻與我們連絡是很重要的，以避免日後的麻煩。

　　如果我們在此電子郵件日期之15日內沒有收到您的回音，則我們將會以Elsevier Science的方式出版你這篇論文，或在學會期刊之狀況，使用適當的學會版權線。

　　由Author Gateway之線上追蹤您論文之狀態請上http://authors.elsevier.com/TrackPaper. htm1.您必須提供以下資料：

- 我們的編號ERGON 1227
- 通訊作者的姓Li

　　如果您是Author Gateway的註冊使用者，您可以從您個人化的首頁來追蹤論文的狀態並在進展中收到電子郵件的提示。您所要做的是在個人化首頁中將您著作的資料加入您已被接受論文的清單中。您也可以不需要設定著作情況就追蹤您的文章，但您將不會收到電子郵件的提示或建立您擁有個人化首頁。

　　請記著在註冊後，您可能在24小時之後才能在追蹤系統上看到您的文章，Author Gateway是滿足您所有投稿需要之新的整合，線上輸入點，這項服務提供處理作者相關資訊與Elsevier Science公司的服務。

　　如果你需要訂購額外的抽印本或帳單地址與表格上端地址不符，請傳真抽印本訂購單給我們否則您不需要將它送回。

　　您論文印刷頁數預估是11頁（這是依本期刊之平均數與圖的大小計算而得的）。

　　Elsevier將會儘可能的修正您的論文並且以最準確而快速的出版，為了能達成（這樣的目標），我們需要您的幫助，當您收到校稿時確定將所有修正一次的資料寄回是很重要的，後續的校正將是不可能的，所以請確認你第一次寄回的（校對稿）是完整的。注意這並不意味您有較少的時間來修改，只是只會有一組的校正會被接受，謝謝。

　　如果遇到任何問題，請不要猶豫與我連絡，最好是由傳真或是電子郵件並在所有通訊中註明ERGON 1227之編號。

誠摯的

Elsevier Science NL

J Baker
Sara Burgerhartstracet 25
105 KV 阿姆斯特丹
荷蘭

11. 編輯以電子郵件催校訂稿

Amsterdam, 08 April 2003
Our reference: ERGON 1227
Editorial reference: 02-24

Re: Ergonomic evaluation of a fixture used for power driven wire-tying hand tool
To be published in: International Journal of Industrial Ergonomics

Dear Dr. Li,

We have not yet received the corrections of the above-mentioned article. If not already sent, please e-mail us your corrections as soon as possible (alternatively you may fax us the relevant pages).

If, by any chance you have not received the proofs of your article (as either paper or PDF delivery), please inform us immediately.

Elsevier Science NL
J. Baker
Sara Burgerhartstraat 25
105 KV Amsterdam
Netherlands

阿姆斯特丹, 2003年4月8號
編號：ERGON 1227
編輯參考：02-24

關於：使用在動力鐵絲綑綁手工具之夾具的人因工程評估

將登載於International Journal of Industrial Ergonomics

親愛的李博士：

　　我們尚未收到您上述論文的校正稿，如果您尚未寄出，請儘快的以電子郵件將您的校正稿寄給我們（您也可以將相關的稿頁傳真給我們）。

　　如果您尚未收到校正稿（紙本或PDF輸出），請立刻通知我們。

Elsevier Science NL

J Baker

Sara Burgerhartstracet 25

105 KV阿姆斯特丹

12. 以電子郵件通知已傳真須校訂部分

Subject: paper ERGON 1227 submitted to International Journal of Industrial Ergonomics

Dear Mr. Baker,

I'm sorry about the late response. I have just faxed four pages of the proof corrections (Author Query Form and 3 pages of manuscript with corrections on them) to you.

I have made corrections on pages 1, 5, and 9. Please let me know if you haven't received these pages.

Best Regards,

Kai Way Li

Associate professor

Department of Industrial Management

Chung-Hua University

主旨：ERGON 1227 投稿至International Journal of Industrial Ergonomics

親愛的Baker 先生：

　　我很抱歉這麼晚回信，我剛剛傳真了4頁校正稿給您（作者詢問表與3頁含有修正之中文稿）。

我在1、5、9頁做了修改，若您尚未收到這些稿頁請通知我。

謹致

李開偉

副教授

工業管理系

中華大學

13. 編輯以電子郵件通知已收到校訂稿

From: <j.baker@elsevier.com>

To: <kwl@chu.edu.tw>

Subject: Your paper ERGON 1227 submitted to International Journal of Industrial Ergonomics

Dear Dr. Li,

I received your corrected proofs, thank you for sending them

Yours sincerely,

Jerry Baker

發件人：<j.baker@elsevier.com>

收件人：<kwl@chu.edu.tw>

主旨：您投稿至International Journal of Industrial Ergonomics 之ERGON 1227號稿件

親愛的李博士：

我收到您的校稿，感謝您的寄送。

誠摯的

Jerry Baker

14. 出版商通知校訂稿之收悉與處理情況

Author article tracking service

Article title: Floor slipperiness measurement

Reference: SAFETY1256

Journal title: Safety Science

Corresponding author: Dr. K.W. Li

First author: Dr. K.W. Li

Proofs returned: 10-SEP-2003

Thank you for returning the proofs of your article. At this moment it is not possible to give you citation information, or the publication date for your article. This depends on the number of papers lined up for publication in the journal.

You will be alerted by e-mail when citation information is available.

Don't forget as a registered user of the Author Gateway you can login at any time and access comprehensive tracking information about your article from your personal homepage at http://authors.elsevier.com.

Please return your copyright form if you have not already done so, if the copyright form is not returned before publication of your article, copyright transfer will be assumed.

For more specific questions about your article or general questions about publishing with Elsevier please contact Author Support at mailto:authorsupport@elsevier.com

Copyright Elsevier

作者稿件追蹤服務

稿件標題：地板光滑程度量度

編號：SAFETY1256

期刊：Safety Science

通訊作者：李開偉博士

第一作者：李開偉博士

校稿寄回：2003年9月10日

　　感謝您寄回您的校稿，此時尚無法給您論文的作者索引資訊與出版日期，這要視期刊等待出版的稿件數目而定。

　　索引資訊產生時，您將會經由電子郵件收到提示。

不要忘了作為一個Author Gateway的註冊使用者，您可以在任何時間登入你的個人首頁於http://authors.elsevier.com來取得關於稿件處理追蹤之資訊。

若您尚未寄回版權表，請將它寄回；若在您的論文出版前，您未將其寄回，我們將假設版權之移轉（是適當的）。

關於更多與您論文出版或在Elsevier出版之一般問題，請聯絡作者支援處於authorsupport@elsevier.com

Elsevier版權部

15. 邀請審查期刊稿件

Dear Professor Li,

Re: Evaluation of hand tools used in construction works: effects on discomfort
and performance

I am hoping you will be prepared to referee the above paper, submitted for *Applied Ergonomics.* As you may already be aware, *Applied Ergonomics* is a scientific journal emphasizing the practice of ergonomics rather than the development of its theoretical basis. Our intention is to publish material which demonstrates the benefits of using ergonomics or illustrates the variety of ways ergonomics can be applied. Papers with a substantial theoretical or experimental component are not excluded, however, providing application-related aspects are highlighted sufficiently.

If you are able to review the manuscript, I would appreciate one of four recommendations: accept the paper as it stands, accept with minor modifications, resubmit with major modifications, or reject. Your views on the scientific quality, clarity of presentation and suitability for *Applied Ergonomics* would also be useful, together with any advice that will help the authors improve their paper. It would help with administration if your comments (anonymous), intended to be seen by the authors, could be kept separate from any confidential remarks for me regarding publication.

We aim to complete the refereeing process in a timely manner. With this in mind, if you will be unable to review the paper within four to five weeks, say by 31 August, please do let me know and return it. In these circumstances, any suggestions you can provide for an alternative reviewer would be most welcome.

Yours sincerely

Dr. Raymond Harsey

Scientific Editor

Applied Ergonomics

親愛的李教授：

關於：用於營建工作之手工具評估：在身體不適與績效的影響

　　我希望將您準備好的審查上述投到Applied Ergonomics的稿件。正如你所知Applied Ergonomics是一份強調人因工程實務而非其理論基礎發展的科學期刊，我們的目的是出版能說明使用人因工程的好處或說明人因工程不同應用的材料。但是，如果能夠提供充分強調應用相關問題，我們也不排除實質上是理論或實驗性的論文。

　　如果您能審查此稿，我將感謝您能做出下列四種建議之一：如目前情況接受該文、小幅修正後接受、大幅度修正後再送審、退稿。您在科學品質、文稿清晰與適合於Applied Ergonomics方面的意見，併同任何能幫助作者改善其文稿的建議將會很有幫助。我們的目標是適時的完成審查作業。因此，若不能在4～5週內或8月31日前審查此論文，請告訴我並將其退回。這種情況下，很歡迎您能建議任何可以替代的審查委員。

誠摯的

RaywondHarsey博士

Scientific Editor

Applied Ergonomic

16. 回覆審查期刊稿件信

August 12, 2003

Dr. Raymond Harsey

Health & Safety Ergonomics Unit

Department of Human Science

Loughborough, Leicestershire, LE253WR

United Kingdom

Dear Dr. Harsey,

Re: Evaluation of hand tools used in construction works: effects on discomfort and performance

I have reviewed the above-mentioned manuscript, submitted to Applied Ergonomics. I think the manuscript provides a good example about ergonomic evaluation of hand tool designs. I would recommend acceptance of the manuscript with minor modification.

My comments for the manuscript are enclosed in a separate sheet.

Best regards,

Kai Way Li, Ph.D.

Professor

Department Industrial Management

Chung-Hua University

2003年8月12日

親愛的Harsey博士：

　　關於：使用於營建工作之手工具評估：對身體不適與績效的影響

　　我已經審查過上述投到Applied Ergonomics之稿件了，我覺得這份稿件提供了手工具設計之人因工程評估的一個很好的範例，我建議在小幅度修正後接受該稿之刊登。我對於稿件的意見附於另外一頁中。

謹致

李開偉博士

教授

工業管理系

中華大學

 ## 6-5　徵求同意轉載圖片

1. 徵求同意

Dear Dr. Gongist,

I am an associate professor with the Department of Industrial Management, Chung-Hua University, in Taiwan. I visited Liberty Mutual Research Center this summer as a visiting scholar and had worked with four other researchers on a field measurement of slip resistance project.

I am revising my book "Practical Human Factor Engineering" (in Chinese, published by Chuan-Hwa publishing Inc. in Taipei). In the revised version I am thinking to use one of the figures in your article:

Figure 4, Gongist et al., Human-Centered approaches in slipperiness measurement, Ergonomics, 2002, 44, 13, 1167-1199.

The same figure appeared in chapter 19 of Biomechanics in Ergonomics (ed. S. Kumar), Taylor & Francis, 1999.

I'll be appreciated and acknowledged if you grant me the permission to use this figure in my book.

Very best regards,

Kai Way Li
Associate Professor
Department of Industrial Management
Chung-Hua University
Taiwan

親愛的Gongist博士，

　　我是臺灣中華大學工業管理系的副教授，我今年夏天到Liberty Mutual研究中心擔任訪問學者並與其他四位研究員一起從事一個抗滑性現場量測的研究計畫。

　　我目前正在修訂我的書《實用人因工程學》（中文，由臺北的全華出版公司出版）；在修訂版中，我希望能使用您論文中的一張圖：

　　圖四，Gongist et al., 以人為中心的光滑程度量測，Ergonomics, 2002, 44, 13,1167-1199.

　　同一張圖也出現在，《人因工程之生物力學》一書第十九章（S. Kumar主編），Taylor & Francis, 1999

　　如果您同意我在我的書中使用此圖，我將會非常感謝並且在書中誌謝。

敬致
李開偉
副教授
工業管理系
中華大學
臺灣

2. 告知同意轉載圖片

Dear Dr. Li,

With pleasure, you'll have my permission when you use the appropriate citation to the original source (Gongist et al, 1989, Ergonomics, vol. 32, pp. 979-995). For this original figure, I combined the information in two previously published figures by Murray (1967; gait phases) and Perkins (1978; gait forces). The citations to these two papers appear in the above Ergonomics article from 1989.

Good luck with your book project. It would be nice to receive the complete citation to your forthcoming book.

Very best regards,

Ron Gongist

親愛的李博士，

　　我很榮幸且願意授權給您，只要使用適當原始出處的引用資料（Gongist et al, 1989, Ergonomics , Vol. 32 , 979-995頁），在這個原始的圖，我合併了兩個先前Murray（1967；步伐階級）與Perkins （1978；步伐力量）已發表之圖上之資訊而成的。這兩篇文章的索引顯示於上述1989之Ergonomics文章中。

　　祝您出書計畫順利，我希望能收到您將出版書籍的完整索引。

謹致

RonGongist

3. 徵求同意

From: <kai@chu.edu.tw>

Date: Thu, 24 Oct 2002 12:07:41

To: <bettyschindle@astmsu.com>

Subject: copyright

Dear Ms. Schindle,

I am asking permission of using FIG- 4 (in "Development of SATRA slip test and tread pattern design guidelines," Slips, Stumbles, and Falls: Pedestrian Footwear and Surfaces, ASTM STP 1103, B.E. Gray, Ed., ASTM, Philadelphia, 1990,113-123.) in a revised version of my book "Practical Human Factor Engineering" (in Chinese), which will be published in Taiwan. If you are not responsible for copyright affairs, could you please forward my mail to the corresponding department and/or personnel. Thanks for your help.

Sincerely,

Kai Waly Li, Ph. D.

Department of Industrial Management

Chung-Hua University

Hsin-Chu, 300

Taiwan

發件人：kwi@chu.edu.tw

日期：2002年, 10月24日, 星期四, 12：07：41

收件人：<bettyschindle@astmsu.com>

主旨：版權

親愛的Schindle女士：

　　我要申請使用圖4（〈ATRA防滑測試與鞋底紋路型式設計的指引〉，滑倒、絆倒與跌倒：行走之鞋材與地板表面，ASTM STP 1103 , B.E., Gray, 主編, ASTM, 費城, 1990, 113-125）在我將於臺灣出版的《實用人因工程學》（中文版）的修訂版上。如果您不負責版權事務，請您將此信轉給相關之部門或人員，感謝您的協助。

誠摯的
李開偉博士
工業管理系
中華大學
新竹市300
臺灣

4. 告知同意轉載圖片

Dear Dr. Li:

This is in response to your e-mail message yesterday to Betty Schindle.

As requested, ASTM permission is granted to reproduce figure 4 from the article, "Development of SATRA Slip Test and Tread Pattern Design Guidelines," from STP 1103 provided the following credit line is used:

Reprinted, with permission, fromSTP 1103 - Slips, Stumbles, and Falls: Pedestrian Footwear and Surfaces, copyright ASTM International, 4200 Frankland Drive, West Conshohocken, PA19728

Should you have any questions, please contact me.

Sincerely,

Christopher Harper

ASTM International

4200 Frankland Drive

West Conshohocken, PA 19728

親愛的李博士：

　　這是您昨天給Betty Schindle電子郵件的回信。如您的請求，ASTM同意您使用由論文STP113〈SATRA防滑測試與鞋底紋路設計指引的發展〉之圖4如果您以下列的方式在引用處標示：

Reprinted , with permission , from STP 1103 - Slips , Stumbles , and Falls：Pedestrian Footwear and Surfaces, Copyright. ASTM International, 4200 Frankland Drive, West Conshohocken, PA19728

有任何問題請與我連絡

誠摯的

Christopher Harper

ASTM International

4200 Frankland Drive

West Conshohocken , PA19728

6-6 其他信件

1. 請協助編修英文

Dear Mr. Johnson,

Please check the English for my manuscript attached to this mail. I'll be appreciated if you may finish editing this manuscript in two weeks. Thanks.

Sincerely,

Kai Way Li

親愛的Johnson先生：

　　請幫我檢查附件中稿件的英文，如果您能在二個星期內完成稿件的編修，我將會非常的感謝，謝謝。

誠摯的

李開偉

2. 請協助編修英文

From: Li Kai Way

Sent: Monday, May 12, 2003

To: Marcy, Tom

Subject: check English

Tom,

Are the following two sentences ok? If not, can you rewrite them?

  "The higher the cadence, the higher the NEMG(%)."

  "Reports on high-heeled shoe slip resistance assessment together with a discussion on leg muscular activities when wearing high heels are, however, rare in the literature."

Best regards,

Kai Way

發件人：李開偉

寄件日期：2003年5月12日，星期一

收件人：Marcy, Tom

主旨：檢查英文

Tom：

     以下的兩個句子是否妥當？如果不妥，您可否將其重寫？

  "The higher the cadences, the higher the NEMG(%)."

  "Reports on high-heeled shoe slip resistance assessment together with a discussion on leg muscular activities when wearing high heels are, however, rare in the literature."

敬致

開偉

3. 回函

From: Marcy, Tom
To: Li Kai Way
Sent: Monday, May 12, 2003
Subject: check English

Kai Way,

Second one is long, not necessarily poor.

First one, suggest as "Higher cadences resulted in higher NEMG (%)."

Tom

發件人：Marcy, Tom

收件人：李開偉

寄件日期：2003年5月12日,星期一

主旨：檢查英文

開偉：

　　第二個句子還可以，只是有點長，第一個句子建議改為"Higher cadences resulted in higher NEMG(%)."

Tom

4. 邀請參與問卷調查

Dear Dr. Li,

We would like to invite you to participate in a survey about the quality of the search results, found by the scientific search engine Scirus.

Taking part in the survey is simple: we ask respondents to perform 5 searches in their area of interest and rate each search result. Please take five minutes of your time to rate the Scirus search results. It is very important for us to receive as much feedback as possible, because only then we can make the search engine work better in your field of interest.

All respondents will receive a summary of the end results of the survey, if they opt for that. If you have any questions or remarks in regard to the above, you can send an email to survey@scirus.com. We appreciate your feedback very much and would like to thank you in advance for your cooperation.

Best regards,

Chris Cambridge

Scirus

親愛的李博士：

　　我們想邀請您來參加一項關於研究成果品質的調查，此調查由科學搜尋引擎Sciras創辦的。

　　參與這個調查很簡單：我們要求回應者執行5項他們有興趣領域的搜尋並對每個搜尋結果評分，請花5分鐘來對Sciras搜尋結果評分，儘可能收到更多的回饋對我們是很重要的，因為只有這樣我們才能讓您有興趣領域的搜尋工作做得更好。

　　所有的回應表將會收到調查結果的摘要，如果他們需要的話。如果您對上述有任何問題或是評論的話，請以電子郵件寄至survey@sciras.com我們感謝您的回饋與您的合作。

謹敬

Chris Cambridge

Sciras

5. 通知同意擔任訪問學者事宜

January 25, 2002

Dr. Kai Way Li, Associate Professor

Department of Industrial Management

Chung-Hua University

Taiwan

Fax: 886-3-537-3771

Dear Dr. Li,

On behalf of our Vice President and Director, Dr. Raymond Levy, I am pleased to inform you that, on the basis of competitive review of your application, you have been selected as the 2002 Visiting Scholar of our laboratory. Congratulations!

As you are aware this is a three-month, collaborative research, resident fellowship commitment. During this period the laboratory will arrange for support to be provided consistent with our Visiting Scholar program policies and procedures and applicable United States immigration and tax regulations.

As the 2002 Visiting Scholar, you will also receive an appointment at the Harvard University School of Public Health in Boston under the shared faculty provisions of the Program between our laboratory and Harvard in Occupational Safety and Health.

As soon as possible, I would be grateful if you could confirm your acceptance of offer so that we may jointly proceed with the research activities and planning your time in residence with us. As soon as I receive your confirmation, I can initiate the necessary procedures to facilitate your visit.

Thank you.

Best regard,

John K. Marcy MS, CSP

Associate Director

Cc. R. B. Levy

Enc.

2002, 1月25日

李開偉博士，副教授
工業管理系
中華大學
臺灣

傳真：886-3-537-3771
親愛的李博士：

　　本人很高興的代表我們副總裁兼院長Raymond Levy博士通知你，你的申請在經過具有競爭性基礎的審查後，您已經獲選為本實驗室2002年的訪問學者，恭喜！

　　如您所知，這是一個承諾為期三個月與在地一起進行的合作研究，在這段期間中心會安排與我們訪問學者計畫政策、程序相符的支援、美國移民局與稅務法規方面等的幫助。

身為一位2002年訪問學者，您將會在我們實驗室與哈佛職業安全衛生分享資源的計畫下，收到位於波士頓哈佛大學公共衛生學院之委任。我希望您能儘快的確認願意接受此推薦以便我們能同步進行研究活動與計畫您到這邊與我們在一起的時間。

在我收到您的確認之後，我可以開始進行必須的程序來協助您的到訪。

謝謝

致敬

John K. MarceyMs, CSP

副處長

副本 R. B. Levy

附件

6. 通知訪問學者任命事宜

HARVARD SCHOOL OF PUBLIC HEALTH

Office for Academic Affairs

July 25,2002

Kai Way Li

Environmental Health

Building I-l411

Dear Dr. Li :

With this letter, the Office for Academic Affairs begins the practice of writing to new and continuing annual appointees each July to confirm their appointment and to convey some basic policies and procedures relating to annual appointments. While the enclosed policies have long been in effect in practice, we want to be sure that all appointees and their supervisors are aware of them.

I am pleased to confirm your appointment as Visiting Scholar in the Department of Environmental Health at the Harvard School of Public Health. This non-faculty academic appointment is for the period 7/1/02 through 10/15/02,with the option of renewal. Enclosed is information about some policies and procedures pertaining to your appointment.

Congratulations on your appointment and best wishes for a rewarding and successful time here.

Sincerely,

Beth L. Anderson
Associate Dean for Academic Affairs

Enclosure
CC:Helen Marshel

哈佛大學公共衛生學院
學術事務辦公室

2002, 7月25日
李開偉
環境健康
I-1411大樓

親愛的李博士：

　　經由這封信，學術事務辦公室開始每年7月寫信給年度新任、續任被委任的人，來確認他們的委任及傳送一些與年度委任有關的基本政策與程序。儘管所附的政策長久以來一直在實施，我們要確信所有被委任的人與他們的行政上司都明瞭這些政策。

　　我很高興的確認您擔任哈佛大學公共衛生學院環境健康系的訪問學者的委任，這個非教學之學術任命期間是7/1/02到10/15/02，並可選擇延長。隨函檢附與您的委任有關之政策與程序方面的資料。

　　恭喜您的委任並祝福您在此地的時光會很有收獲與成功。

誠摯的

Beth L. Anderson
學術事務副處長

含附件
副本：Helen Morshel.

7. 宣布新任主管

December 3, 2001

Dear Kai Way:

I am very pleased to announce the appointment of Tony Blair, Ph.D., as Director of the Center for Safety Research. Tony, who joins us from Harvard University School of Hygiene and Public Health, will be responsible for the research program investigating the fundamental causes of accidents and injuries.

Following the Research Center's 1999 restructuring and the appointment of Jekins Hugh as director of the Center for Disability Research (investigating post-event and return to work), Tony's appointment completes our management team. The two highly-integrated Centers will continue to share physical and intellectual resources with the ultimate goal of peer-reviewed publication of research findings.

It is an exciting time in the history of our laboratory as we move forward in our science-based endeavors to prevent injury and reduce disability. I look forward to sharing our accomplishments with you and with the rest of the global safety and health community so that together, through research and application of findings, we can help people lead safer, more secure lives.

Sincerely,

John
JBL
Enc.

2001年12月3日
親愛的開偉：

　　我很高興的宣布Tony Blair博士，擔任安全研究中心主任的任命。由哈佛大學衛生與公共健康學院加入我們的Tony將會負責意外事故與傷害基本原因的研究調查。

　　在研究中心1999年徵求並任命Jekins Hugh擔任失能研究中心（調查事故後與回到工作崗位之問題）主任後，Tony的任命讓我們的管理團隊變得完整，這兩個高度整合的中心將會繼續分享實體與智慧方面的資源，並將研究發現以發表經同儕審查的著作為終極目標。

　　這是我們實驗室在歷史上由科學基礎的努力來預防傷害與減少失能，向前邁進的一個令人興奮的時刻，我期望與您和全球其他安全及健康領域同仁共同分享我們的成就；如此，我們可經由研究與應用成果來幫助人們活得更安全與更有保障。

誠摯的

John

JBL

含附件

Chapter 7

履歷表與個人簡歷

7-1 履歷表

履歷表 (resume 或 curriculum vitae) 是應徵工作時需繳交的重要文件，履歷表的內容包括個人的基本資料及應徵工作有關的各項資料：

- 姓名
- 年齡或出生年月日
- 性別
- 聯絡：地址、電話、e-mail、傳真
- 婚姻狀況
- 學歷（包括年分與學位）
- 專業證照
- 工作經歷
- 專業團體會員
- 特殊事蹟
- 推薦人

一般而言，學歷、工作經歷、專業證照是求職時雇主考量的最主要的項目，申請人是否具備擔任申請職位的資格大多是由這幾項決定的。履歷表上的學歷通常僅列大專以上與專業技能有關的部分，高中以下的學歷不需列出。工作經歷則以顯示個人的專業技能為主，太短期工作經歷的列舉對求職者並無太大的幫助，筆者建議工作不到三個月的經歷不必列出。過多的短期工作反而讓人感覺求職者心性不定，無法久任。推薦人則可應要求再提出。

英文的履歷表可分為 resume 與 curriculum vitae（簡稱 CV）。兩種的差別何在呢？在美國，CV 主要使用在學術、科技、醫藥、建築、專業設計與創作等領域中之專業職位（包括教授、訪問學者、研究員、科學家、醫生、建築師、設計師、藝術創作者等）之求職使用。CV 中所需要突顯的是個人的學歷、專業成就、獲得榮譽等項目。教授、學者、研究員、及科學家的專業成就通常是參與過的研究計畫及著作目錄，有些文獻建議這些條列式的研究計畫、著作、及作品可以在履歷表外另外裝訂呈現，但也有許多專家建議這些資料應該直接附在 CV 裡，因為這些資料是

反應申請人資歷與成就最重要的部分。因此資歷較淺的申請人（如碩、博士班剛畢業的）寫的 CV 可能只有一、兩頁，資深的申請人（如資深的教授、科學研究人員）寫的 CV 則可能長達一、二十頁以上。

　　Resume 是除了上述的申請人以外的人求職使用的文件。resume 中應該強調的是個人的經歷、專業技能（例如熟悉特定軟體，包括程式語言或套裝軟體與硬體的操作）、及專業證照。除了高階主管的職位以外，resume 一般都不超過兩頁。

1. Resume

Resume

Name: Keng Way Chen　　　　　　Date of Birth: November 1, 1975

Gender: Male

Address: 5F-2, #15, Lane 28, Chung-Sun Rd, Shin-Chu, Taiwan 300

TEL: 03-535-4281

E-Mail: kcng @chu.edu.tw

Education:

1998　MS, Industrial Management, Chung-Hua University, Taiwan

1995　BA, Business Administration, Chung-Hua University, Taiwan

1992　Diploma, Business Administration, Chung-Hua Junior College, Taiwan

Current Position:

1999- present　Supervisor, Quality Assurance Division, Matek Inc., Taiwan

Working Experience:

1997-1999　Engineer, Risk Management Division, Aaron Technology Inc.

1995-1997　Assistant Engineer, Risk Management Division, Aaro Technology Inc.

1993-1995　Technician, Customer Service Division, Esson Inc.

Qualification:

Certified Quality Control Engineer, License No. xx, Quality Control Society.

Chartered Industrial Engineer, License No xx, Chinese Institute of Industrial

Engineers.

Membership:

Member, Quality Control Society, ROC

Senior Member, Chinese Institute of Industrial Engineers.

履歷表

姓名：陳鏗偉　　　　　　　　　　　　　　出生年月日：1975年11月1日

姓別：男

地址：300臺灣新竹市中山路28巷15號5F-2

電話：03-535-4281

電子郵件：keng@chu.edu.tw

學歷：

1998 中華大學工業管理碩士

1995 中華大學企業管理學士

1992 中華專科學校畢業

現職：

1999 迄今Matek公司品質保證處課長

經歷：

1997-1999　Aaron科技公司風險管理處工程師

1995-1997　Aaron科技公司風險管理處助理工程師

1993-1995　Esson公司客戶服務處技術員

証照：

品質管理學會，合格品管工程師，執照xx號

中國工業工程師學會，註冊工業工程師，執照xx號

會員：

中華民國品管學會

中國工業工程學會資深會員

2. Curriculum Vitae

Curriculum Vitae

Name: Jen-Jen Wang　　　　　　　　　　　　　　　Gender: Female

Date of Birth: November 1, 1973　　　　　　　　Marriage Status: Married

Address: 15, Chung-Sun Rd, Shin-Chu, Taiwan 300

TEL: 03-535-4281 ext 4283 (O)

　　　03-342-2022　(H)

E-Mail: wang @chu.edu.tw

Education:

1999-present   Doctoral Program, Institute of Technology Management,

                       Chung-Hua University, Taiwan

                       Expected date of graduation: June, 2004

1993-1995   MS, Industrial Management, Chung-Hua University, Taiwan

1989-1992   BS, Mechanical Engineering, Chung-Hua University, Taiwan

Working Experience:

1997-1999   Manager, Risk Management Division, Aaron Technology Inc.

1995-1997   Sales Representative, Chung Hua Telecom., Taipei.

1993-1994   Staff, Customer Service Division, Esson Inc.

Specialize in:

Risk Management, Job Shop Management, Hazard Prevention

Publication:

Jen-Jen Wang (2002), Hazard Prevention in Electronic Factories, Asson Publishing Co. Hsin-Chu.

Jen-Jen Wang (2002), Identification of ergonomic risk factors among assembly line workers in electronic factories, Proceedings of the annual meeting of

Ergonomic Society in Taiwan, 45-52.

履歷表

姓名：王珍珍   姓別：女

出生年月日：1973年11月1日   婚姻狀態：已婚

地址：300新竹市中山路15號

電話：03-535-4281分機4283（辦）

        03-342-2022（住）

電子郵件：wang@chu.edu.tw

學歷：

1999迄今中華大學科技管理研究所博士班，預計2004年6月畢業

1993-1995　中華大學工業管理碩士

1989-1992　中華大學機械工程學士

經歷：

1997-1999 Aaron科技公司風險管理部經理

1995-1997 臺北市中華電信公司業務代表

1993-1994 Esson公司客戶服務部組員

專長：

風險管理、現場管理、危害預防

著作：

王文文(2002)，電子工廠之危害預防，Asson出版社，新竹

王文文(2002)，電子工廠裝配線工人之人因工程風險因子之辨識，中華民國人因工程學會年會論文集，45-52

3. Resume

Jen-Jen Wang

15, Chung-Sun Rd, Shin-Chu, Taiwan 300

0933-444-221

wang @chu.edu.tw

EXPERIENCE

1995-1999   Master Production Schedule planning, materials planning, and operation management of the division. Supervising 6 engineers and 30 technicians.

1994-1995   Engineer, Materials Flow Sector, Aaron Technology Inc. Responsible for facilities and equipments maintenance, on-line trouble shooting of the materials flow system.

1993-1994   Staff, Customer Service Division, Esson Inc. Acknowledged as the staff of the year on 1994. Handling customer complains, documentation, communication and follow-up of customer service.

Education:

1995 MS, Industrial Management, Chung-Hua University, Taiwan

Ranked No.1 upon graduation

Winner of Outstanding Thesis Award of the National Science Council, ROC

1992   BS, Mechanical Engineering, Chung-Hua University, Taiwan

Ranked No.1 upon graduation

References: Upon request.

王珍珍

300臺灣新竹市中山路15號

0933-444-221

wang@cc.chu.edu.tw

經歷

1995-1999 Aaron科技公司消費產品部經理負責主生產排程，物料規劃與營運管理，督
導6名工程師與30名技術員

1994-1995 Aaron科技公司，物流部工程師負責設施與設備維護、物流系統之線上偵錯。

1993-1994 Esson公司客戶服務部職員1994年年度最佳員工；處理客戶投訴、客戶服務之
文件、通訊及追蹤處理。

學歷

1995 臺灣中華大學工業管理碩士第一名畢業
中華民國國家科學委員會最佳論文獎

1992 臺灣中華大學機械工程學士第一名畢業

推薦函：應要求提供

4. Resume

Jen-Jen Wang

15, Chung-Sun Rd, Shin-Chu 300, Taiwan

TEL: 0933-444-221

wang @chu.edu.tw

OBJECTIVE

To apply for a managerial position in industrial engineering and/or quality assurance in a
semiconductor manufacturing company.

EDUCATION

1996　MS, Industrial Management, Chung-Hua University, Taiwan

Ranked No.1 upon graduation

Winner of Outstanding Thesis Award of the National Science

Council, ROC

1992　BS, Mechanical Engineering, Chung-Hua University, Taiwan

Ranked No.1 upon graduation

Coordinator, ME undergraduate students groups

EXPERIENCE

2000-present　Director, Industrial Engineering Division, Susex Technology Inc., responsible for establishing standard time, conducting work evaluation and design, process planning, manpower planning, and production cost control.

Supervising 4 engineers and 12 technicians.

1996-1999　Engineer, Quality Control Division, Aaron Technology Inc.

Planning and conducting in-coming and final products spection, troubleshooting, and report the on-line problems to the division manager.

1994-1996　Part-time technical staff, Mechanical and Automation Division,

Industrial Technology Institute assist in computer data input, computer graphing References: Upon request.

王珍珍

300臺灣新竹市中山路15號

電話：0933-444-221

wang@chu.edu.tw

目的

申請半導體製造公司工業工程或品質保證部門之管理階層職位

學歷

1995　臺灣中華大學工業管理碩士第一名畢業

曾獲中華民國國家科學委員會傑出論文獎

1992　臺灣中華大學機械工程學士第一名畢業

機械工程系學會總幹事

經歷

2000　迄今Susex科技公司工業工程部主任負責建立標準工時、工作評估與設計、製程規劃、人力規劃與生產成本控制，督導4名工程師與12名技術員。

1996-1999　Aaron科技公司品質管制部工程師規劃與執行進料與最終產品檢驗、偵錯，並向部門經理報告線上問題。

1994-1996　工業技術研究院機械與自動化處，兼職技術員，協助電腦資料輸入與繪圖。

推薦函：應要求提供

7-2 自傳

除了履歷表以外，我們有時候也需要撰寫個人的傳記或自傳。個人傳記的長短視其用途與刊登的要求而定，而內容則以個人的學術、專業背景、特殊的經歷與工作表現為主。

1. YING-MIN LIU is an lecturer of industrial engineering at Ming-Chi College. He received a Bachelor of Engineering degree from Feng-Chia University in 1994 and an M.S. degree in industrial management from Chung-Hua University in 1996, both in Taiwan. He is currently enrolled in the Ph.D. program in technology management at Chung-Hua University. His current interests include operation management, supply chains, and artificial intelligence. Mr. Liu is a member of the Chinese Institute of Industrial Engineers.

   YING-MIN LIU 是明志學院的工業工程講師，他於1994年由逢甲大學得到工程學士再於1996年由中華大學得到工業管理碩士；兩者皆在臺灣。他目前就讀於中華大學科技管理研究所博士班。他目前的興趣包括作業管理、供應與人工智慧。Mr. Liu 是中國工業工程學會的會員。

2. FU SHIN (JESSICA) CHANG received her B.A. in business administration in 1998 and her M.S. in computer science in 2000 both from Chung-Hua University. She is currently employed at the systematic development division of Sutek Corporation in the Science Park, Hsin-Chu, Taiwan. Previously she worked as a research assistant at Chung-Sun Science and Technology Institute. Her research interests include human-computer interface design and system usability development.

   FU SHIN (JESSICA) CHANG 在1998年得到她的企業管理學士並於2000年得到電腦科學碩士，兩者皆在中華大學。她目前任職於臺灣新竹科學園區的Sutek公司的系統發展部門。之前她曾在中山科學院擔任研究助理。她的研究興趣包括人機介面設計與系統使用性開發。

3. Kristina Sloan received a B.A. degree in psychology from the University of Texas, Austin and an M.A. in psychology (applied experimental/ human factors) from California State University, Northridge, in 1986. She has conducted human factors research at the UT Biotechnology Laboratory, Rockwell International, and Perceptronics Inc. She is currently a consultant to Susex Corporation and is working on Xerox corporation projects that involve designing user interfaces for printer systems. Her research interests in human factors are concerned with consumer products, warning, and human-computer interaction.

Kristina Sloan 由德州大學澳斯汀分校獲得心理學學士，並於1986年由加州州立大學北嶺分校獲得心理學（應用實驗/人因工程）碩士。她曾經在洛克威爾國際公司、Perceptronics公司及UT生物科技實驗室從事人因工程研究。她目前是Susex公司的顧問並正在執行全錄公司之列印系統使用者介面設計的研究計畫。她的研究興趣在與人因工程有關的產品安全、警告標示與人與電腦互動的議題。

4. Raymond Jenkins is the Senior Vice President and Director of Intelligent Information Systems Division at Perceptronics Inc. He received his B.S., M.S., and Ph.D.degrees in engineering with specialization in human-machine system, computer methodology, and artificial intelligence from the University of Wisconsin. Dr. Jenkins has served as principal investigator and program manager on several R&D AI programs for DARPA, the Army, Air Force, Navy, and NASA. From 1972-1980, Dr. Jenkins was the senior member of the Avionics Technical Staff at Rockwell International on NASA's Space Shuttle Program. From 1968 to 1972, he worked as a systems engineer at the Ralph M. Parsons Company on the Safeguard and Sentinel anti-ballistic missile system program. During the last ten years, he has authored some 50 publications and conducted research in the areas of real-time expert system, tactical decision aids, robotics, intelligent tutoring systems, and human performance and workload analysis models. Dr. Jenkins is a member of AAAI, IEEE, the Human Factors and Ergonomics Society, ADPA, AIAA, and ACM.

Raymond Jenkins 是Perceptronics公司資深副總裁兼智慧系統工程部門主管。他在威斯康辛大學專修人機系統、電腦方法與人工智慧並獲得工程學士、碩士與博士學位。

Dr. Jenkins曾經在DARPA、陸軍、空軍、海軍、航太總署之多項AI研發計畫擔任計畫主持人與計畫經理。由1972-1980，Dr. Jenkins擔任洛克威爾國際公司製作航太總署太空梭計畫之資深航電技術服務成員。由1968- 1972，他曾擔任Ralph M. Parsons公司製作防衛義勇兵反彈道飛彈計畫之系統工程師。最近十年，他發行了五十份出版品，並執行了專家即時系統、戰術決策輔助、機器人、智慧監測系統、人員績效與工作負荷分析模式方面之研究。Dr. Jenkins是AAAI、 IEEE、人因工程學會、ADPA、AIAA、與ACM的會員。

5. KAI WAY LI is a professor with the Department of Industrial Management at Chung-Hua University (CHU) in Taiwan. While at the university, he had served as the secretary of the presidential office, chairman of the Department of Transportation Management, and the executive director of the Extension Education Center. Currently, he is also the Director of Environmental Safety & Health office at CHU. Dr. Li was elected as the 2002 visiting

scholar of Liberty Mutual Research Institute for Safety and a visiting scholar in Public Health, Harvard University. In 1991, Dr. Li received his doctorate in industrial engineering from Texas Tech University. He earned his M.S. in industrial engineering from the University of Texas at Arlington and his B.S. in civil engineering from the National Chiao Tung University. Dr. Li focuses his research on the prevention of injuries via ergonomic intervention, including slip/fall prevention, hand tool design, and work design/redesign. Dr. Li has published approximately 100 scientific articles and three books.

KAI WAY LI 是臺灣中華大學工業管理系的教授。在學校裡，他曾經擔任校長室秘書、交通管理系主任與推廣教育中心副主任。目前，他也是中華大學環境安全衛生室主任。Dr. Li被選為2002年Liberty Mutual Research Institute for Safety 與哈佛大學公共衛生學院的訪問學者。在1991年，Dr Li. 由Texas Tech University 獲得工業工程博士學位；他由德州大學Arlington分校取得工業工程碩士及由交通大學取得土木工程學士學位。Dr. Li 的研究專注於經由人因工程的介入來預防傷害的發生，包括滑倒－跌倒預防，手工具設計與工作設計/再設計。Dr. Li出版了大約100篇學術論文與三本書。

7

Chapter 8

備忘錄、傳真暨
其他文件

8-1 備忘錄

備忘錄 (memorandum) 是組織內部或組織間的正式文件，也就是我們一般所謂的公文，因此具備法定的效力，在組織內會建檔保留，以為日後業務執行、追蹤、責任歸屬及績效考核的依據。

備忘錄與中文的公文一樣需寫明發文者、收文者的姓名與職稱、日期及事由 (subject 或 regarding)，備忘錄發出前必須由發文者簽署（或 initial，即簽下 first name, middle name, 及 last name 的第一個字母）以示負責（由電子郵件發出的則不需簽署）。組織中下級人員對上級的備忘錄之事常包括申請、查詢、建議；上級對下級的備忘錄之事則常包括任命、工作分派、指示等。備忘錄在文件的開頭通常以 Memorandum 或 Memo 字樣來標示本文件為一備忘錄。由於備忘錄公文特質的要求，在撰寫時應用字精簡、精準，絕對不可語意不清。

1. 請款備忘錄

Expense Reimbursement Request

Memo

To :   TracyPollak

From :   Dal-Hong Song, Visiting Scholar, DEH/HSPH

Cc :   Ted Corty,Tom Sloason

Date :   25 July 2002

Re :   Expenses for airfare, Rental Car and Housing for May/June

Please find attached the following receipts for fullor partial reimbursement consistent with the position budget:

Roundtrip airfare from Taipei to Boston on Northwest airlines.

Rental car expense from 5-31 to 6-28 totaling$926.10.

Housing expenses from 5-30 to 6-26 totaling$2,517.90.

Notes :

There is an itinerary receipt. The final price is listed on a separate receipt also attached (the ticket was purchased through a discounter).

There is also a exchange rate receipt from the bank in Taipei to validate the rate.

Amount of airfare in Taiwan NT= 37,957.00

Conversion rate on date of purchase = 34.06 NT per US$

Amount to be reimbursed for airfare in US $= 1,114.42

Sincerely,

Dal-Hong Song

請款申請

備忘錄

致：Tracy Pollak

由：Dal-Hong Song、訪問學者、PEH/HSPH

副本：Ted Corty, Tom Sloason

日期：2002年7月25日

事由：五/六月之機票、租車與住宿費用

請核收所附以下之收據並核撥與職位預算相符之全額或部分額度之費用：

女由臺北到波士頓之西北航空來回機票

租車費用由5月31日至6月28日共計926.10元

住宿費用由5月30日至6月26日共計2,517.90元

註：

附有一件旅遊行程收據，最後價格列於所附之另一張收據上〈機票是由折扣商處購得〉。

另有一張由臺北的銀行提示匯率收據以確認匯率值。

機票價格新臺幣37,957.00

購買當日之匯率換算價34.06新臺幣兌一美元

機票應核退金額1,114.42美元。

誠摯的

Dal-Hong Song

2. 報告訓練活動辦理情形暨評估與改善建議

MICROBITE

Memorandum

November 25, 2003

To :   Mark Long, Human Resource

Cc :   TonyBraso, Accounting,

     Joseph Sloason, Operation Management

From : Gordon Smith, Training supervisor

Subject : November management Training Program: Evaluation

     And Recommendations

The November Management Training Session was successful, with training rated as "very good" by most participants. A few changes, beyond the recent innovations, should result in even greater training efficiency and profits.

Workshop Strengths

Especially useful in this session were several program innovations:

- Dividing class topics into two areas created a general-to-specificfocus: The first week's coverage of company structure and functions created a context for the second week's coverage of management skills.

- Videotaping and critiquing trainees' oral reports clarified their speaking strengths and weaknesses.

- Emphasizing interpersonal communication skills (listening, showing empathy, and reading nonverbal feedback) created a sense of ease about the group, the training, and the company.

Innovations like these ensure high-quality training. And future sessions could provide other innovative ideas.

Suggested Changes/Benefits

From the trainees' evaluation of the November session (summary attached) and my observations, I recommend these additional changes:

- We should develop several brief (one-day) on-the-job rotations in different sales and service areas before the training session. These rotations would give each member a real-life view of duties and responsibilities throughout the company.

- All training sessions should have at least 10 to 15 members. Larger classes would make more efficient use of resources and improve class-speaker interaction.

MICROBITE
備忘錄

2003年11月25日

致：Mark Long，人力資源

副本：Tony Braso，會計部

　　　Joseph Sloason，營運管理

發件人：Gordon Smith，訓練課長

主旨：11月份管理訓練計畫：評估與建議

　　11月份的管理訓練場次被大部分的參與者評分為「非常好」（可說是辦理的很成功），在最近的變革下，一些改變將會產生更大的訓練效率與效益。

研討會的強化

這場活動特別有用的是幾項計畫的創新：

- 將課程主題分成二部分以建立一個由一般到特定的聚焦，第一週所涵蓋公司之結構與功能，建立了第二週所涵蓋之管理技巧之前景。
- 攝影與評論受訓者之口頭報告，可讓他們口語能力的強弱變的很清楚。
- 強調人際溝通技巧（傾聽、表現入神的態度與讀取非口語的回饋）建立關於群體、訓練與公司之輕鬆氣氛。

諸如此類的創新可確保高品質的訓練，未來的場次可以提供其他創新的構想。

建議之變更/效益

由受訓者11月場次（附結論）所作之評分與個人之觀察，個人建議以下之額外之變革：

- 我們應該發展幾項短暫（一天）的在職輪調，這些輪調將會給予每個成員對全公司關於責任與職責的真實的全貌。
- 所有訓練場次至少要有10到15個成員，較大的班級能夠更有效率的使用資源並提高講員與班上成員的互動。.

3. 通知一般規定

Memo

From :　　White, Kathy

Sent :　　Friday, August 01, 2003

To :　　All employees

Subject :　　Lunchroom/Bikes

Three bulletin boards as well as a whiteboard have been placed in the lunchroom. These bulletin boards are for the following:

Bulletin boards

1. Employee wage, fair practice, etc information (closest one to the vending machines)
2. Official notices, conference agendas, and meeting information
3. Employee board - any item you wish to post (selling vehicles, newspaper articles, etc.). If posting on this board, please have a "toss by" date on the posting.

Whiteboard

To be used for general use (employee functions/celebrations, etc.) Also, a bicycle rack has been purchased for employee bikes. The bicycle rack is located outside the employee stair tower (Building F) and Building D's side door closest to the rear parking lot.Starting Monday, all bicycles are to be stored at the bike rack, not in the buildings.

備忘錄

發件人：White Kathy

寄送日期：2003年8月1日星期五

致：全體員工

主旨：午餐室/腳踏車

午餐室已新增了三個公布欄與一個白板，這些公布欄與一個白板的用途如下：

公布欄

員工薪資，一般業務等資訊（最接近販賣機的那一塊）。

正式公告，研討會日程與會議資訊。

員工公告－任何你希望張貼事項（賣車、報紙文章等），如果張貼在本布告欄，請寫下「可清除」之日期。

白板

一般用途（員工集會/慶典等），另外，已為了員工採購了一個腳踏車架，車架放置於員工階梯塔（F棟）與D棟側門鄰接停車場的後面，自下一週開始，所有腳踏車必需停放在腳踏車架上，不可放置於建築物內。

4. 通知一般規定

Memo

From :　　White, Kathy

Sent :　　Friday, August 01, 2003

To :　　All employees

Subject :　Lunchroom/Bikes

I forgot to mention that there is also a literature rack located in the lunchroom for magazines/newspapers/brochures - all items should also have a "toss by" date posted on them.

備忘錄

發件人：White , Kathy

寄送日期：2003年8月1日,星期五

致：全體員工

主旨：午餐室/腳踏車

　　我忘了提到在午餐室還有一個書報架可以放置雜誌、報紙、小冊子，所有物件上都必須寫上「可清理」日期。

5. 通知稿件處理程序變更

Memo

From :　　Morgado, Amy

Sent :　　Tuesday, July 22, 2003

To :　　All research staffs

Cc :　　Bang, Joan; White, Kathy; Rothwell, Mary; Mik, Jerilyn; Bolsen, Patricia; Gouin, Joanne; Lenis, Diane

Subject :　Change in Papers in Process Procedure

Importance : High

In order to simplify the paper processing system for everyone, we now require that forms, manuscripts, acceptances, etc. be submitted to myself and Diane Lernis electronically instead of hard copy. Please follow the directions on the attached, revised papers in process form for all future paper submittals.

Over the next several weeks, I will contact each of you for electronic copies of manuscripts that are currently in the paper processing system, in order to bring the whole system up to date.

If you have any questions, please contact me.

備忘錄

發件人：Morgado , Amy

寄送日期：2003年7月22日,星期二

致：全體研究人員

副本：Bang , Joan ; White , Kathy ; Rothwell , Mary ; Mik , Jerilyn ; Bolsen , Patricia ; Gouin , Joanne ; Lenis , Diane

主旨：稿件處理程序之變更

重要性：高

　　為了簡化各位之稿件處理系統，我們現在要求表格、稿件、接受函等文件之電子檔，而非紙本，直接交給我與Diane Lenis，未來論文之投稿請遵守附件中修定之稿件處理表中之指示辦理。

　　在未來的幾週裡，為了將整個系統更新，我將會與各位聯絡有關正在處理程序中之論文。

　　有任何問題請與我聯絡。

6. 通知服裝規定

Memo

To :　　　Research Center Staff

From :　　Jerry Smith, Director

Date :　　May 20, 2003

Subject :　Casual Friday dress

Beginning June 1, all staffs may wear casual clothes to work on Fridays. Staffs who have meetings with people who do not work for this center will dress appropriately for the appointments.

Blue jeans and clothing with holes are not appropriate dress and should not be worn. Please acknowledge this memo by initialing and dating it.

備忘錄

致：研究中心員工

發件人：Jerry Smith , 主任

寄送日期：2003年5月20日

主旨：週五可穿便服

由六月一日開始，全體員工週五可穿便服上班，在預期要會見非在本中心工作的訪客，在會客時應穿著適當。

藍色的牛仔衣褲與衣服上有洞不是適當的衣著，請勿穿著。看完後，請簽名與日期以示知悉。

7. 通知電腦系統維護

Memo

From :　　　Desktop Services Communications

Sent :　　　Thursday, August 07, 2003

Subject :　　Broadcast Communication:Scheduled Network Maintenance

Scheduled Network Maintenance For Employees

Due to scheduled maintenance, network services will be unavailable in all offices on Sunday, August 10, 2003 from 7:00 a.m. to 1:00 p.m. EDT.

During this time, you will not have access to e-mail at the office or through remote access (including Outlook Web Access and Blackberry). In addition, you may not be able to print or access other online services. Maintenance is necessary to ensure high availability and quality of network services.

備忘錄

發件人：桌上電腦服務通訊處

寄送日期：2003年8月7日,星期四

主旨：廣播通訊、網路維護時程安排

員工網路維護作業之安排

由於排定之維護作業，所有辦公室之網路服務將會在東部時間2003年8月10日上午七點到下午一點中斷。

在這段時間，您將無法在辦公室或由遙控（包括Outlook Web Access與Blackberry）收發電子郵件。另外，您可能無法從事其它線上服務之列印與存取。維護作業是確保網路服務之高度有效性與品質。

Before the Maintenance Period

Please do the following by the end of day Friday, August 8, 2003:

1. Close all applications, including Microsoft Outlook.
2. Lock your computer by pressing the CTRL-ALT-DEL keys and choosing Lock Computer.
3. Turn off your monitor.

It is good practice to perform these steps at the end of every day. Note: If you do not perform these steps, just restart your computer after the maintenance period.

After the Maintenance Period

On Monday, August 11, 2003, there is no need to restart your computer unless you experience a problem. Follow the directions below if you have to restart:

Windows 2000/NT Users:

1. Close all applications.
2. Choose Start > Shut Down.
3. Select Restart and click OK.

Windows 95 Users:

1. Close all applications.
2. Choose Start > Shut Down.
3. Select Restart your computer and click Yes.

If you experience printing problems, please also turn off/on the printer you use.

For VPN or Dial-in users with an external modem, please restart your modem in addition to your computer.

Below is the list of remaining scheduled maintenance dates in 2003. You will receive a reminder prior to each date.

Sunday, September 14, 2003

Sunday, October 12, 2003

維修期之前

請在2003年8月8日星期五下班前完成以下事項：

1. 關閉所有應用程式，包括微軟之Outlook

2. 經由按CTRL-ALT-DEL鍵與選擇閉鎖電腦來閉鎖您的電腦

3. 關閉螢幕

每天下班前都做這些動作是很好的習慣。註：如果您不執行這些步驟，只要在維護期後，重新啟動您的電腦即可。

維護期之後

在2003年8月11日星期一，除非遇到問題否則不須重新啟動電腦，如果要重新開機請遵守以下指示：

Windows 2000/NT使用者

1. 關閉所有應用程式

2. 選擇開始>關閉

3.選擇重新開機並按OK

Windows 95使用者

1. 關閉所有應用程式

2. 選擇開始>關閉

3. 選擇重新開機並按Yes

如果您遇到列印的問題，也請關閉再打開您使用的列表機，對於VPN或外部數據機撥入之使用者，除了電腦外也請您重開您的數據機。

以下是2003年剩於之排定日期之維護作業清單，您將會在這些日期前收到提醒。

2003年9月14日，星期日

2003年10月12日，星期日

8. 通知電腦安全系統升級

Memo

From： Desktop Services Communications

Sent： Friday, August 08, 2003 2:03 PM

Subject： Critical Security Update for Windows 2000

Importance：High

Critical Security Update for Windows 2000 for all employees

A Microsoft Security Patch will be automatically installed on your computer in the next few days.

Why is it important to have this update?

This critical update, called Microsoft Windows 2000 HotFixKB823980 1.0, is required on all company computers in order to protect our environment from cyber terrorism.

This update requires a restart. A staggered communication will be sent asking everyone to restart his/her computer over a period of days. When you receive this second communication, you should restart your computer during that same business day.This ensures that the Microsoft Security Patch has been successfully installed on your computer.

Note:

• Remote Dial-in users: You will automatically receive this update through your dial-in connection. The installation of this update will take approximately 30-45 minutes (depending on your connection). You should avoid opening or working in applications while the installation is running.

• Remote Broadband users: You will automatically receive this update through your broadband connection. The installation of this update will take approximately 10-20 minutes (depending on your connection). You should avoid opening or working in applications while the installation is running.

If you have questions or experience computer problems, please call the User Support Center at SDN 8-422-2255 or 1-888-873-2217.

備忘錄

發件人：桌上電腦服務通訊處

寄件日期：2003年8月8日星期五

主旨：視窗2000重要安全性更新

重要性：高

所有員工之視窗2000重要安全性更新

在未來的數天內一個微軟安全修補程式將會被自動的安裝在您的電腦。

這項更新有何重要性？

這項被稱為微軟視窗2000 HotFix KB 823 980 1.0的重要更新必須安裝在所有公司的電腦上，以在網路的恐怖攻擊中保護我們的環境。

這項更新需要重開電腦，在為期幾天的時間裡，一個搖晃的訊息將會發送給每個人，要求重新開機，您應該在同一個工作天中重開電腦，這樣能確保微軟的安全修補程式能成功的安裝在您的電腦上。

註：

- 遙控撥號使用者：您將會自動的經由撥號連線收到這項更新，這項更新的安裝將需時30-45分鐘（視連線速度而定），安裝執行時，您應該避免開啟或使用應用程式。

- 遙控寬頻使用者：您將會經由寬頻連線，自動的收到這項更新，這項更新的安裝大約需時10-20分鐘（視連線速度而定），安裝執行時，您應該避免開啟或使用應用程式。

有任何疑問或遇到電腦問題時，請致電使用者支援中心於8-422-2255或1-888-873-2217

8-2 傳真

在許多場合，傳真（fax 或是 facsimile）是文件傳輸常用的方式。傳真的主要內容可能是包括書信在內的各種文件，傳真文件與郵寄及電子郵件的差別在於傳真的雙方必須以傳真機來收發文件。一般機構的傳真機通常是多人共用的，因此傳真時必須以一傳真首頁來說明，否則傳真文件容易遺失：

- 傳送人資料
- 收件人職稱與姓名
- 主旨或事由 (subject)
- 文件頁數

1. 傳真首頁

FAX

To :   Mr. Ted Marsey, Associate Director

Liberty Mutual Research Institute

Fax : 508-416-9673

From :   Kai Way Li

          Department of Industrial Management

          Chung-Hua University

          Fax: +886-3-537-2841

          Jan 10, 2002

Subject :   To apply for the 2002 visiting scholar

The application materials contain 12 pages (including this page):

- application form – one page

- resume & publication records of the applicant – four pages

- research proposal – four pages

- statement of commitment of the applicant – one page

- statement of commitment from the applicant's home institution – one page

傳真

致：Mr. Ted Marcey,副處長

    Liberty Mutual Research Instute

    Fax：508-416-9673

由：李開偉

    工業管理系

    中華大學

    Fax：+886-3-537-2841

    2002年1月10日

主旨： 申請擔任2002年訪問學者

申請資料12頁（包括本頁）

- 申請表- 1頁

- 申請人之履歷與著作紀錄- 4頁

- 研究計畫書- 4頁

- 申請人之承諾聲明- 1頁

- 申請人服務機關之同意聲明- 1頁

8-3　公告

　　公告（announcement）是組織對內或對外之特定人員宣布的事項，其撰寫可以一般敘述的方式陳述，公告也是公文的一種，由組織發布，發布前通常會在內部文件中由負責人簽署；公告本身不需任何人簽署。

1. 公告學術研討會徵文

Call for papers on slips, trips and falls

There will be an International Symposium on slips, trips and falls at the Ergonomics Society Annual Conference 2004 which will be held at the University of Wales, Swansea, UK from April 14 to 16, 2004. The objective of this symposium is to provide a technical forum on slip, trip and fall accidents for safety researchers and consultants around the world to present their latest findings and to exchange research ideas. The symposium will cover all aspects related to the problems from research to practical experience, such as falls from heights, biomechanics, slip resistance measurements, standardization, pedestrian fall prevention, flooring and stairway design and development, design of footwear, anti-skid devices, and housekeeping. Papers may address industrial safety as well as safety at home and during leisure-time.

If you are interested in presenting your papers at this symposium, please follow the guidelines for abstract submission listed at the conference website www.ergonomics.org.uk/events/AC2004Call.htm. Please indicate in your submission that your abstract(s) is (are) for this symposium. The deadline for abstract submission is August 22, 2003. Each paper will be allocated six pages in the Congress proceedings, published by Taylor and Francis. The deadline for the full papers will be December 19, 2003.

For questions about the symposium, please contact:

Harvey McGrory
Health & Safety Unit
Department of Human Sciences
Loughborough, Leicestershire, LE243WR
United Kingdom
Phone : 44-1509-143042
Fax : 44-1509-226240

滑倒、絆倒、跌倒研究徵文

在2004年4月14-16日於英國Swansea的威爾斯大學舉辦的2004年人因工程學會年會,將會有一場關於滑倒、絆倒與跌倒方面研究的國際論壇。這個論壇的目的,是對世界各地的安全研究人員與顧問提供滑倒、絆倒、跌倒事故技術研討會來呈現他們最新的發現與交換研究的構想。這個論壇將會涵蓋所有研究到實際經驗與這些問題相關的議題,包括由高處墜落、生物力學、抗滑量測、標準化、行人跌倒預防、地板鋪設與階梯設計與發展、鞋設計、抗滑器材與維護。論文可以強調工業安全與居家與休閒時間之安全。

如果您有興趣在本論壇展示您的論文,請洽詢www.ergonomics.org.uk/events/AC2004Call.htm研討會網站上所列的摘要投稿之指引來做。請在投稿時指明您的摘要是歸屬於本論壇的,摘要投稿之截止期限是2003年8月22日,每篇論文都會在由Taylor與Francis公司出版的研究會論文集上預留6頁的空間,全文的截稿日是2003年12月9日。

對論壇有問題請洽:

Harvey McGrory

Health & Safety Unit

Department of Human Sciences

Loughborough ,Leicestershire ,LE243WR

United Kingdom

電話:44-1509-143042

傳真:44-1509-226240

2. 徵求短期訪問學者

Visiting Scholar Program

Liberty Research Center for Safety and Health

705 Frankland Road

Hopkinton, CA 01082

Telephone: 528 436-4561

For more than 40 years, the *Liberty Research Center for Safety and Health* has been internationally recognized for its research in the prevention of injury and illness in the workplace. Through broad based research programs, and in close collaboration with customers, universities and researchers around the world, the Center strives to accomplish its primary purpose, embodied in the Liberty Creed, to relieve pain and sorrow and fear and loss in the workplace. A commitment to peer-review publication is at the heart of the Center's ongoing mission.

From Research to Reality^{TM}

The research program embraces both fundamental and applied research towards the improvement of occupational safety and health. The Center aims to determine the causes of accidents and injuries and then proceeds to identify and validate interventions. From investigations which are reported in peer-reviewed literature, the objective is to drive down the incidence rates of injuries and disorders, and to reduce the disabilities which arise from those accidents which do occur. The Center's research findings are used in many applications, including:

- engineering design modifications found in all modern motor vehicles
- manual materials handling criteria used throughout the world
- devices for the field measurement of coefficients of friction, used nationwide
- machine guarding criteria, which have been adopted in a number of national and international standards

The Center's research has also resulted in vibration measurement and analysis techniques, staircase design, field measurement of the attenuation of hearing protective devices, and innumerable workplace redesigns carried out through the interventions of 650 consultants.

On-Site Facilities

The Center's 40th anniversary in 1994 marked the opening of 16,000 square feet of new laboratory space and a significant extension of its capability. With a total of 15 Laboratories in operation, the scope of research has been expanded and now extends from biomechanics to electronics, and from field studies to theoretical modeling. At any given time, approximately 50 projects are operational.

The Liberty Industrial Hygiene Analytical Laboratory provides technical support to Liberty's field consultants and customers, and Liberty Technology produces and continues development of the Liberty Boston Elbow.

Visiting Scholar Program

The Visiting Scholar Program was initiated in 1994 with the objective of establishing collaborative relationships with senior researchers in areas of mutual interest. Each year, one individual is selected to spend three or more months at the Center. In accordance with the ResearchCenter's commitment to peer-review research, a minimum of a joint peer review publication is expected from this collaboration, but a longer term relationship between the Center and the Scholar's home institution would be encouraged.

Application Procedure

The Liberty Scholar Application should consist of:

A. A brief outline of less than two pages of the research proposal, indicating whether the proposal is part of an ongoing program or a new initiative.

B. *A resume, including publication record and the current position held by the applicant.*

C. *The identification, where possible, of potential contributions to LibertyResearchCenter for Safety and Health .*

D. *The anticipated period and dates of the visit.*

E. *A provisional commitment from the Scholar's home institution for participation in the program or a statement from the applicant which addresses this issue.*

Initial proposals will be reviewed for scientific and business relevance, and a confidential, external review may be used as appropriate. Following the identification of the successful applicant, the Scholar will provide a more detailed proposal, which will form the basis of the relationship between the scholar and LibertyResearchCenter for Safety and Health.

Mail or fax applications to :

LibertyResearchCenter for Safety and Health

705 Frankland Road

Hopkinton, CA 01082

Fax : 508-435-5426

Stipend

The Scholar will be provided with a stipend for three months. However, if this stipend is used to supplement the existing base salary of the Scholar, the period of residence may exceed three months and extend up to one year, making it suitable as a location for sabbatical leaves for academic researchers. A vehicle will be provided for three months.

Air Fare

Air fare will be provided to cover the cost of one return air trip, or its equivalent, based upon the lowest, commercially available fare from an established carrier.

Research Costs

Research costs identified in the detailed proposal will be subject to negotiation, but the expectation is that this will form part of an ongoing LibertyResearchCenter program. Because the Scholar will become part of the LibertyResearchCenter staff, access to computing, office support, etc., will be the same as all staff researchers.

Visa

Where appropriate, Liberty will assist the Scholar in seeking the appropriate work visa as requested by the Department of Naturalization and Investigation.

Liberty Harvard Program in Occupational Safety and Health

Through the Center's relationship with HarvardUniversity, opportunities will be provided for the scholar to make presentations to a wider academic audience and to discuss potential collaboration.

The Campus

The campus consists of 86 wooded acres, including a small lake, and is located 26 miles west of Boston, at the junction of Route 495 and the Boston Turnpike.

Physical Facilities

40,000 square feet office and laboratory space：26,000 sq. ft. Research; 3500 sq. ft. Liberty Technology; 10,500 sq. ft. AIHA accredited Industrial Hygiene Analytical Laboratory

15 Research Laboratories:

- 3-acre DrivingRange
- Acoustics Laboratory
- Biomechanics Laboratory
- Cognitive Psychology Laboratory
- Cumulative Trauma Laboratory
- Driving Simulator
- Electronics/Computer Laboratory
- Environmentally Controlled Chamber
- Epidemiology Laboratory
- Human:Machine Systems Laboratory
- Low Back Pain Laboratory
- Occupational Physiology Laboratory

Prosthetics

Semi-Anechoic Chamber

Tribology Laboratory

Computing Capabilities

Hardware :

Apple and IBM PC's; Digital Equipment VMS workstations; UNIX workstations; Liberty nationwide network.

Software :

SAS; ProCite Library System; Microsoft Word and Excel; PageMaker; PowerPoint; 4D; Informed Manager; ETS; ARTS; BoComp; DEBRA

訪問學者計畫

Liberty安全與健康研究中心

705 Frankland Road

Hopkinton, CA01082

電話：528 436-4561

超過40個年頭，*Liberty安全與健康研究中心*在職業場所疾病與傷害預防上之研究獲得了國際上的聲譽。經由廣泛基礎的研究計畫及與客戶、大學及世界各地學者間等密切合作，中心致力完成深植於Liberty 信念的主要目標來減輕職場中之疼痛、不幸、遺憾、恐懼與損失，承諾發表經同儕審查的出版品是本中心進行中任務的核心。

經由研究來達到務實™

研究計畫涵蓋能改善職業安全與健康的基礎與應用研究，本中心致力於決定意外與傷害的成因並進一步來找出與實證介入的方案。經由報導於同儕審查文獻的調查，（本中心）之目標在於降低傷害與疼痛的事故率，並減少由那些會發生之事故所造成之失能。

本中心的研究發現被應用在許多地方，包括：

- 於所有現代化汽車的工程設計改良
- 應用於世界各地的人工物料處理準則
- 使用全國的現場摩擦係數量測器材
- 許多國家與國際標準曾持用的機器防護準則

中心的研究也發展出了震動量測與分析技術、階梯設計、聽力防護具減音的現場量測及經由650位顧問師介入之無數的工作場所再設計的執行。

現地設施

1994年本中心40週年標記了16,000英呎全新實驗空間的啓用與（研發）能量之顯著擴充。經由15個實驗室的營運，研究的範圍現在已由生物力學到電子學，由現場調查至理論模式已被擴充。在任何時間，大約有50個研究計畫同時在進行。

Liberty工業衛生分析實驗室提供Liberty的現場顧問師與客戶技術支援，Liberty技術部生產與Liberty波士頓手臂的持續發展。

訪問學者計畫

基於與有共同興趣的資深學者建立合作關係的目的，訪問學者肇始於1994年。每年有一位學者被挑選來花三個月或更長的時間在中心，為了配合中心發表同儕審查著作的承諾，這種合作預期至少發表一篇經同儕審查之著作，但中心鼓勵與學者服務機關進行長期的合作。

申請程序

Liberty學者申請資料應包括：

A. *一份不超過兩頁的簡短的研究計畫書，要指明該計畫書是進行中計畫的一部分或是全新的開始。*

B. *一份履歷表，包括申請人之著作記錄及目前職位。*

C. *可能的話指出對Liberty 安全與健康研究中心會有之潛在貢獻。*

D. *預期訪問的期間與日期。*

E. *學者服務機關對於參與本計畫之承諾，或者申請人之承諾聲明。*

初步的計畫書將會被審查其科學與商業之相關性。如果需要的話，隱密的外部審查也可能會進行。在找出成功的申請者之後，學者將需要提出一份詳細的計畫書，它將成為學者與Liberty安全健康研究中心的合作基礎。

郵寄或傳真申請資料：

　　　Liberty安全健康研究中心

705 Frankland

　　　Hopkinton，CA 01082

　　　傳真：508-435-5426

薪資

學者將會有三個月的薪資,但如果這分薪水是用來彌補學者的現有底薪,訪問期可由三個月延長最多至一年,以配合學術界的學者成為一個適合休假訪問的所在。本中心將提供一輛汽車為期三個月。

機票

本中心提供同於一般商業航空客機最低費率之往返機票之費用。

研究費用

詳細計畫書中明列之研究支出將可研議,但本中心期望(那些支出)將成為Liberty 中心進行計畫之一部分。因為學者將會成為Liberty 研究中心之一員,其使用電腦、辦公室等的權利將和全體研究人員相同。

簽證

適當情況下,Liberty將會協助學者取得由歸化與調查部要求的適當工作簽證。

Liberty -哈佛職業安全與健康計畫

經由本中心與哈佛大學之關係,中心將提供學者對更廣泛的學術界作簡報與討論可能合作之機會。

中心園區

本中心園區位於波士頓西方26英哩,495號公路與波士頓高速公路之交會處,包括一個小湖共占地86英畝。

實體設施

40,000平方英呎之辦公與研究空間;26,000平方英呎研究空間;3,500平方英呎Liberty技術部;10,500平方英呎之AIHA權工業衛生分析實驗室。

15個研究實驗室包括:

    3英畝駕駛場

    聲響實驗室

    生物力學實驗室

    累積性傷害實驗室

    駕駛模擬器

    電子/電腦實驗室

    環境控制室

    流行病學實驗室

    人機系統實驗室

    下背痛實驗室

    工作生理實驗室

    義肢

　　半-無迴聲實驗室
　　潤滑學實驗室
計算能力
硬體：

Apple與IBM電腦；Digital設備VMS工作站；UNIX工作站；Liberty全國網路。

軟體：

SAS；Pro Cite Liberty系統；微軟WORD與Excel；Page Maker；

Power Point 4D；informed Manager；ETS；ARTS；Bo Comp；DEBRA。

3. 公告訪問學者來訪

Visiting Scholar Program Enters It's Eighth Year

Since its inception, the Visiting Scholar Program has offered unique collaborative experiences for senior researchers from around the world. In keeping with the tradition, the Center has selected Kai Way Li, Ph.D. as the 2002 Liberty Research Center Visiting Scholar. This summer, he will collaborate with Center researchers on a slips and falls research project.

Dr. Li is an associate professor with the department of industrial management at Chung-Hua University in Taiwan. While at the University, he has served as special assistant to the president, chairman of the Department of Transportation Management, and the executive director of the Extension Education Center. In 1991, Dr. Li received his doctorate in industrial engineering from Texas Tech University. He earned his M.S. in Industrial Engineering from the University of Texas at Arlington and his B.S. in Civil Engineering from the National Chiao Tung University.

"I'm honored to be selected as the 2002 Visiting Scholar," states Dr. Li. "To visit the Center and to participate in the slips and falls research project will be a great experience for me. This joint project is an exciting one. I'm looking forward to collaborate with the Center researchers this summer."

While at the Center, Dr. Li will work with four other researchers to investigate the role of friction level and friction variation in worker reports of slipperiness in restaurants. Through this study, researchers hope to find a link between friction variation or friction level and factors influencing worker reports of slipperiness. The results should increase knowledge of the interactions between physical surface measures and human-centered measures- a key theme of 2001's special issue of Ergonomics on The Measurement of Slipperiness (Vol. 44 No. 13, October 2001).

訪問學者計畫進入它的第八個年頭

從一開始，本訪問學者計畫提供了由世界各地資深研究人員獨特的合作經驗。為了保持傳統，本中心選出李開偉博士擔任2002年Liberty 研究中心的訪問學者。今年夏天，他將會與中心的研究員合作進行滑倒與跌倒方面的研究計畫。

李博士是臺灣中華大學工業管理系的副教授，在學校裡，他曾擔任校長的特別助理、交通管理學系主任與推廣教育中心副主任。李博士在1991年由德州理工大學獲得工業工程博士學位，他由德州大學阿靈頓分校獲得工業工程碩士及國立交通大學獲得土木工程學士。

「我很榮幸被選為2002年的訪問學者」李博士說：「訪問中心並參與滑倒與跌倒研究計畫對我將會是一個絕佳的經驗，這個合作計畫是很刺激的，我期待今年暑假與中心的研究員一起合作。」

在中心期間，李博士將與其他四位研究員一起調查餐廳裡地板摩擦值之水準與變異在工作人員反應之地板光滑程度上之角色。經由這個研究，研究人員希望找到摩擦變異或摩擦水準間之關連性與會影響工人反應地板滑溜性之因子。研究結果將會增加我們對物理表面量度與以人為中心之量度間互動方面的知識，這是2001年Ergonomics滑溜性量測專刊揭示的一個主要議題（Vol. 44. No.13，2001年10月）。

4. 校友聯絡暨宣布新任國際事務主管

Greetings from University of Texas!

I am pleased to write you that United States Ambassador William R.. Endsley, Jr. is the new Associate Vice Provost for International Affairs and Director of the International Cultural Center at the University of Texas. Below is some biographical information about him. We in the Office of International Affairs are most pleased with his appointment.He is a wonderful advocate for international education. He is aware of our Alumni Abroad program and wants to strengthen our connections with our alumni and looks forward to welcoming many of you to our 2005 Homecoming Reunion.From those who responded to the survey, either the first or second weekend in April 2005 seems to be best time for the Reunion.Let me know your preferred date for the reunion in April 2005 and if you would be interested in participating in an International Golf Tournament.   Chris

Endsley assumes duties at the University of Texas

United States Ambassador William R. Endsley, Jr. named the new Associate Vice Provost for International Affairs and Director of the International Cultural Center, and assumed his duties June 2003.

Ambassador Endsley served as U.S. Ambassador to Ethiopia from 1999-2002and to Guinea from 1996-1999. Prior to his Ambassadorship to Guinea,Endsley attended the Department of State's most prestigious training program, the one-year Senior Seminar. During this time he lectured at educational facilities and to civic groups around the country about U.S. foreign policy, Africa, diplomatic careers and about life in the Foreign Service.

The Ambassador joined the Foreign Service in 1978 as a management analyst in the Bureau of Personnel. His first overseas assignment was as a General Services Officer in Lusaka, Zambia from 1979-1981. He later was assigned to Victoria, Seychelles, for two years as an Administrative Officer.

由德州大學來的問候

我很高興通知你們美國大使 William R. Endsley Jr. 是德州大學新任的國際事務處副處長暨國際文化中心主任。以下是一些關於他的個人資料，國際事務處的同仁都很高興他的任命，他是一位國際教育的先進，他熟悉本校之海外校友計畫並打算強化本校與校友間之連繫並期望歡迎各位在2005年之返校大團聚。經由對問卷回應的校友之反應，2005年4月的第一或第二個週末似乎是最好的團圓時間，請讓我知道你較適合哪一個時間及是否對參與國際高爾夫巡迴賽有興趣。　Chris

Endsley於德州大學任職
美國大使William R. Endsley Jr. 被任命為新任
國際事務副處長暨國際文化中心主任
並於2003年6月就職

Endsley大使於1999至2002與1996至1999年間分別擔任美國駐衣索匹亞大使與駐蓋亞那大使。在擔任蓋亞那大使之前，Endsley參與了國務院著名的訓練計畫：一年之資深研討會；在這段期間他在全國各民間團體與教育機構講授了美國的對外政策、非洲事務與他在海外服務的外交生涯。

大使先生於1978加入海外服務，並擔任人事局之管理分析師。他的第一個海外任命是於1979至1981年間擔任於尚比亞之盧沙卡的一般服務事務員；之後，他被派到維多利亞的Seychelles擔任兩年的行政官員。

He next served as Systems Administrator for the African Bureau in Washington, D.C. from 1983-1984. Afterwards, he returned overseas as the Administrative Officer in Addis Ababa, Ethiopia from 1984-1986. He was the Deputy Chief of Mission in Lome, Togo from 1987-1990; Cameroon from 1990-1993; and Nigeria from 1993-1995.

His most recent assignment involved him serving as a "Diplomat in Residence" for the South-Central region, based out of the University of Oklahoma's International Programs Office.This is a program of the Department of State to bring greater diversity into America's diplomatic corps.Ambass-
adorEndsley used his foreign service experience to promote the work of the various U.S. Foreign Affairs Agencies, and to help students prepare for the Department of State's series of examinations. He also taught a course at the University of Oklahoma entitled *Africa and the World*.

The Ambassador has been the featured speaker at a number of educational and civic events, including as keynote speaker at the most recent graduation ceremonies held in May.

Among Ambassador Endsley's numerous awards are the U.S. Department of State's Superior Honor Award for his role in helping end the recent Eritrean War; the Meritorious Honor Award for helping alleviate the 1984/85 East African famine; and the National Order of Merit of the Republic of Guinea for strengthening bilateral relations. He speaks English, French and Hungarian.

William Endsley was born in Budapest, Hungary and arrived in the United States as a political refugee in 1957.He received his Bachelor of Arts degree in political science and history from the University of Texas in 1974, and his Masters of Administration degree in the management of information technology from George Washington University in 1978.

他隨後於1983至1984服務於華盛頓D.C.之非洲事務局擔任系統管理師；之後，他返回海外，於1984至1986年於衣索匹亞之阿迪斯阿巴巴擔任行政官員。並於下列期間擔任特遣團團長：1987至1990年之東加隆姆；1990至1993年之卡麥隆及1993至1995年之奈及利亞。

他最近的職務是擔任奧克拉荷馬大學國際計畫辦公室之中南區域在地外交官，這是一個國務院引進不同人才進入美國外交團隊的計畫。Endsley大使用他的海外服務經驗來提升各美國海外事務機構的工作，並幫助學生準備國務院辦理之系列考試。他並在奧克拉荷馬大學教授一門課程：非洲與世界。

大使先生曾在不同之教育與民間活動擔任**主講人,包括在五月舉行之最近一次畢業典禮擔任專題演講人**。

大使先生獲得的眾多獎章包括美國國務院為表揚他在協助終止最近的衣索匹亞戰爭所扮演角色之傑出榮譽獎;協助減輕1984年東非大饑荒之褒揚榮譽獎與為強化雙邊關係的蓋亞那共和國的國家褒揚令。他能說英文、法文與匈牙利文。

William Endsley出生於匈牙利之布達佩斯並於1957年以政治難民身分抵達美國,**他於1974年獲得德州大學政治與歷史文學士**,於1978年獲得喬治華盛頓大學資訊管理碩士學位。

The University Interim President, Jeffery R. Haragan said that *Ambassador Endsley would be an asset to the globalization efforts at the university. International education is one of the truly essential areas for any research university today, and we are extremely pleased to have Ambassador Endsley as our new leader to lead the way.*

Provost Jerry Marcy also praised Endsley saying,His personal knowledge of the United States Department of State, together with his international experience, will provide students, faculty and staff with rare insights about the rapidly changing world in which we live. I am thrilled to be associated with him.

Vice Provost Tim Brink said that Ambassador Endsley was the best candidate for the job. I had the pleasure of chairing the committee that sorted through more than 100 applications for the position of head of the Office of International Affairs and Director of the International Cultural Center, he said. We received many outstanding applications, but obviously that of William Endsley stood out. He brings international experience, a diplomatic career, successful administration, utmost professionalism, and other qualities that will make him an ideal person to continue and expand the fine work of that office. We are delighted that Ambassador Endsley has come to our university.

Ambassador Endsley has also made clear his delight at returning to UT. During his commencement address he *stressed the growing importance of international affairs and globalization to the life of all Americans. He also noted the growing prestige of UT around the world and stated his intent to keeping this momentum going.*

Chris S. Barkley

International Recruitment and International Alumni Relations

Office of International Affairs

本校代理校長Jeffery R. Haragan說*Endsley大使將會是學校在全球化努力上的一項資產，今日對任何一個研究型的大學而言，國際教育是一個不可或缺的領域，我們非常高興能有Endsley大使當我們這條道路的新領導人。*

Leamon Scientific Services, Inc.

25 WEST MARKET STREET 1 AKRON, OHIO 44303-2099

Tire Testing & Analysis

Vehicle Testing & Performance Evaluation

Laboratory Testing & Technical Consulting

Management Consulting & Market Research

WORLD HEADQUARTERS

PH : 330/762-7441   FAX : 330/762-7447

Jerry Marcy處長也稱讚Endsley說他對美國國務院的知識與國際經驗將會提供學生與教職員對於我們所處之快速變動世界獨特少有的見解。我很興奮能與他共事。

Tim Brink副處長說Endsley大使是這個職位最佳的候選人。他說：「我很榮幸由一百位申請人中挑選出擔任國際事務主管與國際文化中心主任的委員會主席的職位。我們收到許多傑出人士的申請，但明顯的William Endsley出線了」。他帶來了國際經驗、外交生涯成功管理、高度專業與其他會使他成為理想人選來繼續並延伸那個辦公室優良工作之特質。

Endsley大使也很明白的表示他很高興回到德州大學，在他畢業典禮的演講中他*強調國際事務與全球化對所有美國人的生活日益的重要，他也提到德州大學在世界上日益提升的聲望，並說明他打算持續保持這種動能運行的企圖。*

Chris S. Barlley

國際招生與國際校友關係組。

國際事務辦公室

8-4　報價單

Leamon Scientific Services,

Tire Testing & Analysis

Vehicle Testing & Performance Evaluation

Laboratory Testing & Technical Consulting

Management Consulting & Market Research

To :	Kai Way Li	Fax :	+886-3-542-6521
Company :	Chung-Hua University	Phone :	+886-3-518-5683
From :	Dick Jahant	Date :	November 25, 2003
Subject :	Price Quote	Pages to Follow :	0

Test Specification and Description　　　　　　　　**Price per**

Sample/Box

Blown Rubber

Both used in the ASTM C 1028 Test Method for

Coefficient of Friction

3" x 3" x 1/8" Sheets	$ 65.00 Per Sheet
6" x 6" x 1/4" Sheets	$ 105.00 Per Sheet

Price is plus shipping charge.

TOTAL AMOUNT DUE PRIOR TO SHIPMENT: CREDIT CARDS OR WIRE TRANSFERS ARE ACCEPTABLE METHODS OF PAYMENT.

The following is our Bank Information. When we receive notification that the funds have been wired, I will ship your order. Your invoice will be sent separately after we have received the money transfer. Please let me know if you have any questions. Thank you for your order.

FUNDS MAY BE WIRED DIRECTLY TO OUR ACCOUNT :

BANK NAME :   First City Bank

BANK ADDRESS :   116 Main Street, Akron, OH 42703

BANK ROUTING NUMBER :   0201223555

BANK ACCOUNT NUMBER :   5024-5611

There is a $15.00 Bank Wire Transfer fee for this option.

輪胎測試與分析

車輛測試與效能評估
實驗測試與技術顧問
管理咨詢與市場調查

To :	李開偉	Fax :	+886-3-542-6521
Company :	中華大學	Phone :	+886-3-518-5683
From :	Dick Jahant	Date :	November 25, 2003
Subject :	報價	Pages to Follow :	0

測試規格與描述　　　　　　　　　　　　　　　　**單價**

Sample/Box

發泡橡膠

使用於 ASTM C 1028 測試方法之
摩擦係數

3" x 3" x 1/8" 張	$ 65.00 每張
6" x 6" x 1/4" 張	$ 105.00 每張

價格包括運費

運送前需全額付清：信用卡或電匯是可接受的付款方式

　　以下是我們的銀行資料，當我們收到銀行入帳通知後我將會寄出您的訂貨。我們收款之後將會另外寄送發票。有任何問題請即告知，謝謝惠顧。

費用可以直接匯至我們的帳戶：

銀行：	First City Bank
銀行地址：	116 Main Street, Akron, OH 42703
銀行流通號碼：	0201223555
銀行帳號：	5024-5611

選擇銀行匯款將需支付 $15.00 的往來（手續）費用

8-5 同意書

說明研究目的與受測者的權利，並邀請受測者參與研究之同意書

Chung-Hua University

Informed Consent Form

Purpose of Study

The purpose of the proposed experiment is to explore the relationship between the measured friction and perception of worksite slipperiness. An attempt will be made to establish a link between slipperiness perception and the measured friction at actual worksites.

Benefits

There will be no direct benefit to you from your participation.

Participation

Your responsibility is to answer the questions listed in the perception survey of slipperiness. Your participation in this study is strictly voluntary. You have the option not to answer specific questions or to discontinue your participation at any time without penalty or question. You will be under no pressure to continue.

Risks

No additional risks associated with this survey participation are anticipated.

Confidentiality

Data obtained in this experiment will become the property of Department of Industrial Management, Chung-Hua University. You will not be asked to write your name on the survey. No personal information will go to your employer or supervisors.

Supervision

This study will be directly supervised by Kai Way Li, Ph.D. Questions or comments about participation should be directed to Dr. Li at (03) 537-4281 or 0931-542-450.

Videotaping

In this study, you might be photographed and/or videotaped. These photographic or video records are the property of Department of Industrial Management, Chung-Hua University and may be used at any time for any purpose.

Consent _____

Please read the following statement and sign on the line below if you agree to participate in the study.

 I have read this document and understand the purpose of the study, and what will be expected of me if I agree to participate. By signing this consent form, I agree freely to participate as a research subject without any pressure having been placed on me to do so.

I hereby grant to employees of Chung-Hua University, permission to use still, motion picture or video photography of me. I consent to the use of the photographs or reproductions of them by Department of Industrial Management, Chung-Hua University for any purpose including their use in research presentations, scientific periodicals, newspapers, magazines or other media for advertising or for any other purpose.

_____   _____
Signature   *Date*

中 華 大 學
書 面 同 意 書

研究目的

本（規劃）實驗的目的是要發掘量測到的摩擦與工作現場（人對）地板滑溜性認知之間的關係，（研究）將嘗試建立實際作業現場（人對）滑溜性的認知與地板摩擦量測值間的關連性。

報酬

您將不會由參與（本研究）得到直接的報酬。

研究參與

您的責任是回答滑溜性認知問卷上所列的問題，您的參與完全是志願性的，您有權利不回答特定的問題或隨時中止對問卷調查的參與而不會被懲罰或詢問，您將不會有任何必須繼續參與的壓力。

風險

參與問卷調查不會讓您遭遇任何的（身體傷害）風險。

保密

本實驗所取得的數據將成為中華大學工業管理系的財產，您將不會被要求在問卷上填寫姓名，您個人的資料也不會被透露給您的雇主或上司。

研究指導與管理

本研究由Dr. Kai Way Li直接負責，關於參與的問題或者意見應直接連絡Dr. Li 於(03) 537-4281 或0931-542-450。

影像拍攝

本研究中，您可能被照相或攝影。這些相片或錄影記錄是中華大學工業管理系的財產，（它們）將可能在任何時間使用於任何（研究）目的相片或錄影帶之使用完全以研究分析為主而不會被用在其他任何的目的。

簽名：_____

請閱讀以下聲明並在下方欄位上簽名以示同意參與本研究

本人已閱讀本同意書並了解本研究的目的與若同意參與將須配合的事項。經由本同意書的簽署，本人在沒有任何必須參與的壓力下同意參與本研究擔任受測者。

本人同意中華大學的（研究）人員可以使用本人靜態或動態相片或錄影，本人同意中華大學工業管理系使用這些相片或其再製品於任何用途包括研究展示、科學期刊、報紙、雜誌或其他媒體廣告或者其他（研究）目的。

-

_____   _____
　　　　　　　　　簽名　　　　　　　　　　　　　　　　　　　　　　　日期

Chapter 9
常用字彙

　　英文字彙一般都有多個意思，視其文章的背景而定。本單元所列之字彙的中文解釋是根據筆者的經驗，在技術文件與論文中較常用的解釋。

A

Abbreviation　縮寫 (n)

abnormal　異常的 (adj)

abnormality　異常 (n)

abstract　摘要 (n)

abundant　充足的 (adj)

accept　接受 (v)

acceptable　可接受的 (adj)

acceptance　接受 (n)

access　接近、捷徑、存取 (n)

accessibility　易接近、捷徑、易存取性 (n)

accessible　可取得的、容易理解的 (n)

accident　意外事件 (n)

acclimatization　適應〔氣候〕(n)

accordance　一致 (n)

accordingly　相應的、依據的 (adv)

accounting　會計學 (n)

achievement　成就、進展 (n)

acknowledge　感謝 (v)

acknowledged　公認的、被認可的 (adj)

acknowledgement　致謝 (n)

acoustic　聽覺的 (adj)

acquisition　取得 (n)

acronym　字頭 (n)

activate　驅動 (v)

adaptation　適應 (n)

address　強調 (v)

adequate　適當的、足夠的 (adj)

adequately　適當的、足夠的 (adv)

adjust　調整 (v)

adjustment　調整 (n)

adopt　採用 (v)

adoption　採用 (n)

aerobic　有氧的 (adj)

aesthetic　美學的 (adj)

aesthetics　美學的 (n)

affiliation　相關機構、服務單位 (n)

aggregate　集合 (n)(v)；聚集的 (adj)

aim　目標、目的 (n)；瞄準、指向 (v)

algebra　代數 (n)

algorithm　演算法 (n)

allocate　配置、分配 (v)

allocation　配置、分配 (n)

allowance　容差、寬放 (n)

alternative　選擇、取捨 (n)；選擇的、取捨的 (adj)

ambiguous　曖昧的、不明確的 (adj)

analog　類比、類似物 (n)

analysis　分析 (n)

analytical　分析的 (adj)

analyze　分析 (v)

animated　動畫的 (adj)

animated　漫畫 (n)

anonymosly　匿名的 (adv)

anonymous　匿名的 (adj)

anthropometrical　人體測計學的 (adj)

anthropometry　人體測計學 (n)

anticipate　預期 (v)

anticipate　預期 (v)

appendix　附錄 (n)

applicant　申請人 (n)

application　應用、申請 (n)

apply　應用、申請 (v)

appraisal　評價、鑑定 (n)

approach　途徑、方法、接近 (n)；
　　　　　研討、趨近 (v)

appropriate　適當的 (adj)

approximate　近似的、接近的 (adj)；
　　　　　近似、接近 (v)

approximately　近似的、接近的、
　　　　　大概的 (adj)

arithmetical　算數的 (adj)

article　文章 (n)

articulatory　關節的、分節的 (adj)

artificial　人工的 (adj)

aspect　方面 (n)

assert　主張 (v)

assess　評估 (v)

assessment　評估 (n)

assignment　指派工作、任務 (n)

assistance　協助 (n)

assistant　助理 (n)

associate　伙伴、副的 (n)

association　學會、團體 (n)

attenuate　減弱、稀釋 (v)

attenuation　減弱、稀釋 (n)

attribute　屬性 (n)；歸因於 (v)

auditory　聽覺的 (adj)

author (co-author)　作者 (共同作者) (n)

authorize　授權 (v)

authorship　作者身分、著作具名 (n)

autocorrelation　自相關 (n)

automate　使自動、自動操作 (v)

automatic　自動的 (adj)；自動的機器 (n)

automatically　自動的 (adv)

automation　自動化 (n)

autonomous　自發性的、自律的 (adj)

average　平均值 (n)；平均的 (adj)；
　　　　　平均化 (v)

avionics　航電學 (n)

aware　知道 (v)

B

Background　背景 (n)

basic　基本的 (adj)

basis　基礎 (n)

batch　批次、組 (n)

bearing　軸承 (n)

belief　信念 (n)

benchmark　基準、標竿 (n)

bi-(monthly)　兩 (個月的)

bias　傾斜、偏袒 (n) (adj)(adv)(v)

bibliography　參考書目 (n)

biomechanical　生物力學的 (adj)

biomechanical　生物力學的 (adj)

biomechanics　生物力學 (n)

biotechnology　生物科技 (n)

bivariate　雙變數的 (adj)

brief　簡明的、簡要的 (adj)

browser　瀏覽程式、瀏覽者 (n)

buffer　緩衝器 (n)

c

calculate　計算 (v)

calculation　計算、運算 (n)

capacity　容量、能力限度 (n)

case　個案、情況 (n)

catalog　目錄 (n)

cathode　陰極 (n)

causal　原因的、因果關係的 (adj)

challenge　挑戰 (v)

chapter　章 (n)

chart　圖 (n)；製圖 (v)

chronological　依年代順序排列的 (adj)

circuit　範圍、巡迴、線路、電路 (n)

citation　引用、列舉 (n)

cite　引用、列舉 (v)

clarify　澄清、闡明、瞭解 (v)

clarity　清楚 (n)

classification　分類 (n)

classify　分類 (v)

clutter　雜亂 (n)；弄亂

coefficient　係數 (n)

cognition　認知 (n)

cognitive　認知的 (adj)

coherence　附著、凝聚、一致 (n)

coherent　凝聚的、一致的 (adj)

collaborate　合作 (v)

collaboration　合作 (n)

collaborative　合作的 (adj)

colleague　同僚、同事 (n)

collect　蒐集 (v)

collection　蒐集 (n)

column　直行 (n)

combination　合併、組合 (n)

combine　合併 (v)

commensurate　等量的 (adj)

comment　評論、論述、意見 (n)

commitment　承諾、實行 (n)

common　普通的、一般的 (ad)

commonly　普通的、一般的 (adv)

communicate　溝通 (v)

communication　溝通 (n)

comparable　可比較的 (adj)

comparative　比較的 (adj)；比較級 (n)

compare　比較 (v)

comparison　比較 (n)

compliance　承諾、順從、遵守 (n)

compliant　順從的、遵守的 (adj)

complicate　更複雜化 (v)

complicated　複雜的 (adj)

component　成份、元件 (n)；
　　　　　成分的 (adj)

comprehension　理解、包容 (n)

comprehensive　綜合的、
　　　　　有理解力的 (adj)

computation　計算 (n)

compute　計算 (v)

computerize　電腦化 (v)

concept　概念 (n)

conceptive　有概念的 (adj)

conceptual　概念的 (adj)

conceptualization　概念化 (n)

conceptualize　概念化 (v)

conclude　總結 (v)

conclusion　結論 (n)

concurrent　同時發生的事件 (n)；
　　　　　同步的 (adj)

condition　狀況、情況 (n)

conduct　經營、引導 (n)；
　　　　進行、傳輸 (v)

conference　會議、研討會 (n)

confidence　信心 (n)

confident　有信心的 (adj)

confidential　秘密的；保密的 (adj.)

confusion　混亂、混淆 (n)

consent　同意 (n)；同意 (v)

consistency　一貫、一致、和諧 (n)

consistent　一致的 (adj)

consolidate　使穩固 (v)

constraint　限制 (n)

consult　諮詢 (v)

consultant　顧問 (n)

consumption　消耗 (n)

contaminated　被污染的 (adj)

contamination　污染 (n)

content　內容 (n)

context　來龍去脈、前後關係 (n)

contextual　文脈上的 (adj)

contexture　構造 (n)

contingency　偶發性 (n)

contingent　偶發的事 (n)；
　　　　　暫時的、偶發的 (adj)

contrast　對比 (n)；對照 (v)

contribution　貢獻 (n)

convention　集會、一般約定 (n)

convergence　收斂 (n)

convergent　收斂的 (adj)

conversion　轉換 (n)

convert　轉換 (v)

conveyor　輸送器（帶）(n)

9

convolution　迴旋 (n)

coordinate　協調 (v)

coordinator　協調人 (n)

copyright　版權 (n)

core　核心 (n)

correction　修正 (n)

correlation　關連性 (n)

cost　成本 (n)

counterpart　對應的部分 (或個體) (n)

crank　搖柄 (n)

creative　創作的、有創造力的 (adj)

creativity　創造力、創造性 (n)

criterion　準則 (n)（複數 criteria）

critical　關鍵的 (adj.)

critique　評論、批評 (n)

cumulative　累積的 (adj.)

current　潮流、電流 (n)；
　　　　現在的、現行的

curriculum　課程 (n)

D

deduction　推論、演繹 (n)

deductive　推論的 (adj)

define　定義 (v)

definition　定義 (n)

dehydration　脫水 (n)

delay　延遲 (n)(v)

demand　需求 (n)

demonstrate　說明、示範、實證 (v)

demonstration　說明、示範、實證 (n)

dependent　依附的、應變的 (adj)

deployment　布署、展開 (n)

description　敘述 (n)

descriptive　敘述的 (adj)

descriptive　敘述的 (adj)

design　設計 (v)(n)

determinant　決定因子、行列式 (n)；
　　　　　　決定的 (adj.)

deterministic　固定的、已決定的 (adj.)

develop　發展 (v)

development　發展 (n)

deviation　偏差 (n)

device　裝置、儀器 (n)

diagnostic　診斷 (n)、診斷的 (adj)

diagram　圖、圖形、圖式 (n)

dichotomous　分成兩種的、兩分的 (adj)

differential　微分 (n)；差別地 (adj)

digit　數字、位數 (n)

digital　數字的、位數的 (adj)

discomfort　不適 (n)

discrete　離散的 (adj)

discuss　討論 (v)

discussion　討論 (n)

disease　疾病 (n)

dispatch　派遣 (n)；遞送 (v)

dispersion　散佈 (n)

dispersive　分散的 (adj)

distal　遠端的 (adj)

distribute　分配 (v)

distribution　分配 (n)

division　部門 (n)

document　文件 (n)

documentation　文件、憑證 (n)

dose　劑量 (n)

downtime　停工期 (n)

draft　草稿 (n)

duplicate　複製 (v)、副本 (n)

dynamic　動力的、動態的 (adj)

Dynamically　動力的、動態的 (adv)

E

edit　編修 (v)

edition　版、版本 (n)

editor　編輯、編者 (n)

effect　影響、效果 (n)

effectiveness　有效性 (n)

efficient　有效率的 (adj)

electromyography　肌電圖 (n)

electronic　電子的 (adj)

element　元素、成份 (n)

emphasis　強調 (n)

empirical　經驗的 (adj)

employee　員工 (n)

employer　僱主 (n)

employment　聘僱 (n)

endnote　底標、最後的注記　(n)

engineer　工程師 (n)

engineering　工程 (n)

enhance　增加、提高 (v)

entity　實體、個體 (n)

equation　等式 (n)

ergonomic　人因工程的 (adj)

ergonomically　人因工程的 (adv)

ergonomics　人因工程 (n)

especial　特別的 (adj)

especially　特別的 (adv)

essential　必要的、不可缺的 (adj);
　　　　　　要素、要點 (n)

estimate　估計 (v)

estimation　估計 (n)

ethical　倫理的 (adj)

ethically　倫理的 (adv)

ethics　倫理 (n)

evaluate　評估 (v)

evaluation　評估 (n)

evaporation　蒸發 (n)

evolution　進展 (n)

examination　檢查、檢驗 (n)

examine　檢查、檢驗 (v)

example　例子、範例 (n)

execute　執行 (v)

execution　執行 (n)

executive　執行長 (n)；執行的 (adj)

expect　期望 (v)

9

expectation　期望 (n)

experiment　實驗 (n)

expert　專家 (n)

explicit　明確的 (adj)

exploratory　探測的 (adj)

exponential　指數的 (adj)

extension　伸展、擴充 (n)

extensive　廣大的、多方面的 (adj)

external　外部的 (adj)

extreme　極端（的）、
　　　　　末端（的）(n) (adj)

extremely　極端的、非常的 (adv)

F

fabricate　製造 (v)

fabrication　製造 (n)

fabricative　製造的 (adj)

facility　設施、設備 (n)

factor　因素、因子 (n)

fatal　致命的、決定性的 (adj)

fatality　致命性、死亡 (n)

feedback　回饋 (n)

field　工作現場、野外 (n)

figure　圖、圖表、形狀 (n)

finding　發現 (n)

finite　有限的 (adj)

fixture　夾具 (n)

fluctuation　變動、波動 (n)

footnote　足標、下標 (n)

forecast　預測 (n)

foreman　領班、工頭 (n)

formal　正式的 (adj)

format　格式 (n)

formula　公式、程式、配方、藥方 (n)

forum　研討會、論壇 (n)

framework　架構、體制 (n)

friction　摩擦 (n)

friendly　友善的 (adj)(adv)

function　函數、功能、機能 (n)

fundamental　基本的 (adj)

funding　資金、財源 (n)

furnace　火爐　(n)

fuzzy　模糊的 (adj)

G

gain　增量 (n)

gait　步伐 (n)

gasometer　氣體計量計 (n)

general　一般的 (adj)

generalize　一般化 (v)

genetic　起源的、遺傳學的 (adj)

geometric　幾何的 (adj)

geometry　幾何 (n)

global　全球性的、全面性的 (adj)

globe　球、地球 (n)；使成球狀 (v)

glossary　字彙 (n)

goal　目標、終點 (n)

goggle　護目境 (n)

goniometer 角度計 (n)

grammar 文法 (n)

grammatical 文法的 (adj)

grammatically 文法的 (adv)

grid 格柵、方格 (n)

grind 研磨 (n)(v)

grit 砂粒 (n)

group technology 群組技術

guidance 指引、指導 (n)

guide 指引 (v)

guideline 指引 (n)

H

handbook 手冊 (n)

handle 握柄 (n)

handout 分發的印刷品、講義 (n)

hardcopy 紙本 (n)

hardness 硬度 (n)

hazard 危害 (n)

hazardous 具危害的 (adj)

heuristic 啟發式教學法 (n)；
　　　　　啟智的 (adj)

hierarchial 層級化的 (adj)

hierarchize 層級排列 (v)

hierarchy 層級、體系 (n)

hinge 鉸鍊、樞紐 (n)

homogeneity 均質、同質 (n)

homogenize 使均質 (v)

homogenous 均質的 (adj)

hybrid 混雜的 (adj)

hypothesis 假設 (n)

hypothesize 假設 (v)

hypothetical 假設的 (adj)

hypothetically 假設的 (adv)

I

icon 圖像 (n)

iconic 圖像的 (adj)

identical 完全相同的 (adj)

identifiable 可確認的、
　　　　　　可證明為相同的 (adj)

identification 確認、證明 (n)

identify 指出、確認 (v)

identity 身分、一致、本體 (n)

idle 閒置的 (adj)

illuminance 照度 (n)

illustration 說明 (n)

illustrative 說明的、敘述的 (adj)

impair 損害 (v)

impairment 損害 (n)

impedance 阻抗、電阻 (n)

implement 實施、執行 (v)

implementation 實施、執行 (n)

implication 暗示 (n)

improve 改進 (v)

improvement 改進 (n)

inappropriate 不適當的 (adj)

incentive 誘因 (n)；激勵的 (adj)

incident　事件 (n)

incident　事件 (n)

inclusive　含有的、包括的 (adj)

independent　獨立的 (adj)

index　指數 (n)

indicate　指出 (v)

indication　指示 (n)

indicator　指標、指示器 (n)

individual　個體、個人 (n)

inductive　前提的、前言的 (adj)

industrial　工業的 (adj)

industry　工業 (n)

inference　推理 (n)

inferential　推理的 (adj)

inferior　劣度 (n)；下方的 (adj)

infinite　無窮大 (n)；無限的 (adj)

informal　非正式的 (adj)

information　資訊 (n)

informative　有資訊的 (adj)

initial　最初的 (adj)；
　　　　姓名的第一個字母 (n)(v)

initialize　初始化 (v)

initiative　創新、起始 (n)；起始的 (adj)

innovation　創新 (n)

innovative　創新的 (adj)

innovator　創新者 (n)

innumerable　無數的 (adj)

inquire　詢問 (v)

inquiry　詢問 (n)

inspect　檢查 (v)

inspection　檢查 (n)

inspector　稽查員 (n)

instantaneous　瞬間的 (adj)

institution　機構 (n)

instrument　儀器 (n)

instrumentation　儀器使用 (n)

integer　整數 (n)

integrate　整合 (v)

integration　整合 (n)

intention　意向、意圖 (n)

interchangeable　可互換的 (adj)

interface　介面 (n)

internal　內部的 (adj)

interpret　解釋、翻譯 (v)

interpretable　可解釋的、可翻譯的 (adj)

interpretation　解釋、翻譯 (n)

interpretative　解釋的 (adj)

interpreter　解釋者、翻譯者 (n)

intervention　介入 (n)

interview　會面、會談 (n)；
　　　　會面、會談 (v)

interviewee　被訪問者 (n)

interviewer　訪問者 (n)

introduction　介紹 (n)

inventive　發明的、有發明能力的 (adj)

inventory　存貨、庫存 (n)

investigation　調查、研究 (n)

investigator　調查者、研究人 (n)

invitation　邀請 (n)

invite　邀請 (v)

isometric　等長的 (adj)

isotonic　等張的 (adj)

issue　出版品、爭論點、主題 (n)；
　　　　出版、發佈 (v)

item　項目 (n)

itemize　列舉 (v)

iterative　反覆的 (adj)

itinerary　旅遊 (n)；旅程的 (adj)

J

jargon　黑話、匣語 (n)

jeopardize　危及 (v)

job　工作、職業 (n)

journal　期刊 (n)

justification　辯護、正當化 (n)

justify　辯護 (v)

K

key　關鍵的 (adj)；鍵

keynote　基調、主旨 (n)、
　　　　　會場發表主要講話 (v)

kinematic　運動學的 (adj)

kinematics　運動學 (n)

kinesiology　人體運動學 (n)

kinetic　運動的、動力學的 (adj)

kinetics　動力學 (n)

kurtosis　峰度 (n)

L

lab　研究室、實驗室 (n)

labor　勞工、勞力 (n)

laboratory　實驗室 (n)

lathe　車床 (n)

layout　配置、佈局 (n)

lead time　前置時間 (n)

level　水準、層次 (n)

liability　負債 (n)

liner　線性的 (adj)

link　連結、鏈 (n)

literature　文獻 (n)

local　局部的、本地的 (adj)

longitudinal　縱向的 (adj)

lot　批量 (n)

loudness　響度 (n)

luminance　亮度 (n)

M

machinery　機械裝置、機械作用 (n)

major　主要的 (adj)

manage　管理 (v)

manageable　可管理的 (adj)

management　管理 (n)

manual　手冊 (n)

manufacture　製造 (v)

manufacturer　製造者 (n)

manufacturing　製造 (n)

manuscript　稿子、稿件 (n)

mapping　影像製作 (n)

margin　邊緣 (n)

marginal　邊緣的、邊際的 (adj)

matrix　矩陣 (n)

maximal　最大的 (adj)

maximization　最大化 (n)

maximize　最大化 (v)

maximum　最大值 (n)

mean　平均值 (n)

meaning　意義 (n)

meaningful　有意義的 (adj)

measure　量測、量度 (v)

measurement　量測、量度 (n)

mechanism　機構 (n)

membrane　薄膜 (n)

memorandum (Memo)　備忘錄 (n)

mental　心智的 (adj)

merit　優點、價值 (n)

metaphor　隱喻 (n)

meter　米、量表、量具 (n)

method　方法 (n)

methodology　方法、研究方法 (n)

metronome　節拍器 (n)

minimal　最小的 (adj)

minimization　最小化 (n)

minimize　最小化 (v)

minimum　最小值 (n)

minor　次要的、不重要的 (adj)

misleading　誤導的、令人誤解的 (adj)

mission　任務 (n)

mode　模式 (n)

model　模式、模型 (n)

modeling　模式建立 (n)

modernization　現代化 (n)

modification　修改、修飾 (n)

modify　修改、修飾 (v)

module　模組 (n)

monitor　顯示器 (n)；監控 (v)

monochrome　單色畫面 (n)

monthly　每月的 (adv)

multiple　多的 (adj)

multiplier　乘數、放大器 (n)

multivariate　多變量的 (n)

muscular　肌肉的 (adj)

musculoskeletal　肌肉骨骼的 (adj)

N

native speaker　說母語者 (n)

negative　負的、否定的、陰性的 (adj)

network　網路 (n)

neural　神經的 (adj)

noise　噪音、雜訊 (n)

nominal　名義的、名目的 (adj)

nomogram　計算圖 (n)

norm　準則、標準 (n)

normal　普通的、常態的 (adj)；

　　　　常態、垂直線 (n)

normality　常態、標準 (n)；

normalize　常態化 (v)

null　無效的、不存在的、虛無的 (adj)

O

objective　目標、目的 (n)；

　　　　客觀的、實體的、目標的 (n)

observation　觀察、觀測值 (n)

observe　觀察 (v)

observer　觀察者、觀測者 (n)

obtain　取得、得到 (v)

occupation　職業 (n)

occupational　職業的 (adj)

olfactory　嗅覺的 (adj)

operate　操作 (v)

operation　經營、操作、作業 (n)

operator　操作員、作業員 (n)

optimal　最佳的 (adj)

optimization　最佳化 (n)

optimize　最佳化 (v)

optimum　最佳 (n)；最佳的 (adj)

oral　口述的、口語的 (adj)

ordinal　順序的 (adj)

organization　組織 (n)

organize　組織 (v)

orient　定位、使適應 (v)

orientation　定位、適應 (n)

origin　起源 (n)

original　最初的、起始的、原創的 (adj)

orthogonal　直交的 (adj)

outcome　結果 (n)

outlet　銷售通路、市場 (n)

outline　大綱、輪廓 (n)；

　　　　簡述、描繪輪廓 (v)

P

pallet　墊板、棧板 (n)

panel　小組討論會 (n)；分成格子 (v)

paper　文件、文章 (n)

paradigm　範例、典範 (n)

parameter　參數 (n)

parametric　參數的、母數的 (adj)

participant　參加者 (n)

participate　參加 (n)

particular　特別的 (adj)

partition　分割 (n)；分割 (v)

partner　伙伴 (n)

peer　同事、同等級者 (n)

percentile　百分位 (n)

perform　執行 (v)

performance　績效、性能 (n)

period　期間 (n)

periodic　週期的、定時的 (adj)

periodically　週期的、定時的 (adv)

pervade　蔓延、擴大 (v)

9

phenomenon　現象 (n)

（複數 phenomena）

phonemics　音素學 (n)

photochemical　光化學的 (adj)

photoconduction　光電傳導 (n)

photoconductive　光電傳導的 (adj)

photolithography　光學照相 (n)

photometer　光度計、光表 (n)

photometry　測光學 (n)

physical　身體的 (adj)

pictorial　圖畫 (n)；插畫的 (adj)

pilot　示範的、先導的 (adj)

pixel　圖素、光點 (n)

plagiarism　抄襲 (n)

plot　略圖 (n)；計劃 (v)

population　母體、人口 (n)

positive　正的、肯定的 (adj)

postscript　附錄、後記 (n)

potential　潛力、電位 (n)；潛在的 (adj)

practical　實際的、實用的 (adj)

practice　實務 (n)；練習 (v)

practitioner　業者 (n)

precise　精確的 (adj)

precisely　精確的 (adv)

predict　預測 (v)

predictable　可預測的 (adj)

predictive　預測性的 (adj)

predictor　預報器 (n)

preface　序、前言 (n)

prefatory　前言的 (adj)

prerequisite　先決條件 (n)；

　　　　　　　必要的、先決條件的 (adj)

present　呈現、報告、展示 (v)

presentation　報告、展示 (n)

presenter　報告人 (n)

press　出版社 (界)、印刷 (n)

prevalence　盛行、流行 (n)

prevention　預防 (n)

primary　主要的、最初的 (adj)；

　　　　　主要者 (n)

principal　主要的 (adj)

principle　原理、規則 (n)

printout　印出品 (n)

priority　優先順序 (n)

probabilistic　機率的 (adj)

problem　問題 (n)

problematic　有問題的 (adj)

proceeding　會議記錄、學報 (n)

process　處理 (v)

processor　處理器 (v)

product　產品 (n)

productive　多產的；有生產力的 (adj)

productivity　生產力 (n)

profession　職業、專業 (n)

professional　職業的、專業的 (adj)；

　　　　　　　專業人員 (n)

professionalize 使專業化 (v)

profile 輪廓、斷面 (n)

profilometer 斷面量測器 (n)

program 計畫、學程、程式 (n)

project 計畫 (n)

proliferate 增加、擴散 (v)

pronounced 明顯的 (n)

proofread 校正、校對 (v)

proportion 比例 (n)

proportionate 使成比例 (v)

proposal 計畫書、提案 (n)

proscriptive 禁止的 (adj)

prospective 未來的、期望的 (adj)

protocol 程序、協定、約定的過程 (n)

provide 提供 (v)

provision 供應 (n)；供應 (v)

provisional 暫時的 (adj)

proximal 近端的 (adj)

psychology 心理學 (n)

psychophysical 精神物理學的 (adj)

publication 出版品、著作 (n)

publish 出版 (v)

publishable 可出版的 (adj)

publisher 出版者、出版商 (n)

purpose 目的 (n)

purposive 有目地的、故意的 (adj)

Q

quadratic 二次方程式 (n)；方形的 (adj)

qualitative 計質的、性質的 (adj)

qualitatively 計質的、性質的 (adv)

quality 品質 (n)

quantify 量化、數值化 (v)

quantitative 數量的 (adj)

quantitatively 數量的 (adv)

quantity 數量 (n)

quarter 四分之一、一季 (n)

quarterly 季刊 (n)、每季的 (adj)

quartile 四分位 (n)；四分位的 (adj)

question 問題 (n)

questionable 有問題的；有爭議的 (n)

questionnaire 問卷 (n)

queue 排隊 (n)；排隊 (v)

quota 配額 (n)

quotation 引用、報價單、價格行情 (n)

R

random 隨機抽樣 (n)；隨機的 (adj)

randomization 隨機化、隨機決定 (n)

randomize 隨機化 (v)

randomly 隨機的 (adv)

range 範圍、全距 (n)

rank 等級、類別、評價 (n)；排序 (v)

ranking 等級、順序 (n)

ratchet （防倒轉之）棘齒 (n)

rate 評定、等級鑑定 (v)

rating　考核、評分 (n)

ratio　比例 (n)

rationale　原理、理論 (n)

react　反應 (v)

reaction　反應 (n)

reactive　反應的；反作用的 (adj)

reactor　反應器 (n)

readability　可讀性 (n)

readable　可讀性 (adj)

reality　真實 (n)

receptor　感受器 (n)

recognize　辨認、任可、表揚 (v)

recommend　建議 (v)

recommendation　建議 (n)

recruit　招募 (v)

recruitment　招募 (n)

reduce　減少 (v)

reduction　減少、縮減 (n)

redundant　多餘的 (adj)

refer　引用、參考 (v)

referee　仲裁者、調停者、審查者 (n)；
　　　　審查 (v)

reference　參考、參考文獻 (n)

refine　改善 (v)

reflectance　反射比 (n)

reimburse　償付 (v)

reimbursement　償付 (n)

reject　拒絕 (v)

rejection　拒絕 (n)

relevance　關聯、相關性 (n)

relevant　相關的 (adj)

reliability　可靠性、可靠度 (n)

reliable　可靠的 (adj)

repetition　重複、反覆 (n)

repetitive　重覆的 (adj)

replenish　補充 (v)

replenishment　補充 (n)

replicate　反覆、複製 (v)

replication　複製 (n)

report　報告 (n) (v)

representation　描繪、陳述、代表 (n)

representational　代表的 (adj)

reproduction　複製、仿造 (n)

require　要求 (v)

requirement　要求、需求 (n)

research　研究 (n)

researcher　研究者 (n)

resolution　決議、解析、解析度 (n)

resolve　解析、分解 (v)

resonance　共振、共鳴 (n)

resource　資源 (n)

respective　個別的 (adj)

respectively　個別的 (adv)

respirator　防毒面具 (n)

response　反應、回應 (n)

responsive　有反應的、回應的 (adj)

result　結果 (n)

resume　履歷 (n)

retain　保留 (n)

retrieval　取回、修補 (n)

retrieve　取回 (n) (v)

review　檢視、審查、回顧 (n)；
　　　　檢視、審查、回顧 (v)

reviewer　審查委員、評論者 (n)

revise　修訂 (v)

revision　修訂、校定 (n)

risk　風險 (n)

robot　機器人 (n)

robotics　機器人學 (n)

role　角色 (n)

roughness　粗糙度 (n)

route　路徑 (n)

routing　流程安排 (n)

S

sagittal　矢狀的 (adj)

salary　薪水 (n)

sample　範例、例子 (n)

scale　比例、尺度 (n)；按比例做 (v)

scenario　情節 (n)

schema　輪廓、概要 (n)

scheme　圖解、方案 (n)

scholar　學者 (n)

scientific　科學的 (adj)

scope　範圍 (n)

score　分數 (n)

search　搜尋 (n)

section　節、部分 (n)

selection　選擇 (n)

semantic　語意的 (adj)

seminar　研究班、研討會 (n)

sensory　感覺的 (adj)

service　服務 (n)

set　組、集合 (n)

shift (night shift)　班次 (n)（晚班）

shop　工廠 (n)

significance　重要性、顯著性、含意 (n)

significant　重要的、顯著的 (adj)

significantly　重要的、顯著的 (adv)

simulate　模擬 (v)

simulation　模擬 (n)

simultaneous　同時的 (adj)

simultaneously　同時地 (adv)

situation　情況 (n)

skew　傾斜 (n)
　　　　歪斜的、不對稱的 (adj)；
　　　　使偏移 (v)

skewness　偏度 (n)

slipperiness　滑溜性 (n)

slippery　滑的 (adj)

social　社會的 (adj)

society　學會 (n)

socket　插座、凹槽 (n)

solid　實體 (n)；實體的 (adj)

solution　解答、溶液 (n)

source　來源 (n)

specific　特定的、明確的 (adj)

specification　規格 (n)

9

specimen　樣品 (n)；做為樣品的 (adj)

spell　（英文）拼字 (v)

spindle　紡錘 (n)；紡錘狀的 (adj)

sponsor　負責人、贊助者 (n)；
　　　　發起、贊助 (v)

spreadsheet　試算表 (n)

square　正方形、平方 (n)；
　　　　正方形的 (adj)

staff　職員、幕僚 (n)

standard　標準 (n)

standardization　標準化 (n)

standardize　標準化 (v)

static　靜態的 (adj)

statistically　統計的 (adv)

statistics　統計、統計量 (n)

stepwise　逐步的 (adj)

stimulus　刺激 (n)

stipend　津貼、薪俸 (n)

stochastic　隨機的 (adj)

stock　存貨、股票 (n)；庫存的 (adj)

strain　應變、變形 (n)

strategy　策略、戰略 (n)

stratification　分層、層次 (n)

stratify　分層 (v)

stress　應力、壓力 (n)；著重、強調 (v)

study　研究、調查 (n)

style　格式、風格 (n)

subject　主題、受測者、實驗品 (n)；
　　　　受制於 (adj)

subjective　主觀的 (adj)

submission　提出、遞交、投稿 (n)

submit　提出、遞交、投稿 (v)

subset　子集合 (n)

subsidiary　子公司、附屬機構 (n)；
　　　　　附屬的 (adj)

subtle　敏銳的 (adj)

suggest　建議 (v)

suggestion　建議 (n)

superior　上等的 (adj)

supervisor　管理人、監督人 (n)

supplement　補充 (n)；補充 (v)

supplementary　補充的 (adj)；補充物 (n)

supplier　供應者、供應商 (n)

supply　供應 (v)

surveillance　監測、管制

surveillant　監測者、管制者

survey　調查、研究 (n)；測量、考察 (v)

symbolic　象徵的、符號的 (adj)

symbolism　符號、表象 (n)

symposium　論壇、座談會、評論集 (n)

synchronization　同步化 (n)

synchronize　使同步 (v)

synonym　同義字 (詞) (n)

synthesis　綜合、合成 (n)

synthetic　綜合的、合成的 (adj)

system　系統 (n)

systematic　系統化 (adj)

systematically　系統化 (adv)

T

table　表 (n)

tactile　觸覺的 (adj)

task　工作、任務 (n)

technical　技術的、科技的 (adj)

technician　技術員 (n)

technique　技巧、技能、方法 (n)

technological　技術的、科技的 (adj)

technology　技術、科技 (n)

term　項目 (n)

terminology　術語、專業名詞 (n)

test　測試、試驗 (n)(v)

tester　測試器 (n)

testimony　聲明、證詞 (n)

text　文字 (n)

theoretical　理論上的 (adj)

theoretically　理論上的 (adv)

theorist　理論家 (n)

theory　理論 (n)

therapy　理論家

thrcshold　閾值 (n)

title　標題 (n)

tolerance　公差 (n)

topic　主題 (n)

ttrackball　軌跡球 (n)

trainee　受訓者 (n)

trajectory　軌跡、軌道 (n)

ttransform　改變、使轉換 (v)

transformation　改變、變形 (n)

transformer　使改變的人或物、
　　　　　　　變壓器 (n)

transition　轉變 (n)

trauma　創傷 (n)

treatment　處理 (n)

tribological　摩擦學的 (adj)

tribology　摩擦學 (n)

turnover　周轉、(人事) 異動

U

ultimate　最終的、極限的 (adj)；
　　　　　終極 (n)

unbiased　無偏差的 (adj)

unnecessary　不必要的 (adj)

usability　可用性 (n)

usable　可用的 (adj)

usage　使用、用法、用處 (n)

user　使用者 (n)

utility　效用、效益、共用事業 (n)

utilization　利用、使用 (n)

utilize　利用、使用 (v)

V

vague　不清楚的、含糊的 (adj)

vagueness　含糊 (n)

validate　確認、實證 (v)

validation　確認、實證 (n)

value　數值、價值 (n)；評價、估價 (v)

valve　活塞、瓣膜 (n)

9

variance　變異數 (n)

variation　變異 (n)

variety　變化、多樣性 (n)

various　各樣的 (adj)

vector　向量 (n)

verification　確認、証實 (n)

verify　確認、証實 (v)

version　版本、敘述 (n)

versus (v.s.)　對應 (prep)

violate　違反 (v)

violation　違規 (n)

virtual　實際上的、虛擬的 (物理) (adj)

viscosity　黏度 (n)

vision　視力、洞察力 (n)

visual　視覺的 (adj)

vita　傳記、履歷 (n)

vital　核心 (n)；
　　　致命的、維持生存必備的 (adj)

W

wafer　晶片 (n)；黏貼 (n)

wage　工資、報酬 (n)

warehouse　倉庫 (n)

waste　廢棄物 (n)；
　　　浪費、消耗、濫用 (v)

wasteful　浪費的、不經濟的 (adj)

weld　鎔接 (n)；焊接 (v)

welder　焊接器、焊接工 (n)

workplace　工做場所 (n)

Y

yield　產量、收益 (n)；屈服、支付 (v)

參考資料

參考文獻

一、書籍、期刊、論文

1. 季健(2002), 科技英語結構分析與翻譯(2nd ed), 高立圖書有限公司

2. Chang, W.R., Matz, S. (2001), The slip resistance of common footwear materials measured with two slipmeters. Applied Ergonomics 32, 549-558.

3. Ciriello, V.M, McGorry, R.W., Martin, S.E. (2001), Maximum acceptable forces of dynamic pushing on high and low coefficient of friction floors, International Journal of Industrial Ergonomics, 27, 1-8.

4. Cook, C., Burgess-Limerick, R., Chang, S.(2000), The prevalence of neck and upper extremity musculoskeletal symptoms in computer mouse users, International Journal of Industrial Ergonomics, 26, 347-356.

5. De Cerio, J., Merino-Diaz. (2003), Quality management practices and operational performance: empirical evidence for Spanish industry, International Journal of Production Research, 41(12), 2763-2786.

6. Degarmo, E., P, Sullivan, W.G., Canada, J.R.(1984), Engineering Economy, 7th ed., Macmillan Publishing Company, N.Y.

7. Garver, M.S.(2003), Best practices in identifying customer-driven improvement opportunities, Industrial Marketing Management, 32, 455-466.

8. Gibaldi, Joseph (1999), MLA Handbook for Writers of Research Papers (5th ed), The Modern Language Association of America, N.Y.

9. Grant, F., H. (1988), Simulation in Designing and scheduling manufacturing systems, in Design and Analysis of Integrated Manufacturing System, National Academy of Engineering, Washington, D.C.

10. Kanellaidis, G., Golias, J., Zarifopoulos, K.(1995), A survey of drivers attitudes toward speed limit violations, Journal of Safety Research, 26(1), 31-40.

11. Lannon, John, M. (1991), Technical Writing (5th ed), Harper Collins Publishers, N.Y.

12. Leamon, T.B., 1992. The reduction of slip and fall injuries: part II- the scientific bassis (knowledge base) for the guide. International Journal of Industrial Ergonomics 10, 29-34.

13. Li, K.W. (2002), Ergonomic design and evaluation of wire-tying hand tools, International Journal of Industrial Ergonomics, 30, 149-161.

14. Li, K.W. (2003), Ergonomic evaluation of a fixture used for power driven wire-tying hand tools, International Journal of Industrial Ergonomics, 32, 71-79.

15. Li, K.W. (2003), An ergonomic assessment of four female shoes: friction coefficients of the soles on the floors and electromyographic activities in the shank when walking, Journal of Chinese Institute of Industrial Engineers, 20(5), 472-480.

16. Li, K. W., Chang, W-R, Leamon, T. B., Chen C. J.(2004), Floor slipperiness measurement: friction coefficient, roughness of floors, and subjective perception under spillage conditions, Safety Science, in press.

17. Mills, G., H., Walter, J., A. (1978), Technical Writing, 4th Ed, Holt, Rinehart, Winston, N.Y.

18. Sanders, M.S., McCormick, E. J. (1993), Human Factors in Engineering and Design, 7th ed, McGraw-Hill International.

19. Snook, S.H., Ciriello, V.M.(1991), The design of manual handling tasks: revised tables of maximum acceptable weights and forces, Ergonomics 34, 1197-1213.

20. Suri, R. (1988), A new perspective on manufacturing system analysis, in Design and Analysis of Integrated Manufacturing System, National Academy of Engineering, Washington, D.C.

21. Tipnis, V., A. (1988), Process and economic models for manufacturing operations, in Design and Analysis of Integrated Manufacturing System, National Academy of Engineering, Washington, D.C.

22. Wilson, W. P. (1990), Development of SATRA slip test and tread pattern design guidelines, in Slips, Stumble, and falls: pedestrian footwear and surfaces, ASTM STP 1103, B.E. Gray, Ed., American Society for Testing and Materials, Philaselphia, 113-123.

23. Zhang, L., Helander, M.G., Drudy, C.G. (1996), Identifying factors of comfort and discomfort in sitting, Human Factors, 38, 377-389.

國家圖書館出版品預行編目（CIP）資料

科技英文寫作 / 李開偉編著. -- 五版. -- 新北市：
　全華圖書, 2019.03
　　面；　公分
　ISBN 978-986-503-050-6(平裝)

1.英語 2.科學技術 3.應用文

805.17　　　　　　　　　　　　　　108002362

科技英文寫作

作　　　者 / 李開偉

發 行 人 / 陳本源

執行編輯 / 黃上蓉

封面設計 / 楊昭琅

出 版 者 / 全華圖書股份有限公司

郵政帳號 / 0100836-1號

印 刷 者 / 宏懋打字印刷股份有限公司

圖書編號 / 0547004

五版一刷 / 2019 年 5 月

定　　　價 / 新臺幣 360 元

Ｉ Ｓ Ｂ Ｎ / 978-986-503-050-6

全華圖書 / www.chwa.com.tw

全華網路書局 Open Tech / www.opentech.com.tw

若您對書籍內容、排版印刷有任何問題，歡迎來信指導book@chwa.com.tw

臺北總公司（北區營業處）

地址：23671新北市土城區忠義路21號

電話：(02) 2262-5666

傳眞：(02) 6637-3695、6637-3696

中區營業處

地址：40256臺中市南區樹義一巷26號

電話：(04) 2261-8485

傳眞：(04) 3600-9806

南區營業處

地址：80769高雄市三民區應安街12號

電話：(07) 381-1377

傳眞：(07) 862-5562

選擇題

以下各題請指出畫底線者，為以下中之何者？

名詞、名詞片語、動詞、動詞片語、形容詞、形容詞片語、副詞、副詞片語、主要子句、從屬子句。

（　）1. Three hypotheses regarding the cultural dimension of power distance were rejected.

(A) 名詞　(B) 動詞　(C) 形容詞　(D) 副詞

（　）2. Much of the empirical research concerns the effect of spirituality on employee attitudes.　(A) 形容詞片語　(B) 動詞片語　(C) 名詞片語　(D) 連接詞片語

（　）3. Grant & Stephens (2004) found that a large majority of employees in a university hospital nursing staff believe their work practices are spiritual.　(A) 名詞　(B) 動詞　(C) 形容詞　(D) 副詞

（　）4. Fernando & Chow (2010) surveyed executives in organizations listed on the Australian Stock Exchange.　(A) 名詞　(B) 動詞　(C) 形容詞　(D) 副詞

（　）5. This article discusses the concept of governmentality in relation to practices and policies of western systems of governance that focus on youth and sport.　(A) 形容詞片語　(B) 動詞片語　(C) 名詞片語　(D) 連接詞片語

（　）6. To answer the question of which problem to address, decision makers may rely on intuition, insight, or rational decision making in valuing an opportunity.　(A) 主要子句　(B) 從屬子句

（　）7. Management is a limited resource and cannot spend an inordinate amount of time in problem identification.　(A) 主要子句　(B) 從屬子句

（　）8. Strategy implementation is defined as an operations-oriented make-things-happen activity aimed at shaping the performance of core business activities in a strategy supportive manner.　(A) 形容詞片語　(B) 動詞片語　(C) 連接詞片語

(　)9. Leadership, as it pertains to strategic management, requires equal attention to both path-finding and culture-building.　(A) 主要子句　(B) 從屬子句

(　)10. In this paper, success is operationally defined as the realization of the specific objectives set by the organization.　(A) 名詞　(B) 動詞　(C) 形容詞　(D) 副詞

(　)11. Commercial drone use is a particularly good example of how public debate and ethical concerns can influence innovation success.　(A) 主要子句　(B) 從屬子句

(　)12. The search period is limited to the past five years in order to focus on recent developments in commercial drone use.　(A) 形容詞片語　(B) 動詞片語　(C) 連接詞片語

問答題

請指出以下句子中的錯誤。

1. D. McGregor，one of the earliest and most prominent advocates of the modern approaches to management，proposed two concepts of worker motivation.

_____

2. Chang et al.【2001b】reported that the $\frac{F_N}{A^2}$ ofBrungraber Mark II is the smallest【0.07 N/cm^2】among the four slip measurement devices compared.

_____

3. 『Specific written consent』means a written authorization containing the name and signature of the employee authorizing the release of the medical information to the public.

_____

4. The rating procedure developed by M. E. Mendall is known as "objective rating"。

_____

5. The means of the participants' age, length of tenure, and working hour per week were 22.55 years、13.12 months、and 37.86 hours.

_____

6. A two/tailed test was performed to examine the difference between the two groups.

_____

問答題

下列句子指出不當之處並加以改正：

1. In the experiment, all the subjects reported to the research personnel after he finished his assembly task as soon as possible.

　　_____

2. How the experiment was accomplished was described in the approach section.

　　_____

3. The times to complete the task by the two groups were about the same.

　　_____

4. Specification measurement using this device may not be proper.

　　_____

5. The performance of this machine is mainly decided by the time to complete the task.

　　_____

6. The travel distance and the time for the two conditions were, on average, 15.2 m and 5.42 min.

　　_____

7. After each subject had decided their maximum acceptable load for each condition, a further three pushes were completed to enable horizontal and vertical forces to be measured.

　　_____

8. CNC grinding machines are widely used to obtain a good surface finish. Hence, these machines are expensive, particularly when used for low production volumes.

---

9. One hundred and fifty workers, from 3 semiconductor manufacturers, took part in the study.

---

10. A set of questions was administered to measure the behavior of the employees.

---

11. All the machine questions will be solved by the technicians immediately.

---

12. Two of the subjects were not able to completed the experiment.

---

13. We designed and distributed a questionnaire to all the employ ees and to collect the response of our employees in implementing the ISO 14000 in our factory and to measure whether they were satisfied with the new company regulations or not.

---

14. As far as the application of Petri nets in assembly system and planning is oncerned, its place-transition and token move-ment together offer a specific graphical epresentation to delineate operational planning knowledge and in modelingalternative process plans

---

問答題

請將以下中文句子翻譯成英文句子

1. 本研究的目的在探討不同服務時間分布對於加工排程的影響。

＿＿＿＿＿＿＿＿＿＿＿＿＿＿＿＿＿＿＿＿＿＿＿＿＿＿＿＿＿＿

2. 本研究的目的在發展一種新的演算法 (algorithm) 來分析最短路徑問題。

＿＿＿＿＿＿＿＿＿＿＿＿＿＿＿＿＿＿＿＿＿＿＿＿＿＿＿＿＿＿

3. 員工對於作業環境溫度與溼度的反應的調查是本研究的主要目的。

＿＿＿＿＿＿＿＿＿＿＿＿＿＿＿＿＿＿＿＿＿＿＿＿＿＿＿＿＿＿

4. 問卷收集到的數據將以敘述統計來分析。

＿＿＿＿＿＿＿＿＿＿＿＿＿＿＿＿＿＿＿＿＿＿＿＿＿＿＿＿＿＿

5. 數據的分析將以 SAS 8.0 統計軟體來進行。

＿＿＿＿＿＿＿＿＿＿＿＿＿＿＿＿＿＿＿＿＿＿＿＿＿＿＿＿＿＿

6. 公司所有的員工都參與了無記名的問卷調查。

＿＿＿＿＿＿＿＿＿＿＿＿＿＿＿＿＿＿＿＿＿＿＿＿＿＿＿＿＿＿

7. 實驗是以完全隨機化集區 (block) 設計來進行的。

＿＿＿＿＿＿＿＿＿＿＿＿＿＿＿＿＿＿＿＿＿＿＿＿＿＿＿＿＿＿

8. A 工具是否適用可經由操作員的主觀反應來調查。

＿＿＿＿＿＿＿＿＿＿＿＿＿＿＿＿＿＿＿＿＿＿＿＿＿＿＿＿＿＿

9. 兩種演算法計算出來的服務時間與最小成本分別為 15.3 分鐘與 53.5 萬美元。

＿＿＿＿＿＿＿＿＿＿＿＿＿＿＿＿＿＿＿＿＿＿＿＿＿＿＿＿＿＿

（請沿虛線撕下）

10. 表 5 列出了受測者的平均年齡、身高、體重與工作年資。

_____

11. 圖 1 顯示了所有實驗變數的平均值、標準差與全距。

_____

12. t 檢定的結果顯示兩種樣本間的差距並不顯著。

_____

13. 本研究的結果與 Smith(1997) 的結果並不一致。

_____

14. 本研究結果與 Smith(1997) 的發現間差異的成因並不清楚。

_____

15. X 公司員工對本研究的參與，作者深表謝意。

_____

16. 兩位匿名的審查者的意見是非常有幫助的。

_____

17. 兩種機器之間的差異似乎是無法比較的。

_____

18. 本研究的限制之一就是樣本數太小。

_____

1. You have worked out a manuscript entitled "Effects of temperature and humidity on employees' performance" and are submitting the manuscript to *Performance Evaluation Journal*. Write a cover letter to the editor, Dr. Eric Blair, to submit 4 copies of your manuscript to the following address: 65 Haslam Hall, Indiana Ave, London 12T4RS, U.K.

2. Write a letter to Dr. M. K. Tong, the program coordinator of the 5th International Industrial Management Conference which will be held in Hong Kong on December 15, 2008, to show your interest in participating the conference. You may ask for more details and/or submit an article.

1. There are recruitment advertisements announced in the United Daily News. Find one position that is most appropriate for you and write a resume and a cover letter (in a separate sheet) to apply that position.

From: United Daily News, Ed. 32, May 24, 2003

Daton Instruments Inc.

Position available:

Purchasing Engineer

- Bachelor degree or above, major in science/engineering or related
- responsible for managing suppliers, sourcing vendors and handling cost reduction projects.
- Good analysis, communication, and English capability

Qualified individual should send his/her resume to:

Recruitment

Human Resource

Applied Instruments

P.O. Box 26541

Hsin-Dian 116

Kestle, Good Food, Good Life

We are looking for …

Graduates with a Bachelor or Master degree in Business Administration or related field who are eager to pursue challenging career and gain extensive professional experience in marketing and sales.

Qualifications…

• Good English skill

• An entrepreneurial spirit and ability to adopt to change

• A communicative, creative and enthusiastic personality

• Familiar with MS Office

If you think you are ready for the challenges and meet our criteria, send a resume with a photo immediately to the following address:

Ms. Y.S. Liu

Human Resource, Nestle

180, 15F, Chung-Hsiao E. Road, Sec 4

Taipei 106

2. Write a biography about yourself.